PRAISE FOR *THE FORGETTING*

'*The Forgetting* is mysterious, deeply moving, impossible to put down – and its killer twist left me gasping. Brilliant. Hannah Beckerman's best book yet.'

—Alex Michaelides

'*The Forgetting* had me absolutely gripped from start to finish, and has one of the best story twists I have ever read. This brilliant and disturbing tale grabbed me from page one and I was completely hooked. I love Hannah's writing – clever, insightful, eloquent and empathetic. Utterly compelling, compulsive reading and superb writing. I could not put it down!'

—Ruth Jones

'I'm SO wowed! I literally gasped when I realised the twist. How clever, how very clever. It's brilliant. So very effective. This is an excellent, important novel.'

—Marian Keyes

'This book is amazing! It's deliciously sinister, deeply twisty, and HUGELY addictive. I love the disquietness of it so much, and Hannah writes into the dark corners of the characters' minds so beautifully.'

—Joanna Cannon

'A tense, stylish thriller. Beautifully written and utterly compelling, with an important message at its heart. It's fantastic.'

—Louise O'Neill

THE
FORGETTING

ALSO BY HANNAH BECKERMAN

The Dead Wife's Handbook
If Only I Could Tell You
The Impossible Truths of Love

THE
FORGETTING

HANNAH
BECKERMAN

LAKE UNION
PUBLISHING

Published by Lake Union Publishing, Seattle

www.apub.com

Amazon, the Amazon logo, and Lake Union Publishing are trademarks of Amazon.com, Inc., or its affiliates.

ISBN-13: 9781542030380
ISBN-10: 1542030382

Cover design by Liron Gilenberg

Printed in the United States of America

For Adam and Aurelia:
the loves of my life

ANNA

LONDON

When I open my eyes, nothing is familiar.

Light falls in parallel strips across the ceiling. Square white tiles, puckered with small black holes, form neat grids. A metal rail hangs above me, curved like the broad sweep of an arm.

My eyes blink against the too-bright light. My head is heavy, as if I have awoken from a leaden sleep.

Muffled sounds become louder in my ears, more distinct: the clatter of metal, the ringing of a phone, the murmur of voices.

I breathe, and my breath is hot against my face.

On the periphery of my vision, a plastic dome curves above my nose. I breathe again, watch the transparent mask mist over, feel the heat rebound against my skin.

'Hello, my love. How are you feeling?'

A man's face hovers over me, so close his features are blurred at the edges.

I try to swallow, but there is no moisture in my mouth, the muscles in my throat contracting without purpose: tensing, tightening, a sensation of choking.

'You're okay. Just breathe normally.' The man rests a hand on my arm and it is hot, clammy, my skin flinching in response.

'Where am I?' The words are like sandpaper in my throat.

'You're in hospital. I'm going to get someone to come and look at you. I'll be back in a minute.' The man's fretful tone is at odds with the reassurance of his words.

As he leaves, the dial is turned up on my senses: the pale blue curtain surrounding my bed; the beeping of a monitor beside me; the rigidity at the back of my neck, aching and stiff.

There is a swish of the cubicle curtain, a change in the direction of air. A new face appears above mine: young, female, wearing a blue nurse's tunic with white piping around the collar. Behind her, the man hovers, knitting his fingers, a frown pinching the bridge of his nose.

'Can you hear me, Anna?' The nurse speaks loudly, enunciating every syllable as though testing the shape of them in her mouth.

I nod, not wanting the sandpaper to scratch the walls of my throat again.

'Anna, my name's Fran, I'm one of the nurses here. Do you know where you are?'

I shake my head. I am in a hospital, that much is clear. But I do not know where, which one.

'You're in Charing Cross Hospital, in Hammersmith. Do you remember what happened?'

The question snags in my mind, like the sleeve of a jumper caught on a rusty nail. I close my eyes, search for the drawer containing the answer to the nurse's question.

'Anna? Do you know why you're here?'

Opening my eyes, the skin tightens across my forehead. Looking at the nurse, then at the man standing behind her, fear pools in the back of my throat.

I do not know why I am here.

Air sucks in through my lips, leaks out into the mask covering my nose, my mouth. Particles of moisture settle on my skin: damp and hot. I search in my mind for words to form an explanation but find only a blank slate.

The nurse smiles. 'Don't worry. You were involved in a road traffic accident earlier today. You've been unconscious for . . . just over four hours. But you're awake now, so that's a really good sign. Let's take a look at you, shall we?'

She bustles around me – shining a light in my eyes, pushing buttons on the monitor, writing notes on a clipboard – but I cannot concentrate on what she is doing because there is something amiss and I do not know what it is, only that there is a void in my head, a vacant space that I sense was once full but has now been emptied. It is a feeling of being untethered from my thoughts, as though something was stolen from me while I was sleeping and I do not know what it was or how to get it back.

'That's all looking fine. Your blood pressure and pulse are good, and your pupils aren't dilated. How does your head feel – pretty sore, I imagine?'

There is such heaviness in my head I am not sure where the weight ends and the pain begins. I nod, and my brain seems to lurch from one side of my cranium to the other.

'And what about your vision? Any blurriness?'

I blink to be sure, slide my eyes slowly from left to right, manage a meagre shake of the head.

'Okay, well, don't try to sit up just yet. Let's take the oxygen mask off and see how that feels.'

She slides a hand beneath my head, lifts the mask from my face, cool air rushing to meet my skin.

'Is that okay?'

My head is too heavy to nod again. I pull my lips towards reassurance, blink forcibly by way of response. The nurse's eyes return to the monitor, studying the numbers, and she writes again on the clipboard.

'Is she going to be okay?' The anonymous man stands at the end of my bed, his voice hesitant, cautious.

'There's nothing immediately concerning. All her vital signs look good. But she's had a significant concussion so we'll want to keep her under observation for a while.' The nurse turns back to me. 'I'll get the doctor to come and look at you now. Try not to worry – you're over the worst.'

The nurse disappears through the blue curtain. The man steps towards the side of the bed, takes hold of my hand, raises it to his lips. I snatch my hand free, not wanting this stranger to touch me, aware suddenly of my vulnerability beneath the thin hospital gown and stark white single sheet. 'Who are you?' The words scrape at my throat, as if hauling their way up the scree slope of a mountain.

The man looks at me with mournful eyes, breathes deeply before replying. 'It's me, Anna. I'm your husband.'

I stare at the face of the man leaning over me – the lines around his eyes, the thick eyebrows, the firm slant of his nose – and panic tightens its grip around my throat.

I have no recollection of ever seeing him before.

LIVVY

BRISTOL

'*Happy Birthday dear Bea-ee,*
   Happy Birthday to you!'

Livvy looked around the gastropub table at a dozen of her sister's closest friends, Bea sitting at the head, basking in the attention.

A hand rested gently on the nape of Livvy's neck, and she turned, found Dominic leaning towards her. He whispered in her ear. 'You look beautiful. You should wear your hair up more often. It really suits you.' He kissed her, just above her collarbone, his breath warm against her skin.

'Honestly, you two. Most couples forget how to be affectionate the moment they have kids. You're still like a pair of newly-weds. It's very cute.' Bea's oldest school friend, Sara, smiled at them.

'What can I say? I'm a very lucky man.' Dominic stretched an arm across the back of Livvy's chair, rested his hand on her shoulder. 'Livvy's my rock, my soulmate and my conscience all rolled into one.'

'Stop! You're making me blush.'

'Take the compliment, Livvy.' Sara thanked the waiter as he removed her plate. 'It's rare to see people our age as loved up as you two. It's a good reminder to the rest of us not to get too complacent.'

Livvy turned to look at Dominic, thought about how much her life had changed in the past eighteen months.

Almost two years ago, she had sat on the sofa in Bea's flat, grieving the end of her previous relationship. For five years she had been convinced that she and Tom would one day get married, have children, grow old together. But then Tom had announced his desire for them both to give up work, go travelling overseas indefinitely, and when Livvy had told him she wasn't keen – she loved her job and didn't want to derail her career – Tom had accused her of being unadventurous, had said he'd never seen a long-term future for them anyway. He'd moved out within days, and Livvy had been left with the fear that she might never – having turned thirty-seven earlier that year – get married or have children.

Three months later, she had been attending a conference on sustainable construction, representing the environmental think tank where she worked, when a man – tall, silver streaks in his hair, a slightly weather-beaten face – had struck up a conversation with her. His name was Dominic, he was a structural engineer, and over the course of the weekend he had repeatedly stopped to engage her in conversation.

On the final evening of the conference, he had sought her out, asked if she'd like to have dinner with him the following week. Their first date had been at a Michelin-starred tapas restaurant, Dominic having remembered Livvy mentioning her love of Spanish food.

Everything with Dominic had been uncomplicated from the outset. There had never been any fears about whether he was going to call, whether or not she would see him again. He had worn his heart on his sleeve, made it abundantly clear how much he liked her. His attentiveness was unlike anything she'd experienced before.

He'd listened intently to everything she'd had to say and asked questions in order to hear her opinions, not – like so many other men she knew – so that he could glaze over until it was his turn to speak again. His genuine interest in her thoughts and feelings had been almost revelatory.

By their third date, they had begun to confide in one another with an intimacy that belied the length of their acquaintance. Dominic was charming, funny and emotionally honest, and the ten-year age gap between them was barely noticeable.

But discovering she was pregnant twelve weeks into their relationship had not been part of the plan. It had been Bea to whom Livvy had first turned, arriving at her flat one morning, panic-stricken and bleary-eyed. And it had been Bea who had advised caution. '*I know you've always wanted a child, but is this really the best way? Do you really want to tie yourself for the rest of your life to a man you hardly know? You could be co-parenting with him for the next eighteen years. That seems like a pretty big risk given you've only known him a few months.*'

That evening, Livvy had arrived at Dominic's two-bedroom Georgian house in Clifton, mouth dry, hands shaking, and delivered the news, fearing rejection. Instead, Dominic had wrapped his arms around her, reminded her that he loved her, and asked her to marry him.

Now, just over a year later, and with a six-month-old son, Livvy sometimes felt that she had packed more into the past eighteen months of her life than the previous eighteen years.

'Bea mentioned that you're going to be working away for a while, Dominic. How are you both going to manage that with a young baby?'

Dominic shrugged. 'It's not ideal, obviously, and I'm going to miss them both. But it's not forever. And we'll still have weekends together.' Dominic's smile was wide, encouraging, and Livvy tried not to think about the fact that tomorrow, Dominic would begin a new job that would take him away from her and Leo every week for the next four months.

'I'm sure it'll be fine. As you say, it's only temporary, and you're such a solid couple.' Sara took the napkin from her lap and laid it on the table. 'And Leo's still so young, he'll be fine.'

As if in Pavlovian response, Livvy glanced down at the screen of her phone, checked that there were no messages from her mum. It was the first time she'd ever left Leo for an evening. A few times recently, Bea had suggested that she and Livvy go out for dinner, but Livvy had wavered, wondered if it was too soon, and Dominic had reassured her there was no rush. She couldn't have missed tonight though; she hadn't missed a single one of Bea's birthday celebrations since they were children. And yet, even though she knew Leo would be fine with her parents, the experience of being apart from him was like having twine wrapped around her heart and tugged with gentle persistence.

Next to her, Dominic pushed back his chair, got to his feet, chimed his knife against his glass.

He smiled broadly, looked down one end of the table and then the other. 'I know you've all known Bea a lot longer than I have, but I just wanted to say that it's a real pleasure to be here tonight, celebrating my sister-in-law's birthday with you all. So please join me in raising a glass and wishing Bea the happiest of birthdays, and many more to come.'

Dominic raised his glass to a chorus of well-wishing. Livvy glanced across the table in time to see a tight smile stiffen the corners of her sister's lips. Disappointment twisted in Livvy's stomach. She didn't understand the tension between Dominic and Bea, wished they could like each other as much as she loved them both. But ever since Livvy had first introduced them sixteen months ago, she had been aware of an underlying friction between them, valiantly shrouded beneath exaggerated politeness.

Dominic sat back down, tilted his head towards Livvy. 'What do you think about heading off soon?'

'We can't leave before dessert.'

'Straight after then?' He kissed her cheek, skimmed a thumb across her bare knee. 'I'm sure Bea will understand, given the circumstances.'

Livvy felt a knot pull taut inside her chest at the thought of Dominic's departure the next day. 'Soon after, I promise.'

ANNA

London

The man looks at me, and I cannot tell whether he is angry or sad.

'Take a deep breath, my love. Don't get upset. Everything's going to be fine.'

I try to breathe but it is as though something is pressing down hard on my windpipe and I cannot get sufficient air into my lungs. There is a part of me that does not want to be instructed what to do by this man who claims to be my husband but whom I do not recall ever having seen before. I just want someone to explain why I am here and what is going on.

The curtain is pulled back and a young woman enters, hair knotted in a bun at the nape of her neck, stethoscope slung around the shoulders of her white coat.

'Mrs Bradshaw? My name's Dr Okonjo. I understand you've had a sustained period of concussion. How are you feeling now?'

The words reverberate in my ears, and my eyes dart towards the man who says he is my husband.

'My wife's very confused. She doesn't seem to know who I am. I'm not sure she remembers anything about what happened.'

Dr Okonjo turns towards the man. 'Mr Bradshaw?'

The man nods.

'It's very common for there to be some level of confusion after a head injury. Do you want to stand back and I can take a closer look?'

The man steps away from the bed, his back brushing against the curtain, a ripple undulating across its pleats. From somewhere outside the cubicle, a woman calls out for a nurse, her voice loud and aggressive, and something inside me cowers from the sound.

The doctor picks up the clipboard hanging at the end of my bed, reads whatever observations have been written about me, eyes darting across the page. Then she looks up, smiles, tucks the clipboard beneath her arm.

'Mrs Bradshaw, can you tell me what happened to you?'

The question crouches in my ears as if waiting to see what I will do with it. I understand its meaning but cannot get the part of my brain that needs to answer it – the part of me that must surely know the answer – to open up and let me in. It is as though there is an impenetrable black box in my head, like the flight recorder of a crashed plane, but it is locked and tightly sealed and there is no way for me to access it. 'The nurse told me I'd been in a car accident, but other than that . . . I don't know.'

'Don't worry. Can you tell me your full name?'

I look at the doctor, wonder if it is a trick question. 'Anna Bradshaw.' The name feels strange on my tongue, as though waiting for me to confess that the only reason I know it is because, between them, the nurse and the doctor have already told me.

The doctor glances down again at the notes, then back at me. 'That's good. And can you tell me your middle name?'

A thick fog swirls inside my mind and I am aware of panic eddying in my chest. I shake my head.

'That's fine. Can you tell me where you live?'

I close my eyes, implore my brain to hone in on whatever part of it holds that piece of information. But it is like stumbling in the dark, flailing for a switch to turn on the light, and finding nothing but a blank, empty wall beneath my fingers.

Opening my eyes, I tell the doctor that I am sorry, I can't remember.

Behind the doctor, the man stands with arms folded across his chest, an expression on his face that I cannot decipher.

'Not to worry. Can you tell me what year it is?'

Without any effort, the answer is there, as easily as if someone had written it on a piece of paper and handed it to me. The doctor smiles and I feel like a child passing a test.

'And what about the prime minister of the UK – can you tell me who that is?'

Again the answer materialises, as if by magic, and it seems almost miraculous to me that it should be waiting to be plucked from wherever it has been stored.

'That's excellent. Can you count backwards from twenty for me?'

I count with ease and it feels as though something is returning to me, as though words and thoughts are pulling into focus.

'What's this?' The doctor holds up a pen and I tell her what it is – correctly, I am sure.

'What date is Christmas Day?'

It is an easy question and I answer automatically, without any conscious processing of thought.

'That's great. And can you tell me your date of birth?'

I open my mouth to reply, wait for the date, the month, the year to tumble out, but nothing comes. Scrunching my eyes closed, I search in the darkness for some thread of memory, like Theseus in the Labyrinth securing a safe exit, but however diligently I hunt, there is nothing there.

The apology stings as I open my eyes.

'That's okay.' The doctor issues me with a sympathetic smile. 'Mrs Bradshaw, as the nurse has already told you, you were involved in a road traffic accident earlier today. You were the passenger in a car, driven by your husband . . .' She pauses, looks over her shoulder, confirming that the man standing behind her in navy blue trousers and a checked grey shirt is the man to whom I am married. 'I don't know the precise details – I'm sure your husband can tell you more – but you sustained a head injury, for which you've had a CT scan, and there's no visible damage. But you suffered a concussion and a period of unconsciousness. Now that you're awake, we'll find you a bed on a ward and keep you in overnight for observation. But there's nothing immediately to worry about, okay?'

I find myself nodding even as a sense of disquiet creeps across my skin.

'What about her memory? There must be something on the scan – some kind of damage to her brain – to explain why she can't remember anything?' The man has stepped forward, his voice filled with urgency.

The doctor clasps the clipboard to her chest. 'Issues with memory rarely show up on brain scans. But temporary amnesia is extremely common in cases of concussion. It's very encouraging that her semantic memory seems to be intact.'

'Semantic memory?' The man frowns and I notice the way the skin hooks over the corners of his eyes, as if ready to protect him from something he might not want to see.

'Semantic memory is recall of facts. Common knowledge, if you like. It's different to episodic memory, which is an individual's personal history.'

'And it's my wife's episodic memory that's been affected? That's why she doesn't know who I am?' There is a hairline fracture in the man's voice. I watch the rise and fall of his Adam's apple, watch him steady the emotion on his face just as someone might settle a distressed child.

The doctor glances down at me. 'Like I say, it's very common for concussion to be accompanied by some degree of confusion – memory loss being the most prevalent. It usually only lasts a few hours, so please try not to worry.'

There seems to be an ellipsis at the end of her speech and it is not until the man asks the question that I realise what is missing.

'But it could go on for longer?' His voice is low, as if not quite trusting that saying the words out loud will not jinx the answer.

There is a pause, into which a thousand possible permutations seem to fall.

'Let's not get ahead of ourselves. In my experience, there are as many iterations of concussion as there are patients. It really is a case of taking things hour by hour. Now, let me make a few calls and find you a bed on a ward. It may take a little time, so just get some rest. You're very welcome to stay with your wife, Mr Bradshaw.' Offering me one final, reassuring smile, she sweeps out of the cubicle, closing the curtain behind her.

There is a moment's stillness and then the man lowers himself onto the edge of the bed, the mattress dipping beneath his weight. 'I'm so sorry, my love. It should be me in that hospital bed, not you. I was the one driving when we crashed.'

The man – my husband – strokes the inside of my wrist with his thumb and it sends fresh waves of panic coursing through my veins. There is an instinct to wrench my hand away, as though there is heat in his fingers and I am at risk of getting burnt. I breathe deeply against the feeling, instruct myself to calm down, tell myself it is fine: the doctor has confirmed this man's identity. 'I don't even know your name.' The confession feels both dangerous and absurd. This man is my husband and yet I do not know his name.

The man hesitates and I try to read the sequence of expressions that flit across his face: bewilderment, hurt, fear I think, though I cannot be sure because there are no memories to guide me.

The cubicle curtain rustles behind him and he glances over his shoulder, then back at me, tries to raise his lips into a smile. 'Stephen. My name's Stephen.'

I say the name silently in my head, over and over, hoping the cadence of it will trigger a memory, or at least the echo of a memory. But there is nothing. Just a vast empty space where my memory must once have been.

LIVVY

BRISTOL

Leo's head rested against Livvy's clavicle, his cheek warm with sleep from his afternoon nap. Across the bedroom, Dominic folded newly ironed shirts with meticulous precision before placing them – buttons up, arms tucked beneath the chest as if on the shelves of a high-end tailor – into his suitcase.

'What's the traffic looking like?' Livvy's voice affected nonchalance even as the minutes until Dominic's departure ticked loudly in her ear.

Dominic grabbed his phone, checked Google Maps. 'Not too bad. Just under three hours. I know it's not ideal, heading off on a Sunday afternoon, but I think it would have been too risky, leaving tomorrow. In future, I promise I'll go at the crack of dawn on Monday morning.'

Livvy shook her head. 'Don't be silly. It makes sense to go this afternoon. The last thing you want is to be late on your first day.'

Dominic raised a playful eyebrow. 'Anyone would think you're not going to miss me.'

'Of course I'm going to miss you. It's going to be horrible without you.' She swallowed against the thought of five days and nights of solo parenting. Dominic hadn't even left yet but she could pre-emptively sense how empty the house would feel without him.

'I'm sorry. I didn't mean to be flippant. I know how hard it'll be looking after this one by yourself all week.' He stroked the top of Leo's head. 'You're being amazing. I know I couldn't have taken this job without your support. And I don't want you to think for a second that I don't appreciate it.' He held Livvy's gaze. 'I promise you can have a lie-in until lunchtime every weekend, okay?'

Livvy laughed. 'I'm not sure Leo will sign up to that.' She handed Dominic his book from the bedside table – a collection of philosophical essays by John Gray that he'd been ploughing through for weeks – and watched him slip it into the side pocket of his suitcase.

As Dominic squeezed the collection of toiletries into his wash-bag, Livvy recalled him telling her about the job eight weeks ago. He'd been so excited by the offer of a four-month contract as senior structural engineer on the building of a new out-of-town super-market in Sheffield and she'd understood immediately that it was a big role, too good an opportunity to turn down. They knew the weekly commute from Bristol would be challenging, but Livvy still had another four months' maternity leave before returning to work, and they'd both reasoned that if he was ever to take a job away from home, this was probably the best time.

'So what will you get up to while I'm away?'

Livvy flicked through the week in her mind, reassuring herself that she had sufficient activities to anchor her time. 'Baby sensory class tomorrow and playgroup at the children's centre on Thursday. I'll see Mum and Dad a couple of times, and Bea's coming over for dinner on Wednesday. You know my family – they'll all rally round.'

'Right, of course. Give them my love, won't you?'

There was the slightest strain in Dominic's voice, as though his words were being squeezed through the holes of a sieve, and Livvy silently berated herself for her insensitivity.

It had been their third date when Dominic had confided in her about his estrangement from his family. Livvy had been chatting breezily about her closeness to Bea, and about how much she loved living ten minutes away from her parents. Dominic had fallen silent, colour draining from his cheeks, and Livvy had paused, asked what was wrong. '*I'm sorry. It's not you. It's just hard, hearing about other people's happy families.*' He had stopped abruptly and Livvy had encouraged him to continue, asked him what he meant. He'd looked at her intently before the story had emerged. '*I didn't have the happiest of childhoods. My dad was . . . a bit of a tyrant. Everything had to be done his way. I can't remember a time when I didn't know that the best way to survive was to keep silent and hope he didn't really notice I was there. He made my life a living hell. And my mum was no help. She never stood up to him, never tried to protect me, even when he was violent.*' The bitterness in Dominic's voice had been sharp, astringent. '*I haven't seen them for almost thirty years. The day I left for university, I knew I'd never go back. I've barely had any contact with them since.*' He had paused, shaken his head. '*I never tell anyone about this usually. I don't know what's come over me today.*'

Sometimes, when Livvy looked back on that conversation now, she saw it as the first major turning point in their relationship: the moment their trust in each other had been cemented. It was as though Dominic had offered her a cross-section of his deepest traumas and had faith that she would handle it with care.

It hadn't been until three months later, when Livvy announced her pregnancy, that Dominic had confessed the reason he'd resisted becoming a parent until then: his fear that, in having a child, he would inadvertently become his own father. And yet Dominic was fantastic with Leo: loving and affectionate, engaged and nurturing, wanting to pass on his passions and interests to their son even at Leo's young age.

Ever since that first conversation about his parents, Livvy had been mindful never to press Dominic for more details. Since moving in with him, she'd been aware of Christmas and birthday cards arriving from his mother, of Dominic ripping them up and throwing them in the bin: not the bin under the kitchen sink but the bin outside the front door, as though even the shredded remains within the walls of their home were too close for comfort.

'Come here, little man. Are you going to miss your daddy this week? Because I'm going to miss you.' Dominic took Leo from her arms, held him against his chest. 'How about, next weekend, you and I go to the museum, look at the mummies, and I can teach you all about Egypt?'

Livvy laughed. 'He might be a bit young for lessons in ancient history just yet.'

'Nonsense! He'll love it, won't you?' Dominic raised Leo into the air, flew him over his head, making aeroplane noises, and Leo laughed, colour filling his cheeks.

Handing Leo back to Livvy, Dominic unplugged the phone charger from his side of the bed. 'That's the last thing I want to forget.' He smiled, wrapped the lead around the plug, tucked it between his socks and pants. Taking a final glance at the spreadsheet on which he'd listed everything he'd need, he zipped up the case. 'Come and see me off?'

With Leo wedged securely against her hip, Livvy followed Dominic down the wooden staircase, past seascapes and brooding skies that Dominic had photographed and hung on the walls long before Livvy had moved in.

'I'll video-call at seven on the dot every evening, okay? *And you, little man, need to make sure you're asleep so that Mummy can have a proper conversation.*' He placed the flat of his palm against Livvy's cheek. 'And I'll call every morning as well, okay? Eight o'clock, en route to the site.'

'I've already said, you don't have to phone twice a day. I know how busy you'll be.'

'Don't be silly, of course I will.' He smiled before a frown knotted across his forehead. 'Are you sure you're going to be okay?'

Livvy swallowed against the tightness in her throat. 'Honestly, we'll be fine. This little one will keep me busy.' She tickled Leo's tummy, watched him laugh, held on to him as he wriggled in her arms.

'Remember to bolt the front door at night. And you can put the burglar alarm on as well, just to be safe. But don't forget to turn it off before you go downstairs in the morning or the neighbours will be cursing you.' He smiled. 'I do know how lucky I am to have you.' He leant forward, kissed her, straightened up again as if bracing himself for an inspection. 'Right, I'd better get going. The traffic's only going to get worse on a Sunday afternoon. I love you.'

'I love you too.' Livvy pulled her lips into a wide, confident smile.

Picking up the suitcase, Dominic headed out to his car, put the case in the boot, lowered himself into the driver's seat. Starting the engine, he turned and waved before pulling away from the kerb.

Tightening her arms around Leo, Livvy held her son's hand, waved back. She watched the black Toyota Prius shrink until it turned the corner at the far end of the road and disappeared out of sight.

For a few seconds she stood still, watching, as if awaiting a magic trick in which Dominic's car might spring back into view like a rabbit pulled from a hat.

Turning to re-enter the house, she heard another car ignite its engine further along the quiet residential street. A blue Ford Fiesta drove towards her, and Livvy noticed the driver – an elderly lady with pure white hair, wearing a bright blue cardigan – staring at her as she neared. The car slowed as it passed, the driver's concentration flitting between the road and Livvy's front door, and for a moment their eyes locked. And then the elderly lady looked away, accelerated, and within seconds she had reached the end of the street and was gone.

For a few seconds, Livvy stood on the doorstep, contemplating Dominic's departure, thinking about the days ahead. And then she headed back inside, into the kitchen to start preparing Leo's dinner, and opened the BBC Sounds app to fill the room with the comforting music of Radio 2.

ANNA

LONDON

I glance up at the clock on the wall: five to two. In a few minutes, Stephen should arrive for visiting time. I am anxious for the seconds to move quickly, so numerous are the questions I have to ask him. Yesterday evening, as he sat with me in A&E, I was overwhelmed by the need for sleep, and awoke to find myself on the ward, the clock blinking into the darkness, telling me it was a little after midnight. This morning I stirred just before eight, my head still heavy as though someone had encased it in lead. Even now, there is effort in lifting it from the pillow, a constant pressure at my temples as if my brain is trying to squeeze into too small a space.

I close my eyes, try to expunge the pain, but it is like trying to shift concrete.

'Anna. Are you okay?'

I open my eyes and Stephen is standing beside my bed, holding a bouquet of pure white flowers – freesias, roses, gerberas, gladioli, their names coming back to me without a second thought – and he is smiling broadly, trying to mask the concern ploughing a series of furrows across his forehead. He looks tired, dark rings haunting the skin beneath his eyes, and I feel a stab of guilt that I may be the cause.

'It's me, Stephen. Do you remember me from yesterday?'

I nod, and a wave of relief washes across his face. There is relief for me too. Even though the doctor on his rounds this morning assured me that my short-term memory appears unscathed, I still worried that I might not recognise Stephen when he arrived, as though we are two adults on a blind date and our descriptions may not match reality.

For the first time I allow myself to examine my husband's face properly. It is a kind face. Handsome, I think, and I assume I must have believed so once if I married him. There are lines around his eyes and I do not know whether they have deepened in the hours since the crash. His expression is thoughtful, thin lips accentuating the strong line of his jaw.

Scrutinising Stephen's face, I realise something suddenly. 'Have you got a mirror?'

Stephen looks at me, confused.

'Please, I need a mirror. Can you find me one?'

Something shifts in Stephen's expression and he nods, tells me he'll be back in a moment. He returns with a small, square compact I assume he must have borrowed from one of the nurses.

I open it, bring it level with my eyes, look at my reflection for the first time since the crash.

The woman staring back at me is in her mid-thirties – older, perhaps, if her genes have been kind to her – and beyond the pale skin and anxious expression, she is, I think, attractive. Her chestnut hair is cut short, and there is something gentle in her face. It is the face of someone I would trust if I needed to call on the goodwill of a stranger.

Except the woman in the mirror is not a stranger. The woman in the mirror is me. And yet I would not have recognised myself had someone handed me a photograph.

The sense of dislocation is overwhelming and I part my lips, encourage the air in and out of my lungs.

'Shall we put this away?' Stephen does not wait for an answer as he prises the mirror from my fingers, snaps it shut, places it on the cabinet next to my bed. 'How did you sleep last night?'

'Really well, thanks. I slept for ages.'

'That's good. You need plenty of rest.'

There is a politeness to our interchange, like we are two strangers, each eager to make a good impression.

'And do you . . . Have any memories come back to you?' His question is hesitant, as though unsure it wants to be heard.

I shake my head, the knowledge of my impotence like a boulder lodged in my chest.

An expression I cannot read flashes across Stephen's face before he pulls his lips into a purposeful smile. 'Try not to worry. I'm sure they'll come back soon.' He pauses, holds out the bouquet of flowers to me. 'I brought you these.'

I do not know why my hands do not immediately reach out to take them, why I feel myself shrink from them.

'You've always loved white flowers and these are some of your favourites. I thought they might . . . help you remember.' He looks awkward suddenly, as though he had been standing on stable ground but has just lost his footing.

'They're lovely. Thank you.'

He pulls up a chair, sits down, puts the flowers on the slim cupboard beside my bed. 'Have any doctors been to see you today?'

I nod. 'Just one. He asked me more questions to assess my memory. I don't think I did very well.'

'I'm sure you did.'

Stephen smiles reassuringly, but I cannot help feeling that this situation is topsy-turvy, that my brain has got its priorities confused. Because the more I manage to recall impersonal things – the name of a queen, the year of the Battle of Hastings – the greater the frustration that I cannot remember information that really matters. Cannot remember how long I have been married, where I met my husband, why we fell in love. Cannot remember where we live, what our house looks like, how we spend our weekends. Cannot remember my work, my friends, my family. It feels like a cruel act of fate to be able to remember facts about people I will never meet, moments in history I have never experienced, when I cannot recall a single detail about my own life.

'So no one else has been to see you?'

I shake my head and then remember. 'The police came to talk to me.'

'The police? What did they want?'

I feel myself squirm as I recall the male officer's impatience with me. 'To know if I remembered anything about the crash.'

'And do you?'

I shake my head. 'I asked if they could tell me anything about it but they said they couldn't because their enquiries are ongoing.' It feels strange, having this quotidian conversation with Stephen, as though this is a normal Sunday and we are simply sharing our daily news. 'The female officer did say you were lucky to get away with only a few bruises. She said it often happens in car crashes – that the driver walks away unharmed.'

I did not mean to sound pointed, but Stephen looks sad, and I feel something snag deep inside me: a scooping out, an excavation, panic whistling through me like wind between the trees. A sense of being lost, unable to grasp hold of anything that might help steer me in the right direction. I close my eyes, force myself to breathe against the narrowing in my throat, implore myself to remember something that might help me find my way back to myself.

When I open my eyes, Stephen is watching me, and I feel self-conscious suddenly. 'How long have we been married?' The question blurts from my lips and I see the same expression on Stephen's face as when I confessed yesterday that I didn't know his name: hurt, anxiety and something else I cannot put a name to. 'I'm sorry. I just . . .' I try in my head to articulate this feeling of disorientation, as though I have been dropped in a foreign location and do not know my route home. 'I just can't remember.'

Stephen takes hold of my hand. 'Don't apologise. Ask me anything. All I want is for you to get better. And you will, I promise.' There is an earnestness in the way he speaks but also a trace of something else: a hint of doubt, like the faint remnant of an erased pencil mark, and I wish I hadn't heard it, that I could believe wholeheartedly this will soon be over.

Stephen rubs the pad of his thumb along my wrist and there is a powerful instinct to pull my hand away, thrust it beneath the hospital sheet. It is a feeling as impulsive as jerking my hand away from a naked flame. Guilt nettles my skin and I glance at Stephen, at the concern with which he is watching me, remind myself that he is my husband. He loves me, and intimacy like this is normal.

I study this man I do not recall marrying – his freshly ironed shirt, neatly clipped fingernails, gently tousled hair – and wonder what this must be like for him: to find himself married to a woman who does not remember who he is. I wonder what our marriage was like, thirty-six hours ago; whether we were happy, whether we were passionately in love or whether we had settled into a prosaic, comfortable rhythm of domestic life. I wonder whether we make each other laugh, whether we have the same interests, whether we are one of those couples who do everything together or lead largely independent lives.

Stephen continues to stroke my wrist, and I resist the urge to withdraw my hand.

'What do you want to know?'

I'm unsure how to answer. Because I know it is impossible for him to tell me everything. There is no way he can fill every blank page, no way he can narrate the detail of every thought, every feeling, every hope, every dream I've ever had. There is no way for him to remake me as I was before, reinstall my memory as one might reboot the hard drive of a computer. He cannot, I know, deliver me back to myself. And yet that is what I need him to do.

'Tell me everything about us. About our relationship. From the beginning.'

LIVVY

BRISTOL

Livvy closed Leo's bedroom door with a muffled click, tiptoed away, looked at her watch. Ten past one. She should have time before he woke to clear her emails: reply to friends, deal with some life admin, confirm her meeting at work next week to discuss her return to the office.

As she made her way down the stairs, her phone pinged in her back pocket and she pulled it out, opened a WhatsApp message from Dominic.

> *How are my two favourite people? Hope all's okay. Lots going on here. One of the architects made a mistake with some calculations and tried to pin the blame on me, but unsurprisingly I had all the paperwork to prove her wrong. Not a great end to the first week though. I miss you both. Let's try to make sure Leo's asleep when I get home tonight so we can have some proper time together. D x*

Livvy tapped out a swift reply, wanting Dominic to see it before he went offline and back to work.

Sorry it's stressful there. That's the last thing you need. We miss you too. I'll do my very best to get Leo down on time, but he doesn't always do as he's told! Can't wait to see you later. I love you. Xxx

She watched the two grey ticks turn blue, saw Dominic go offline, knew he'd phone or text when he was on his way home.

Entering the sitting room, she thought about the letter she'd written for him last weekend and slipped into the outside pocket of his suitcase before he'd left for his first week away: *The bed will be so empty without you. I hope you know how much I'll miss you.* He hadn't mentioned it until she'd raised it during their video call last night, and he'd apologised, told her his head had been so full of the new job that he'd forgotten to thank her. '*I loved it. Feel free to leave a surprise letter in my suitcase every week.*'

Livvy's eyes roamed over the clutter of toys strewn across the sitting room floor. Tidying away the finger puppets, wooden building blocks and cloth books, she wondered how she and Leo managed to make quite so much mess in a single morning. When she'd first moved in with Dominic just over a year ago, she'd loved how immaculately uncluttered his house was, with its impeccably co-ordinated furniture and subtle colour scheme. Her previous boyfriend, Tom, had lived in Livvy's flat for two years and she couldn't remember a single occasion he'd offered to clean up or hang out the washing. Sometimes she wondered why she'd put up with his laziness for so long and felt a quiet sense of relief that he'd broken up with her when he had. She still loved the tidiness of Dominic's house – their house – but sometimes it did feel like an uphill battle, trying to keep things in order with a six-month-old baby in tow.

Her phone pinged again and she glanced at the screen, saw a message from Bea.

Hey. Hope you're okay. I just bought two tickets for that Cuban jazz band we saw a few years ago – remember, that night we didn't get home until 3am and you were presenting at that conference the next morning! ☺ They're playing on the 8th at 9pm. Do you fancy it? I'm sure Mum and Dad will babysit. We are WAY overdue a proper night out! Xx

Livvy read the message, remembered the night her sister was referring to. She felt as though it belonged to a different life: pre-marriage, pre-motherhood, when she and Bea would hang out two or three nights a week. She was aware of a pang of nostalgia for those days, a sense of freedom she simply didn't have now.

Rereading the message, she thought about how much she'd love a night out with Bea. But with Dominic away, she knew it just wasn't practical. And these days, by nine p.m. she was invariably heading for bed.

Hey! That gig sounds fab and you're right, we are way overdue an evening out, but I'm just not sure I can at the moment. I'm sorry. We'll have a proper night out soon, I promise. Xxx

She sent the message, watched the ticks turn blue, saw that Bea was replying. She waited, thirty seconds, then a minute, wondering what kind of lengthy communication her sister was composing. And then a message appeared.

No worries. I'll see if Sara's free. Xx

It was short, terse, disproportionately brief given the time it had taken Bea to write it. Livvy was aware of a knot of tension in her stomach, guilt and self-justification vying for attention. She knew it must be odd for her sister – how the tenor of their relationship had changed since Livvy had got married and had Leo. Most of the time, Livvy couldn't decide if she felt guilty about it, or frustrated that sometimes Bea didn't seem to appreciate just how exhausting motherhood could be.

The doorbell chimed into the silence and Livvy jumped to her feet. She didn't want Leo to wake when he'd only just gone down for his nap.

Opening the door, she experienced a moment's confusion, like seeing an old school photograph and having only the vaguest recollection of a face.

Standing on the doorstep was an elderly lady with short white hair neatly blow-dried, her black patent shoes polished to the point of reflection. She wore a merlot cardigan over a cream blouse, and navy cotton trousers. It was only when the woman opened her mouth to speak that Livvy remembered where she'd seen her before: it was the woman from the blue Ford Fiesta that had dawdled past their house on Sunday afternoon.

'I'm sorry to bother you. I'm looking for Dominic.'

The woman was well-spoken, assertive, but there was something beneath the confidence, like a crack in a pane of glass not yet shattering but at risk, any moment, of doing so.

Livvy stepped onto the edge of the doorframe, pulled the door almost closed behind her. 'He's not here. Can I help you?'

There was a moment's hesitation. 'Are you his wife?'

Caution prickled the back of Livvy's neck. 'I'm sorry, who are you?'

The woman clasped one hand inside the other, kneaded her knuckles. 'My name's Imogen. I'm Dominic's mother.'

Livvy felt herself take an instinctive half-step back.

'You're Livvy, aren't you?'

Livvy was aware of a chill inching down her spine. 'How do you know my name?'

Imogen looked at her, unblinking. 'One of your neighbours was kind enough to tell me.' She held up the palms of her hands as if in a gesture of peace. 'I'm sorry. I know it's rude, just turning up like this, but I didn't know what else to do.'

Imogen kept her hands raised, and Livvy tried to steady her racing thoughts.

Dominic's mother was not what she'd imagined. When Dominic had spoken about her, Livvy had envisaged someone frail, feeble, like a baby bird fallen from its nest. Instead, the woman in front of her was tall – about five foot eight, a good couple of inches taller than Livvy – with broad, capable shoulders: swimmer's shoulders, Livvy thought. There was a certain vigour to her that belied the crevices lining her face.

'I don't want to cause any trouble. It's just . . . I urgently need to get hold of Dominic and he's not replying to any of my messages.'

Livvy tried to recalibrate what she knew about Dominic's mother with the woman standing in front of her. Dominic hadn't mentioned that she'd been in touch. As far as Livvy knew, the only contact from her came twice a year, with the Christmas and birthday cards that found their way straight to the bin.

'It's his father. He's very ill. He's in hospital . . . he doesn't have long left. I think Dominic should come to say goodbye.'

The news landed with a thud. Whenever Livvy thought about Dominic's parents, she always imagined them in their thirties and forties, the age they'd been when they were making Dominic's life a misery; not elderly people at the end of their lives. 'I'm really sorry to hear that. But like I say, Dominic's not here at the moment.'

Imogen paused, as if weighing something up in her mind. 'The thing is, I can't get through to Dominic. I was hoping that you might pass on the message. That perhaps you might be able to persuade him to visit?'

There was an upward inflection at the end of Imogen's sentence and yet somehow it sounded less like a question and more like a statement. And suddenly Livvy understood the real purpose of Imogen's visit. 'Did you know Dominic wasn't here? You saw him leave on Sunday, didn't you?'

There was a moment's fluster, a crimson blush in Imogen's cheeks. And then the determined composure returned as though she had wiped the embarrassment clean from her face. 'I just want to be sure that Dominic knows, that he understands this may be his last chance to heal the rift between them.'

His last chance to heal the rift. Livvy felt her hackles rise, assumed this was what Dominic meant by his mother's capacity for denial. 'I'm sorry, but it's not my place to get involved. How Dominic deals with his family is up to him. I have to go.'

Livvy took a step back, began to swing the door closed, felt a hand resisting the pressure.

Imogen was as close to the threshold as it was possible to be without actually stepping inside, the flat of her palm pushing against the door. 'You must understand. I've got a grandchild I've never been allowed to meet, who I didn't even know existed until I saw you standing on the doorstep last week. My only grandchild. Can you imagine how that felt? To discover by accident that I'm a grandmother and that my son didn't see fit to tell me?' Imogen's voice was belligerent and imploring at the same time, her hand still pressed firmly against the wooden door.

Livvy's fingers gripped tighter around the Yale lock. She thought about the night Dominic had confided in her about the misery of his childhood. She had seen the cost of him disclosing even the barest outline of what had happened, understood that he had spent years working through his trauma in order to form a relationship of his own. And now here was his mother, standing on their doorstep, complaining that she hadn't been welcomed into her grandson's life.

Livvy felt her voice harden, consonants solidifying in her mouth. 'It's not my place to get involved. It's up to Dominic whether he replies to you or not.'

'But you must understand, as a mother, wanting to know what's happening in your child's life, whatever's passed between you?' Imogen slid the black leather handbag from her arm, pulled out a piece of paper. 'Please will you speak to him? You might be able to persuade him. It's important he sees his father before it's too late.' She held out the piece of paper and Livvy glanced down, saw a phone number written on it, realised that Dominic's mother had it all planned: the visit while Dominic was away, the emotional blackmail, the piece of paper prepared with her phone number so that there was no chance of the door being shut in her face as she scribbled it out.

Livvy shook her head. 'I can't. This is between you and Dominic. I'm sorry.' She did not wait for a response as she took a step back and pushed the door closed, hand on the lock until she was sure it had clicked into place.

Running upstairs, she tiptoed into Leo's bedroom with a sudden yearning to check on him. Finding him sound asleep, she left his room and made her way back down the stairs.

Passing the open door to the hallway, she noticed something on the grey coir mat. Bending down, she picked it up, turned it over, heard herself inhale sharply.

A phone number was written in careful handwriting on a piece of plain white paper. The same piece of paper Imogen had offered her just minutes before and which Livvy had refused.

Crumpling it into a ball to put it into the bin, she headed into the kitchen, trying to work out how on earth she would tell Dominic that his mother had made her first impromptu visit in over thirty years.

ANNA

LONDON

Stephen pauses. There is that hesitancy again in his eyes, as though he does not know what to say. Or perhaps I am misreading his expression. Perhaps it is not hesitancy, perhaps it is disappointment.

Clearing his throat, he studies my face as if assessing whether he is about to do the right thing. He glances around the ward, where the other patients are already deep in conversation with their visitors, before turning back to me, his lips inching into a reassuring smile, and I see what perhaps first attracted me to him: there is a quiet confidence about him, an air of competence. A feeling that here is a man you would want with you if you were stranded on a desert island. A man who can take control of a difficult situation and know what needs to be done.

He holds my gaze as he begins to speak, and I listen as he relays the story of our relationship. How we met not long after I graduated, got married six years later, have been happily married now for twelve years. He tells me about his job as a university lecturer, about our two-bedroom cottage in north-west London, about our weekend walks around Hampstead Heath, Richmond Park, Kew Gardens. Stephen talks, and it is like listening to an audiobook or a story on the radio: I am intrigued by events, want to know what happens next, but I have no greater affinity with the details than if they were the lives of fictional characters. I wait for something to spark a recollection: a phrase, a sentence, or even just a word to unlock some fragment of memory. But the story of our marriage might just as well be a novel I've picked up in a bookshop, or a drama I'm watching on TV: however hard I try to translate the events Stephen is describing into images of real life – my life – I find myself stumbling in the dark, not even a pinprick of light to help guide my way.

'I brought this to show you.'

From a brown leather messenger bag, Stephen pulls out a white wooden frame, hands it to me. Behind the glass is an arrangement of dried white flowers. 'They're from your wedding bouquet. Dendrobium orchids. You've had this up on the wall in our bedroom for the past twelve years. I thought it might help you remember.'

I stare at the flowers – all the moisture long since evaporated – and scour my brain for some wisp of memory. But if there's anything there, it doesn't want to be found.

I shake my head, cannot look Stephen in the eye. He rests a hand on my shoulder and I flinch instinctively, watch him withdraw his hand as though he has placed it in a hive of bees. Turning to face him, I expect to see frustration but find only sadness.

He leans forward in his chair but is careful to keep his hands away from the edge of the bed. 'I know this must be so hard for you, my love. You don't remember who I am. I'm sorry – I should be more sensitive to that. Would it help if I showed you some photos of us together?'

It is only now he says it that the fear dares to make itself known to me: Stephen has told me that he's my husband, the hospital has confirmed it, but a part of me still cannot trust in the fact when I cannot remember for myself.

I nod, and Stephen pulls out his mobile phone, swipes at the screen, flicks for a few seconds, and then turns the phone to face me. 'This was last year, for our anniversary – we had a weekend away in Bath.'

From Stephen's phone gleams a selfie of the two of us together, Stephen's arm around my shoulders. The sun is warm on our faces and behind us the houses of a narrow residential street peter out into the distance.

'It was just a couple of nights but the weather was great and we had a lovely time visiting the baths and the Abbey.'

I feel his eyes hot on my face, but I cannot tear my gaze away from the photo. It is like looking at a parallel reality, one which I know must be real, but which seems to exist in a different realm of experience, one I cannot grasp hold of.

He takes the phone away, scrolls some more, turns it back towards me. 'These are just some silly ones from a while back, taken at home.'

It is a portrait of me, pouting like a model in a magazine – clearly tongue-in-cheek – in front of a well-stocked bookcase.

Stephen bends his head towards mine, looks at the photo with me, swipes to the next, and then the next, all variations on the same theme. In the last one, Stephen joins me in the frame, both of us adopting faces of mock surprise, and I cannot decide whether these photos are encouraging or dispiriting – whether they speak of a happier time to which we will soon return, or whether they are a stark reminder of all I have temporarily lost.

'Are you okay? Is it too much?'

I shake my head, swallow against the tightness in my throat. 'I'm fine.' I hear the uncertainty in my voice, look down at my nails, bitten to the quick, wonder what it says about me that I still chew my fingernails.

'It must be so overwhelming. I thought it might help, showing you things, but perhaps it's too soon.' His voice is soft, placatory, the voice one might use to comfort a frightened child separated from their mother in a department store.

'I'm sorry. I want to remember, I really am trying . . .' My voice fractures and I do not know if it is from frustration or fear. I feel cut adrift, as though set loose in a dinghy in the middle of the ocean with no means of navigating my way back to land.

I look down at my hands and a thought jars in my head. 'Why aren't I wearing a wedding ring?'

Stephen follows my gaze down to my bare fourth finger. 'That's odd. You never take it off usually.' He frowns, thinks for a moment. 'Perhaps the nursing staff took it when you had your scan. Don't worry, I'm sure they've got it safely stored somewhere. I'll speak to them for you, get it back.'

I touch the bare skin of my finger, wonder whether, when my ring is returned, it will be like a talisman, restoring the memory of my marriage to me.

I glance across at Stephen, cannot hold back the question any longer. 'What happened?' Just two words and yet they feel dangerous in my mouth.

Stephen's head tips slightly to one side, a pair of vertical ridges sculpting the skin between his eyebrows. 'What do you mean?'

A part of me is unsure I want to know. I do not want to cast aspersions, have no interest in apportioning blame. But it feels important to understand the circumstances, to comprehend the events that have brought me here. 'The accident. What actually happened?'

Stephen's eyes flit down towards his hands, fingers interweaved as if in prayer. 'We were driving along the A4 and a lorry careened into our lane. I had to swerve to avoid it, and we mounted the pavement and smashed into a brick wall. It all happened so quickly . . .'

'Was anyone else hurt?'

Stephen shakes his head. 'Thankfully not. But it should be me in that bed, not you. I was the one driving.' He squeezes my hand. 'I'm so sorry. I hate seeing you like this.'

I return the squeeze, and it feels odd to be comforting a man with whom I must have shared much greater intimacies in the past and yet who is now little more than a stranger. 'It's not your fault. It sounds like it could have been a lot worse if we'd collided with the lorry.'

He responds with a grateful smile and we sit in silence as I try to pull some thread of recollection from my memory. But the imagined scene in my head is like a Hollywood movie, all screeching brakes and crunching metal, and I cannot locate any tangible detail.

In the cubicle opposite, a woman wipes the mouth of an elderly man I assume to be her father, and there is such tenderness in the gesture that it jolts something in me: not a memory but a visceral sensation of love and affection. Turning back to Stephen, the words spring from my lips before I know they are coming. 'What about my parents? My family? Can you tell me about them?'

There is a pause, a stillness, an almost imperceptible twitch of the muscles across Stephen's forehead. 'What do you remember about your parents?'

The question sits in my head, waiting to see what I will do with it. I close my eyes, peer into the darkness, try to shine a light on images of people who must be there, hiding in the shadows. But I find nothing.

Opening my eyes, I squint against the glare of the sun, shake my head. 'I don't remember anything.' It is there again, that feeling of excavation, as though the contents of my chest have been quarried, leaving behind an empty, gaping void.

Stephen inhales a long, deep breath, lets it out again. Light from the window moves across his face and I notice the flecks of silver in his stubble, like crystals of hoar frost on the branch of a tree. Time seems to expand as I wait for him to reply, clinging to the hope that, when he does, his response will unlock the riddle of my amnesia.

The shrill demand of a telephone clamours in the muted air. Stephen glances at the screen of his mobile, then back at me. 'I'm really sorry. I have to take this. I won't be long.' He does not wait for a reply before hurrying out of the ward. I watch him go, through the glass window, pressing the phone to his ear as he heads along the corridor and out of sight.

I close my eyes, think about all Stephen has relayed, hoping that if I concentrate enough on the details he has told me – about the evening we met at a piano recital at Wigmore Hall, about the floor-length silk dress I wore on our wedding day, about our honeymoon in Florence – I may begin to remember for myself. But my mind is like a black hole into which every personal memory has been sucked and I cannot imagine when or how they might be retrieved. I think about Stephen, about how patient he is being with all my questions, and there is a moment's panic about whether he will stick by me in sickness and in health.

'Anna?'

Opening my eyes, I find the doctor from this morning's rounds standing by my bed.

'How are you feeling?'

It is the standard question, one which should be easy to answer. But when I search for words to describe my state of mind, I find only a convenient platitude. 'Okay, I think.'

'Good. As you know, the scans on your brain have been clear, so medically you're fine. I know there are still some issues with your memory, and it might take a few days or even weeks for that to be fully restored. But I don't want to keep you here any longer than necessary, and I suspect that getting back home will aid your recovery much better than staying here. The best place for you right now is in familiar surroundings.'

There is an ellipsis at the end of his sentence, but I hear the unspoken words anyway. 'You're sending me home?'

The doctor nods, smiles, as though he is the emissary of good news. 'There are a few final tests I want to run, which might not happen until later today, but we should be good to send you home in the morning.'

Panic flutters in my chest. I am not yet ready to go home. I don't even know where home is. The only world I know is here, inside the hospital, and I do not want to leave.

Stephen walks back into the ward, anxiety flitting across his eyes when he notices the doctor beside my bed. 'Is everything okay?' His cheeks are flushed, his voice slightly breathless.

'I was just giving Anna the good news that she can go home tomorrow.'

I see my own panic reflected in Stephen's face and it dawns on me that the prospect of my homecoming must be equally unnerving for him. Yesterday morning he had a wife who could remember the dress she wore on her wedding day. Today he is married to someone who doesn't know how old her husband is or when they will be celebrating his next birthday.

'So soon? Are you sure she's ready?'

The doctor appears not to hear the doubt in Stephen's voice, or perhaps chooses to ignore it. 'Absolutely. The best place for Anna now is at home.'

The doctor continues, advising on what I should expect over the coming days: the importance of rest, the avoidance of sport, the need to refrain from driving a car, and I realise I have no idea whether I even have a licence. Looking down at my charts, he informs me not to drink alcohol or take drugs, suggests limiting time spent on computers, tells me I should expect the headaches to continue for a few days at least, possibly longer, and to manage them with regular painkillers. His monologue is so well rehearsed there is no space between his words for me to know what questions I want to ask, let alone voice them.

The doctor pulls some leaflets from a beige cardboard folder, hands them to me. 'There's a lot of information here about recovering from a head injury and what to expect over the coming days and weeks. And there are details of various organisations who can help. I've put in an urgent referral for a short course of therapy to aid with your memory loss and deal with any issues that may arise from the amnesia.'

'Do you really think that'll be necessary?' Concern bleeds through Stephen's voice. 'Yesterday the doctor told us the amnesia would probably only last a few hours.'

The doctor holds Stephen's gaze for a few seconds before turning back to me. 'To be honest, waiting lists for therapeutic services are pretty horrendous at the moment. It may well be that your memory is fully restored before the first appointment comes through, but at least we've got you in the system in case you need it.' Pulling back the cuff of his sleeve, he glances at his watch. 'I'm sorry, I need to get going. Any more questions, don't hesitate to ask one of the nurses. But you're doing really well, Anna.' He pats my arm and offers a reassuring smile before turning and walking away.

Stephen moves into the space where the doctor had been, lowers himself onto the edge of the bed. 'It's great that you're well enough to come home.' He does not sound convinced, or perhaps I am projecting my own anxieties onto him. 'But if I'm going to take tomorrow off work to collect you, I'm afraid I'll need to crack on with a few things this afternoon.'

I pull the stiff, white bed sheet high across my chest. 'Of course. I'm sorry. I don't want to make you miss work.'

'Don't be silly. It's fine. But there's just some stuff I'll need to get done today if I'm not going in tomorrow. I'll talk to the nurses, find out what time I can take you home.' He places a hand against the side of my face, leans forward, kisses my forehead. His stubble is rough against my skin, somewhere between a prickle and a scratch. It is the most intimate interaction we've had since the accident and my whole body stiffens in response. I'm certain Stephen must be able to feel the tension in my muscles, the rigidity of my limbs. I want to apologise, tell him that I don't mean it, that it just all feels so new.

'Get some rest, okay? And I'll see you tomorrow.' He smiles, eyes crinkling at the edges, and I watch him leave, heart gently thudding at the thought that within twenty-four hours I will be going home to a house I cannot remember with a man I do not recall marrying.

LIVVY

BRISTOL

Livvy watched the emotions chase each other across Dominic's face: shock, disbelief, alarm.

'I can't believe my mother was actually here, on our doorstep. Asking you to persuade me to visit my dad. The audacity of it, after all they've put me through . . .' His voice trailed off and he rested his elbows on his knees, sunk his head into his hands.

Livvy sat beside him on the sofa, the flat of her palm on his back, knowing he needed time to absorb the information.

He had been home less than fifteen minutes from Sheffield. All afternoon Livvy had played the conversation with Imogen over in her mind, wondering how best to tell Dominic: whether to let him settle in after his first week away, or get the news over with quickly, like the swift ripping off of a plaster. She had made sure Leo was asleep by the time Dominic arrived and, in the end, the decision had been taken from her: he had known, immediately, that something was wrong, had pressed her to tell him what it was, and she had confessed the story of his mother's visit.

'I'm sorry you had to go through that. My mother should never have put you in that position.'

Livvy rubbed a hand across Dominic's shoulders. 'It's not your fault.' She paused, wondering whether he might be ready for questions. 'So, did you know your dad was ill? I wasn't sure if you'd seen her messages.'

Dominic did not lift his head from where it was pitched in his hands. 'I'd seen them.'

Livvy waited a moment, needing to tread delicately this tightrope between her desire to help him and his need to process events. 'Why didn't you tell me? I hate to think of you dealing with that on your own.' She felt the rise and fall of his shoulder blades beneath the weight of her hand.

'I'm sorry. I should have. It's just . . . My parents have infected so much of my life, I didn't want them infecting us too.' He breathed deeply, emptied his lungs.

Livvy contemplated how she would feel if her father were in hospital, dying. It was unthinkable that she would not want to be by his side, ensuring that he knew how much she loved him. And the knowledge that Dominic's experience was so different from hers made her wish that she could take his past away and rewrite it as a different, happier story. 'I know you have really complicated feelings about your dad and I completely understand why you haven't replied to your mum's messages. But putting aside what's best for them, do you think it might be good for *you* to see him before he dies?'

Dominic raised his head, stared at her as if perhaps she hadn't understood anything he'd said about his family. 'Absolutely not. There's *no* way I'm going to see him.'

Livvy allowed herself a beat, knew the conversation ahead was littered with landmines. 'I don't mean because your mum's asked you, or for your dad's sake either.' She reminded herself of the articles she'd read online that afternoon, about coping with the demise of an estranged or abusive parent. 'The overriding memory you have of your dad is this all-powerful, tyrannical man. And that's the version of him you're still carrying inside you. But that's not who he is any more. He's an old man. He's frail and weak. And perhaps if you saw him like that, it might . . . I don't know . . . take away some of his power.'

Dominic was shaking his head before she had even finished speaking. 'I can't do it.'

Livvy consciously softened her voice. 'I can only imagine how difficult this must be for you, and obviously I don't know everything that went on in your childhood. I'm just trying to think about what's best for you.'

When Dominic spoke, his voice was low, flat. 'He doesn't deserve a visit from me. Neither of them do.' He drew in a deep breath, looked at Livvy and then away again. 'One day, when I was twelve, I got home from school to find that my parents had cleared out my bedroom of everything I'd ever owned.'

He stopped abruptly, and his words took a moment to settle in Livvy's head. 'What do you mean?'

Dominic rubbed at a small stain on his trouser leg. 'They'd got rid of everything. Thrown it all away. My books, my toys, my Lego, all the Airfix models I'd spent hours making and painting. Everything except my clothes – all gone.'

The explanation stumbled in Livvy's mind, like a stuttering car engine that wouldn't ignite. 'Why? Why on earth would anyone do that?'

Dominic raised his shoulders to his neck and back down again, the movement slow, laborious, as though it had taken an inordinate effort. 'I don't know.'

'But they must have given you a reason?'

Dominic shook his head. 'My mum wouldn't tell me. When I asked her, she just said, "*You don't need any of that any more.*" Completely deadpan. She wouldn't even look at me. I remember tugging on her sleeve, crying, begging her to tell me why they'd done it, but she just stood there, like a rod of iron, and wouldn't tell me anything.' Dominic exhaled slowly through a small gap in his lips.

'But that's . . . barbaric. Why would anyone do that, least of all to their own child?'

Dominic shook his head. 'I still don't know to this day. I asked my mum so many times when I was still living at home and she just refused to tell me. She said once that she'd go to her grave without ever telling me the reason why.'

The story swam in Livvy's head, too restless to stay still. 'What about your dad? Did you ever ask him?'

'I wouldn't have dared. I'd have probably got a beating just for daring to ask.'

Livvy tried to imagine the scene: a twelve-year-old boy discovering that all his worldly possessions had been disposed of, and the sense of bewilderment when nobody would tell him why. 'I'm so sorry. I can't imagine how awful that must have been. Or why any parent would be so unspeakably cruel.'

Dominic shrugged. 'It wasn't as if that was the only cruel thing they ever did.' He paused, and Livvy resisted the urge to fill the silence. 'Every meal was like an endurance test. My dad couldn't abide people talking during dinner so we had to eat in silence, every single night. I'd get sent to my room if I so much as coughed. And I can't remember a time my mum ever tucked me up in bed, or read me a story. They were both just so . . . cold. I learnt to take care of myself and tried to avoid my dad's rages.'

Livvy reached out, took hold of Dominic's hand. 'Why have you never told me all this before?'

There was a small shake of Dominic's head, so slight she might have missed it had she blinked. 'I think I was ashamed.'

'Of what?'

47

For a few moments, Dominic said nothing, and when he began to speak, he kept his eyes trained firmly on the rainbow of spines lining the bookshelves. 'It's not easy to acknowledge that your parents hated you so much that they wanted to eradicate every trace of you.'

Livvy moved closer to Dominic, folded her body against his. 'Whatever your parents did, it wasn't your fault. You were a child. They were supposed to protect you and they failed. You have nothing to feel ashamed of.' She felt him wince beneath her embrace. 'What's wrong?'

He shook his head. 'Nothing. I walked into a piece of machinery on site and whacked my shoulder. I'm fine – just a bit bruised.' He offered her a valiant half-smile. 'I'm sorry – I didn't mean to dump all this on you on a Friday night when we haven't seen each other all week. It's not exactly the ideal homecoming, is it?'

'Don't apologise. It's your mum's fault for turning up unannounced. I didn't know whether I should even tell you, but I didn't think I could keep something like that from you.'

Dominic squeezed her hand. 'Of course you were right to tell me. But can you promise me one thing?' He paused. 'The stuff I've just told you, about how my parents treated me. Can you promise to keep that to yourself?'

'Of course.'

'I mean, don't tell anyone, not even your parents, or your sister.' He hesitated. 'I've never told anyone those stories before. And the thought of people talking about them behind my back . . . I honestly can't imagine ever telling anyone other than you.'

'I won't say a word, I promise. I'm just so sorry you had to go through all that.'

A faint murmur emerged from the baby monitor and Livvy glanced at the screen, watched Leo turn his head from one side to the other.

'So what do you want to do about your mum? Just ignore her and hope she doesn't come back?'

'I think so. I don't want to give her the oxygenation of contact – it's what she wants, having me enmeshed in her life again. If she doesn't get a response, she's more likely to leave us alone.'

Leo cried out through the monitor. Livvy looked apologetically at Dominic. 'I should go and see to him. He's clearly not going to self-settle. Will you be okay?'

Dominic nodded and Livvy headed upstairs, lifted Leo out of his cot. As she held her son in her arms and rocked him back to sleep, she thought about the events Dominic had just described – like scenes from a horror film which, once viewed, could never be forgotten – trying and failing to understand how any parent could enact such cruelty on their child.

ANNA

LONDON

I stand in the centre of the sitting room, waiting for memories to emerge. I sense Stephen watching me, but I do not turn to look at him, am not yet ready to confront the weight of his expectation.

The sitting room of our house is small, slightly gloomy, despite a bay window at one end and a second window onto a small patio garden at the other. The floors are wooden, somewhat scuffed. Neatly packed bookcases fill the alcoves. A sofa and two armchairs are arranged around a cast-iron fireplace as if in preparation for a cold winter's night, but they seem too big for the room somehow, as though they have fantasies of belonging to a much larger house. And there's something austere about the room, unhomely almost, though I cannot put my finger on what it is.

'Anna?'

I shake my head. There is nothing I remember about this room. No spark of memory. The house I have stepped into might as well be the home of a stranger.

'Come through to the kitchen.' Stephen's voice hovers in a hinterland between encouragement and disappointment. He cups a hand around my elbow, guides me towards the door like I am an elderly relative unsteady on her feet.

The kitchen is a sea of white: white cupboards, white work surfaces, white tiles. Even the floorboards have been painted white. Only the oak table pushed against one wall breaks up the visual monotony. Every inch of the room is sparkling clean and the effect is almost dazzling, like stepping off an aeroplane into the glare of foreign sun. It strikes me that I cannot imagine cooking in here, cannot imagine daring to chop tomatoes or slice a loaf of bread for fear of creating a mess. And then the thought springs to mind that I do not know whether I am a competent cook, whether it is something I enjoy doing or if it is a daily chore. Whether, in fact, it is Stephen who takes responsibility for our meals.

'How do you feel?'

My breath quickens and I wish I were able to respond truthfully without disappointing him. 'A bit . . . strange.' It is an understatement, but I do not know how to describe this sense of disorientation.

'Shall I show you upstairs? Perhaps you'll remember something up there?' His voice is hesitant and I sense his optimism dwindling.

I nod, and he leads me up the stairs, highlighting the narrowness of the tread and the extra lights in the hallway to mitigate against falls in the dark, as if he is an estate agent and I a potential buyer.

At the top of the stairs, a square hatch looms above our heads.

'The loft ladder's pretty treacherous – I need to get someone to come and fix it – so don't venture up there if I'm not here.' He ushers me into the bathroom directly ahead, another room all in white: a toilet, a sink, a shower over the bath. Functional, compact.

Next door is a tiny bedroom – the second bedroom, Stephen tells me – with a window overlooking the patio garden. The houses that back onto ours are so close that I can see a family photograph

– a man, a woman, a babe in arms – hanging on a neighbour's wall. Our second bedroom is full of cardboard boxes, each sealed with parcel tape.

'I know, you don't have to say it. How have we still not got around to unpacking all these boxes despite having lived here for over a year?' There is a smile in Stephen's voice and I feel a sudden rush of reassurance that he is here, by my side, that I am not having to manage this alone. 'Every weekend we promise ourselves that we'll finally tackle all this' – he swoops an arm across the room – 'and every weekend we somehow manage to find something more interesting to do. We could probably just throw the lot away – we clearly don't need it.' He laughs and I find myself smiling in spite of the worry churning in my stomach.

'Let's look next door and then the tour's complete.' He takes hold of my hand, squeezes my fingers, and I hope he knows how grateful I am for his patience. How sorry I am that he is having to guide me around our home as if I am viewing it for the first time.

The walls in our bedroom are painted pale blue and it would be tranquil were it not for the bed taking up most of the floor space. It seems that a lot of our furniture has delusions of grandeur.

The room smells of fresh linen and I am touched that Stephen has been so thoughtful, putting on new sheets for my return. And yet, at the sight of the bed, with its high wooden headboard and crisp white duvet cover, I am aware of something pulling taut across my chest.

I realise with a sudden jolt that tonight – in less than ten hours' time – I will be climbing into bed with the man currently standing next to me. We will spend the night side by side, on the same mattress, beneath the same duvet, in almost unimaginable intimacy. And the thought of it – the thought of sharing a bed with a man whom I can no more remember than if I'd met him for the first time two days ago – fills me with such overwhelming panic that my lungs seem to shrink, my chest contracting, the walls of my throat narrowing until I am struggling to breathe.

'What's wrong? Are you okay?'

Stephen wraps an arm around my shoulders, guides me towards the edge of the mattress, and I sit down, try to slow my racing heart.

'There was always a chance that coming back home was going to be difficult. I know how much you'd hoped it would help you remember. But you've got to let things take their course. Like the doctor said, it may just take time. But I'm here for you. We'll get through this together.'

Stephen's words swim in my ears and I know he is being kind, but his kindness exacerbates my sense of failure.

'God, I forgot to give you this.' He fishes in his trouser pocket, pulls out a piece of tissue folded into a small square. 'I was right, the nurses had kept it safe while you were having your CT scan and just forgot to give it back.' Unwrapping it, he reveals a slim platinum band. It takes a moment for me to realise what it is, but then I take it from him, feel the weight of it in my hand, heavier than it looks, shinier than I expected. Easing the ring over the knuckles of my fourth finger, I wait for something to happen: some burst of memory, some flash of recollection. Twelve years I have been wearing this ring and I feel sure that it must contain some residual memory. I close my eyes, willing something to come – the music to which I walked down the aisle, the cutting of the cake, our first dance – but there is nothing. Just a dark, empty chasm where my past should be.

The tears are warm as they slip down my cheeks. Stephen holds my hand and I let him, his touch like that of an intimate stranger. We sit quietly on the bed, in a house that does not feel like my home, while a voice whispers in my ear: *What if your memories never return? What then?*

LIVVY

BRISTOL

'So, you're definitely happy to come back after ten months, as planned? You don't want to take a full year's maternity leave?'

Livvy sat opposite her boss in the glass-walled meeting room of the environmental think tank where she had worked for the past six years. 'Honestly, I'll be more than ready to come back. I love hanging out with this little one . . . ' She turned her head to where Leo was asleep in the buggy beside her. 'But I'll start going stir-crazy if I'm away from work for much longer.'

Aisha smiled. 'I remember that feeling, as though your brain might turn to mush if you don't get back soon.' Aisha's phone pinged and she apologised, picked it up, scanned her messages. 'Just give me a sec.'

Livvy nodded, glanced over her shoulder into the open-plan office, where some of her colleagues were tapping at keyboards, reading documents, speaking on the telephone. It was strange being here, with Leo in tow; as though she had stepped through the back of a wardrobe, into a parallel world both familiar and unknown. She knew she was the same person she'd been before Leo was born – the same Deputy Policy Director, wearing the same black ballet pumps and cream blouse she'd regularly worn to the office – and yet a part of her felt completely different.

When she'd first started thinking about maternity leave, just under a year ago, she'd been surprised by how ambivalent she felt. Having hoped for so long that she would one day become a mother, she'd assumed that when it finally happened, her feelings would be uncomplicated. But so much of her identity was linked with work that it had felt inconceivable to give that up, even temporarily. She'd originally suggested six months' leave, anxious not to lose her professional foothold, but Dominic had persuaded her to extend it: '*Six months will fly by. Be kind to yourself, take a bit longer. You've still got decades of work ahead of you.*' He'd wanted her to take a full year, while Bea had counselled her to get back to work as soon as possible: '*You know how energised you are by your job. I honestly think you'll enjoy your time as a mum more if you get back to work. Your brain needs feeding too.*' Livvy had felt they were both right in different ways, and in the end she and Dominic had compromised on ten months. And yet being back here today, a part of her felt eager to return, like an itch she wasn't yet allowed to scratch.

Catching sight of her reflection in the glass wall, she wished she'd managed to stick more stringently to the diet she'd set herself, wished she'd managed to shift the extra half-stone of baby weight she was still carrying. She thought about the note she'd discovered last night when, in a moment of slipped self-discipline, she'd found herself rifling through the drawer where the biscuits were kept. *Dear Squidge. TAKE A STEP BACK AND DO NOT TOUCH THE BISCUITS!! You did ask me to stop you eating them! I love you. D xxx*. It hadn't been the only square of neatly folded paper she'd discovered since Dominic had left for his second week in Sheffield. In her make-up bag had been a note written in so tiny a font that she'd had to squint to read it: *There's no need to make yourself TOO beautiful while I'm away! xxx.* And tucked inside the Agatha Christie novel she was reading had been another slip of paper: *Don't let Leo*

steal my place in bed when I'm not here. He needs to stay in his cot! Xx.
She had tucked the note back inside *The Hollow*, a book Dominic
always teased her for having read countless times before: '*What's the
point in reading a crime novel when you already know who did it?*'

'Sorry about this – won't be a moment. Christian just needs
a quick answer to something – he's at a select committee hearing
today.' Aisha smiled apologetically and Livvy was aware of a feeling she'd been trying to repress ever since she went on maternity
leave: a sense of being out of the loop, uninvolved, fearful of losing
a reputation she had worked so hard to earn.

While Aisha typed a response, Livvy glanced at her phone,
saw a WhatsApp notification from Dominic. Looking up briefly to
where Aisha was still concentrating on her message to their CEO,
she swiped it open, read it swiftly.

> *Hello you. Hope your work meeting's going okay. Just a
> quick one to tell you that I love you and that Leo thinks
> you're the best mum in the whole world (he told me at the
> weekend). Speak later. Xxx*

Smiling to herself, she wondered what Dominic was doing right
now. Whether he was in the midst of a site inspection, talking to
contractors about building materials, or writing a progress report for
the developers. Since starting the Sheffield job ten days ago, he'd sent
her plenty of photographs of the supermarket under construction
– giant steel girders, sky-reaching cranes, industrial-sized diggers –
but she still couldn't quite visualise him there. All the projects he'd
worked on since she'd known him had been smaller, local, domestic:
kitchen extensions, loft conversions, home offices in people's gardens. The Sheffield build was in a different league entirely.

'Sorry about that. Hopefully that's dealt with, but apologies
in advance if there are any more interruptions.' Aisha placed her

phone, screen up, in front of her. 'So have you managed to sort out childcare? I know good nursery places are like gold dust these days. You practically have to put your child's name down before they're even conceived.'

Livvy laughed. 'I've got some good leads, but I know I need to get it sorted. Don't worry – it'll all be in hand by the time I come back.' She heard the assurances in her voice, felt a renewed sense of urgency that she must phone the nursery some friends had recommended, get the wheels in motion.

'Great. I really am thrilled you're coming back as planned. Because I've got some news of my own.' Aisha paused, like a judge on a TV talent show. 'I'm leaving.'

The revelation stuttered in Livvy's head. 'What? Why?'

'Stewart and I are going to work for an NGO in Namibia for a couple of years. We've always wanted to work overseas, and now the kids have flown the nest, we just felt it was the right time.'

Livvy let the news sink in. Along with Christian, Aisha had been one of the founders of the think tank fifteen years ago and had been its Policy Director ever since. She'd been Livvy's boss for the past six years and the thought of her leaving just as Livvy was returning from maternity leave was disconcerting. 'When are you going? And who'll replace you? Not that you are replaceable, as far as I'm concerned.' In the buggy beside her, Leo stirred, snuffled, rolled his head from one side to the other, and Livvy silently implored him to stay sleeping for another twenty minutes, just long enough for her to finish the meeting.

'Well, that's the reason I'm pleased you're coming back. Christian and I have been talking, and we think you should step up into my role, if you're keen. I'm leaving in three months, but Christian's agreed to have a short hiatus until you return. It'll only leave him without a Policy Director for a month, and he agrees that's manageable.'

The words swam in Livvy's head like darting minnows. She'd always imagined that if she ever wanted to get promoted, she'd have to leave this organisation, find a role elsewhere, start again with a new set of colleagues. She'd always assumed Aisha would be in post until she retired.

'What do you think? Can I tell Christian you're interested? You don't have to decide for certain right now. It's a lot to take in, I know.'

'Of course I'm interested. It's just . . . I wasn't expecting to have this conversation. And the thought of you leaving . . .' Livvy took a deep breath. 'Sorry, it's just a bit of a shock. You've been such an incredible mentor to me. I can't imagine this place without you.'

Aisha reached across the table, placed a hand on Livvy's arm. 'That's kind of you to say. I'm going to miss working with you too. But I'll still be on the board, so you don't get rid of me altogether. And I do think it's the right time for you. You'd be brilliant.'

Livvy allowed herself a moment's pause, thought about her feelings arriving here today, worrying whether she would still be perceived as ambitious and committed now that she was a mother.

'So, shall I tell Christian you're interested? Being completely honest with you, he was initially a bit sceptical about being without a Policy Director for a month. You know how closely he and I work, and he'll have to take on a fair amount more in the interim. But we talked it through and he knows you're perfect for the role, so he's prepared to suck it up for a few weeks. It would be good to let him know soonest if you're keen. Why don't the three of us have lunch next week and we can talk it through?'

Livvy nodded, tried to catch her breath. 'That would be great. I'm definitely interested. Thank you, so much.'

In the buggy beside her, Leo awoke, and Livvy lifted him out, held him in her arms, resolved to call the nursery as soon as she got home. Because it was only now, being back in the office, that she realised quite how much she had missed it, and how keen she was to return.

ANNA

LONDON

The house is preternaturally quiet. Since Stephen left for work this morning, I have realised how his voice has filled the space between us since I arrived home yesterday lunchtime.

Popping two painkillers from their foil pouch, I pour a glass of water and gulp down the tablets as though the ferocity with which I take them might expedite their effect. Pressing my fingers to my temples, I rub in concentric circles, try to prise the throbbing pain from my head, but the persistent hammering continues.

Propped up against the kettle is a piece of paper on which Stephen has written his mobile number, told me to call any time I need him. There is a landline telephone in the sitting room, a black handset standing upright in its cradle like a sentry on duty, but I cannot think what circumstances would cause me to interrupt his day. I already feel enough of a burden, and he has phoned twice so far today, to check I am okay.

Last night, I lay awake in bed next to Stephen, listening to him sleep, trying to hypnotise myself with the steady rhythm of his breaths. But the intimacy felt so unnatural – the heat of his limbs under the shared duvet, the breeze of his exhalation on my cheek

– that I watched the digits on the bedside alarm clock click by with unforgiving lethargy. The last time I looked, it had just gone four a.m., and when the alarm on Stephen's phone vibrated three hours later, my head felt sluggish with fatigue.

Lowering myself into one of the armchairs in the sitting room, I curl my feet beneath me. On the coffee table is a trio of paperbacks Stephen has left out for me to read: Dickens, Hardy, Charlotte Brontë – my favourite authors, he has told me, though I remember nothing about the plots of their books. Picking up the copy of *Jane Eyre*, I scan the synopsis, try to ignore the feeling that my brain is trapped in a vice. Turning to the first page, I begin to read the opening lines, but pain smarts behind my eyes. The language feels arcane and I cannot immerse myself in the rhythm of the prose. I put the book down, stare at its cover, try to locate the version of myself for whom it is a favourite novel, but she is elusive, hiding, and I do not know how to entice her out.

Since I got home yesterday, Stephen has been trying to help reconstruct my sense of identity. It is only three days since the crash and yet already there is a clearly delineated before and after, a then and now. A past I cannot remember and a present that feels out of reach. It is as though my life has been fractured in two and I have no way of knowing whether they will ever fuse together again.

I have learnt that I used to be a librarian in a university library but was made redundant last year and have not been able to find another job since. Stephen told me that I was 'brilliant' at my job: '*One day soon you'll be able to remember the speech your boss gave at your leaving party.*' He reassured me that it isn't my fault I haven't yet found another role, that cuts to local services and financial pressures in academia mean that good opportunities are rare. I asked him what I've been doing since – how I've been filling my days – and he replied that I always seemed to be busy doing something, though it wasn't clear exactly what. He told me about my love of cooking, about our shared passion for independent cinema, and about how, most weekends, we head to Hampstead Heath or venture outside London for a long walk. He told me about the galleries we love – the V&A my favourite, Tate Britain his – and the classical concerts we regularly attend at Wigmore Hall, the Southbank Centre, the Barbican. And all the time he talked – with every question he answered, every new piece of information he offered – I felt as though I was drifting further away from myself.

On the bookshelf next to me are tucked the leaflets the doctor gave me at the hospital. Picking one up, I read the first page, learn that memory loss can have a number of different causes, from head injuries and fever to shock and post-traumatic stress. I discover that people with post-concussion amnesia need to be patient during the recovery phase and expect a range of additional symptoms, from mood swings and anxiety to sleep disturbances, fatigue and difficulty concentrating.

Closing the leaflet, I tuck it back into the bookshelf because I know it can't give me the answer to the only question I really need: the question of when I will start remembering again.

Before he left this morning, Stephen asked what I was planning to do today, and I didn't know how to answer. With no reference as to how I usually fill my days, the prospect of the empty hours ahead was like being given the script to a play only to find the pages blank. I told him I might go for a walk, try to reacclimatise myself to the neighbourhood. But he shook his head, the now-familiar furrow of concern forming a deep ridge across his forehead. '*It's still early days, my love. I know your short-term memory has been fine so far, but we just don't know how reliable it is, and I'd be so worried that you might get lost. I know it'll be boring, stuck inside all day, but I'll get home as early as I can. Please just rest up.*'

Getting up from the chair, I stretch my arms above my head, pace from one end of the room to the other like a caged tiger. The watch on my wrist tells me it is just past three o'clock. Stephen has been gone for seven hours already. He has told me he is rarely home before eight, and the next five hours stretch before me like an interminable yawn.

Yesterday, I asked Stephen whether he could show me some photo albums of our life together, and he told me that he will fetch them down from the loft at the weekend, agreed it would be good for me to see them. But I am overcome by a sudden impatience to look at them now, do not want to wait another four days. Heading up the stairs, I pull a chair from the spare room, place it underneath the loft hatch, hear Stephen's voice echoing in my ear: *The loft ladder's pretty treacherous – I need to get someone to come and fix it – so don't venture up there if I'm not here.* I reassure myself that I will be careful, that I need to do this. I cannot just sit around and wait for my memories to return; I have to attempt to coax them back.

With one hand on the back of the chair, I place a foot flat on its seat, check it's sturdy, feel the muscles in my thigh tighten as I lift myself off the ground. Bringing my other foot onto it, I wobble for a moment, and my heart skips as I fling one arm out to the side to steady myself, keep the other firmly attached to the chair's wooden frame. Regaining my balance, I tentatively bring myself to full height, exhale a sigh of relief that I have got this far. Reaching a hand above my head, I look up to where a silver hasp and staple latch sits across the loft hatch, and it is then that I notice it: a small brass padlock hooked through the metal hoop. Releasing my hand from the back of the chair and extending my arm above my head, I tug at it, but it is fixed, the shackle locked tightly in its body, refusing to pull free.

My head begins to spin, as though filled with an eddying rush of air. I grab for the back of the chair, but my vision is blurred, hazy, and my hand flails uselessly. A voice in my head tells me that I shouldn't be up here, standing on chairs, trying to get into lofts when I am only one day out of hospital. The muscles in my legs feel weak and I have a vision of falling, tumbling down the stairs, landing in a slump at the bottom and nobody finding me until Stephen gets home, hours from now. My head reels and I force myself to keep my eyes open, know that if they are closed there will be nothing to anchor me to the material world. My hand manages to find the back of the chair and I seize hold of it, fingers aching with the strength of my grasp. My heart thuds and I order myself to breathe steadily, in and then out, know that I need to sit down but cannot risk climbing off the chair, do not trust my legs to make the necessary moves without stumbling.

The seconds pass, then a minute – maybe more – and gradually the dizziness begins to subside, the contents of my head beginning to feel solid again. I dare to take one foot off the chair, lower it to the ground, instruct the other to follow suit.

When I am sure my legs are stable, I take my hand off the chair, tread slowly down the stairs, clasping the banister all the way. I head into the sitting room, lie on the sofa. Within seconds, the dizziness disappears as though it was never there, and a part of me feels foolish for having become so panicky.

I think about the padlock on the loft, try to imagine why we have put it there, resolve to ask Stephen about it when he gets home later.

On the coffee table in front of me sits the trio of novels, and I feel a stab of guilt like a stitch between my ribs that I have not begun to read them. The claustrophobia of being stuck indoors all day is making me feel trapped, as though I may suffocate by breathing in the same, stale air. Outside, the sun is shining, and as I look out of the window and see the blue sky beyond, I feel a decision being made.

Ignoring the echo of Stephen's voice in my head – *I'd be so worried that you might get lost* – disregarding the dizzy spell I just had, I walk into the hall, slip my feet into my trainers. Pulling my arms through the sleeves of my jacket, I open the front door and head out onto the street.

LIVVY

BRISTOL

Livvy sat on the sofa, laptop open, waiting for her seven p.m. Zoom call with Dominic.

On the video baby monitor, Leo slept soundly, and Livvy watched him on the screen, silently beseeching him not to wake up just as Dominic came online. One day last week, they'd barely said hello before a squawk interrupted them, Livvy rushing upstairs to soothe Leo back to sleep as quickly as she could. Twenty minutes later, she'd come back into the sitting room to find the video connection terminated and a text from Dominic saying he'd had a long day, was going to grab some dinner, and that he'd call her in the morning.

Pulling the laptop onto her thighs, she opened Facebook, scrolled through the home page: a succession of other people's family photos and holiday snaps, news articles and adverts. Clicking on her profile page, her eyes scanned the most recent entries: newspaper features about climate change, friends' JustGiving pages, promotions for local National Trust events. Fingers gliding along the trackpad, she slipped back in time, her postings rare and impersonal. Four months earlier she'd reposted a picture from

Bea's profile, taken of the two of them on Livvy's birthday in the park. Before that there was nothing for weeks. Scrolling further, she found the last photo she'd uploaded: a fortnight after Leo's birth, her newborn son lying in her arms, her parents proudly flanking them on either side. It was soon after she posted it that Dominic had confided how uncomfortable it made him feel having photos of Leo on social media, how he didn't want their son to become one of those babies whose every move was documented online for all the world to see. '*Why would we want complete strangers getting an intimate insight into our lives? And is it really fair to be creating a digital footprint for Leo when he's not old enough to consent to it?*' Livvy had said she hadn't realised he felt so strongly about it, had promised not to post any more personal pictures in the future. These days, she was a Facebook lurker, scrolling through other people's timelines, occasionally reposting articles on things she cared about: the environment, conservation, education. She used Facebook so little, she hadn't even bothered updating her profile since she and Dominic got married.

The waiting Zoom window morphed out of its stupor and there was Dominic, in his office at the construction site. Ten days ago, he'd arrived in Sheffield to find paper-thin walls in the studio flat that had been rented for him – '*If I can hear every word my neighbours are saying, they can hear everything I'm saying too*' – so he preferred speaking to Livvy from the office, or in the car, where they could be guaranteed some privacy.

'Hello you.'

'Hey.'

'What are you up to?'

Livvy's eyes scanned the open tabs at the top of her browser. 'Nothing much. Just scrolling through Facebook.'

Dominic rolled his eyes. 'Oh, Squidge. I thought you weren't doing Facebook any more?'

'I'm not. It's just nice to see what other people are up to.'

Dominic laughed, low and dry. 'You mean what other people choose to tell you they're up to? You know it's all curated nonsense.'

Livvy's finger slid across the trackpad, closed down the Facebook tab. 'I know. I hardly ever look at it these days.'

She watched Dominic unscrew a bottle of water, take a glug, decided not to remind him of the environmental havoc wreaked by single-use plastics.

'So how's my little man been today? It feels like aeons since I left on Monday.'

'He's fine. He was as good as gold at my meeting with Aisha.'

'Of course. How was it?'

Livvy turned the question over in her mind, thought about how unexpected the meeting had been, how much she was looking forward to returning to work. 'It was good. Really good. Aisha dropped a bit of a bombshell though. She's leaving.'

'Really? I thought she was wedded to the place?'

'So did I. But she's off to Namibia with Stewart to work for an NGO.'

Dominic took another swig of water. 'Won't that make your return a bit tricky – getting used to working for someone new?'

Livvy's eyes flicked towards the baby monitor, where Leo was lying on his back in his dinosaur sleeping bag. 'Well, that's the other bit of news. They've offered me Aisha's job. Christian's keen for me to do it, apparently. I'm having lunch with them next week to talk it through.'

'That's fantastic, sweetheart. Congratulations. You absolutely deserve that kind of recognition.' He paused, glanced over the top of his laptop fleetingly, then back at the screen. 'But are you absolutely sure that's what you want?'

'What do you mean?'

Dominic sat forward in his chair, a stack of cardboard folders to one side of him, a window behind placing his face in near-shadow. 'It's just that I know how desperate you were to be a mum. I'd hate for you to feel pressured to take on a big promotion if what you really want is to have more time with Leo.'

Livvy recalled the euphoria she'd felt when Aisha had offered her the job, the certainty that this was what she wanted. 'I don't feel pressured at all. I'm keen to get back.'

'But if you take the promotion, won't you be working even longer hours than before? You'll be frazzled.'

'I'll be fine. And you'll be back by then, so we'll be sharing pick-ups and drop-offs at nursery.'

Dominic fiddled with his trackpad. 'I'm just worried it's not great timing for you, that's all.'

Livvy tried to swallow her impatience, didn't want to have a row on Zoom when it was still two days until he'd be home. 'To be fair, it's not ideal timing you being away four nights a week when we've got a six-month-old baby, but it was a great opportunity for you and I wanted to support you in that. This is no different.'

'I get that, and of course I want to be supportive. But I look at Leo and . . . I don't know . . . He's still so tiny. Can you really see yourself feeling happy leaving him with a complete stranger in a couple of months' time?'

'It's four months. He'll be almost a year by the time I go back—'

'He'll be ten months.'

'And that's pretty standard for women going back after maternity leave.'

'Just because it's standard, doesn't mean you have to do it.'

'Well, if you feel that strongly about it, why don't you take some paternity leave and look after him yourself when I go back?' Livvy's voice was harsher than she had intended, and she watched the muscle at the edge of Dominic's left eyebrow twitch, a tic she had come to read over the past eighteen months as well as a tell in a game of poker. She curbed her irritation, softened her voice. 'What's really wrong?'

There was an almost imperceptible shaking of Dominic's head. 'I'm sorry. I suppose it's just not what I imagined for Leo – being brought up by strangers when he's still so little. I hoped we'd give him the kind of stability and security I never had. I just want him to have a better childhood than I did.' He picked up a pen, prised open the lid, shut it again.

Livvy felt her annoyance slacken. 'I'm sorry too. I didn't realise it was pushing buttons for you in that way. But Leo's upbringing is completely different to yours. You must know that. You're not your dad. I'm not your mum. Leo's loved and cherished and adored. And you know I'd never leave him with someone I didn't trust completely. The nursery I spoke to today sounded really great—'

'And you've done that without even discussing it with me?' There was hurt in Dominic's tone, like the chafed skin of a grazed knee.

Livvy tenderised her voice further. 'It only happened this afternoon. I wanted to talk to you about it in person, not on text. Nothing's been decided yet.'

He looked at her through the screen, eyebrows raised. 'So you're not planning on making all these decisions unilaterally without me?'

'Of course not. It's all up for discussion.'

A noise at Dominic's end caused him to look up and frown. He paused before turning back to Livvy. 'I'm sorry – someone here wants a word. I'll have to go. But, really, well done on the job offer. It's a fantastic achievement. I just want to be sure you make the right decision for you.' He glanced down at his watch and Livvy told him to go, that they'd speak in the morning.

Closing the lid of the laptop and shifting it onto the sofa, she looked at the baby video monitor where Leo was deep in slumber, feeling the particular surge of love for him she always experienced when she watched him sleep. She thought about her return to work, about leaving Leo at a nursery; she knew it would be hard for them both at first. But not accepting the promotion was unthinkable. She'd worked too hard, for too many years, to turn it down. Whatever Dominic's reservations, she would just have to convince him it was the right decision for all of them.

ANNA

LONDON

I walk along quiet residential streets between rows of cottages identical to ours, keeping a mental note of where I am going, ensuring to walk in straight lines until I hit a junction and am forced into a decision as to which way to turn.

Within a few minutes I reach a busy road, feel the traffic fumes hit the back of my throat as a bus trundles past. Without knowing where either direction leads, I turn right, try to memorise the name of the street I have just left and the one I am now entering.

The road I'm walking along is noisier, dirtier than the neighbourhood I'd envisaged we lived in. Graffiti daubs the metal shutters of a charity shop, litter spills from bins, an angry bassline thumps from a cracked window above a tattoo parlour. I keep walking, the street a jumble of contradictions: an elegant delicatessen is nestled between a kebab shop and a hardware store, while vintage clothing boutiques fight for space with grimy carpet shops and pound stores.

Crossing over a railway bridge and passing the entrance to a builders' merchants hugging the railway line, I turn right down the next residential road, eager to escape the exhaust fumes, figuring that if I keep turning right it will make the reverse journey easier.

The houses here are bigger than ours: wide, bay-fronted terraces on one side, three-storey Victorians on the other. I keep walking, the rhythm of my trainers against the pavement spurring me on. I'm aware of a permanent sense of bated breath, anticipating a flicker of recognition, but nothing comes.

I reach the entrance to a tree-lined park set in a square overlooked by houses on all sides and walk through the gate between some metal railings. My head is beginning to ache and I look at my watch, realise I cannot take the next round of painkillers for another two hours. To my left is a children's playground and I go inside, sit on a bench, squint against the sun and the throbbing at my temples.

A woman is pushing her son on the toddler swings, the little boy no more than about three years old. He is wearing a blue jumper with a picture of a tractor on the front, and each time the swing returns for its next push, his mother peers around the edge, says boo, and the boy squeals with delight.

I watch them, and suddenly tears are pooling in my eyes. My throat constricts and I swallow hard against it, shocked at how overwhelmed I feel. I remember the leaflets warning me that my emotions might be heightened, but this tsunami of feeling is so abrupt, so acute, that I wipe the sleeve of my jacket across my eyes, bewildered and embarrassed.

In the pocket of my jacket I find a crumpled tissue and I smooth it out, absorb the tears. After a few deep breaths, the intensity subsides, though a lingering sorrow remains, like the emotional hangover from a bad dream.

As I look back towards the swings, the mother glances in my direction, catches my eye, smiles. My reciprocation is instinctive and for a second I imagine her sitting on the bench beside me, telling me about her son, her family, her life. The sudden yearning for company is so strong that it is like being winded.

The little boy cries out for his mother to push the swing higher, and the woman turns away, propels the swing, and I am left with a feeling of profound loneliness, as though I have woken to discover the world empty of people.

A great sweep of fatigue envelops me and I have an overpowering desire to sleep even though it is still only the middle of the afternoon. Lifting myself from the bench, I cast one last look at the woman and her child as she lifts him out of the swing. He places his chubby hands either side of her face, pulls her head towards him, kisses her lips. My heart twists beneath my ribs and I force myself to turn around, away from emotions I do not understand and cannot control.

Walking out of the park, I get to the end of the street and turn left onto the main road, retracing my steps. I know I need to turn left again, down one of the streets with the small cottages like the one we live in, but I arrive at the first road and it does not look familiar, so I walk on to the next, and then the next, wracking my brain, imploring it to reveal the name of the street I exited earlier, but my mind is blank and all the roads look the same. I cannot recall any identifying feature to help determine which it is. I take a punt on one street, walk until I reach a junction, feel sure this is correct, that when I turn left, I will find my house. But I walk further, and then further still, and my house isn't there, just a small park I don't recall seeing before, and I know this is not right, this is not the way. I turn back, try to retrace my steps, to find the main road and help re-orientate myself, but everything looks different. Panic drums inside my chest, telling me I am lost, that I may never find my way out of this warren. My throat is tight and I feel tears pricking my eyes and I wish I had listened to Stephen, wish I'd never left the house, that I'd stayed at home until he got back. I look behind me and then in front, do not know which way to turn, where to go, shout silently at myself to focus, concentrate, remember. I close my eyes, try to picture what my street looks like, but they are all so similar, these houses, and I cannot think, cannot hear my thoughts, because blood is pounding in my ears. And then I open my eyes and I see a car coming towards me, its blue and yellow colouring so distinctive, and I step to the side of the road, wave my arms in the air, implore it to stop. The police car pulls up at the kerb and the electric window winds down, and before it is all the way open, relief is tumbling from my lips.

LIVVY
BRISTOL

Livvy stopped the pushchair outside the horses' paddock and set the brake. Bending down to crouch beside Leo, she pointed out the horses' long tails, hoofed feet, the way their ears swivelled to detect sound. In his buggy, Leo smiled, kicked his legs, and Livvy laughed at his joy in coming here for a sixth consecutive Friday morning.

Wheeling the buggy on towards the goats, Livvy mentally fast-forwarded to this evening, when Dominic would be home. When they'd spoken last night, he'd seemed stressed: something to do with delays to the construction and an unexpected need to revisit some of the plans. Reading between the lines, Livvy suspected that perhaps there'd been some mistakes in Dominic's calculations, but she hadn't asked him outright, didn't want to compound his anxiety.

Arriving at the goats, Leo squealed with delight as one of them trotted over to the wooden fence, pushed its muzzle through the gap between the slats, low enough for Leo to reach out and stroke it. Watching her son, it was astonishing to Livvy how much he'd changed in the six months since his birth. It seemed, at once, that he had been in her life forever and yet, at the same time, that she had known him for the swiftest blink of an eye. She could no longer remember life without him and yet, some days, it seemed to her only moments since she had first held him in her arms. Friends with older children constantly urged her to savour every moment, commit it all to memory, warned her that so many of the details later disappeared into the ether, like the contrails of an aeroplane evaporating in the sky.

'Livvy?'

Livvy turned around, took a moment to catch her breath, so unexpected was the presence of the person standing beside her, clutching a handbag to her chest as though fearful someone was about to steal it.

'What are you doing here?' Livvy heard the accusatory tone in her voice, did not try to suppress it.

Dominic's mother held Livvy's gaze for a few seconds before her eyes were drawn to Leo in his pushchair. Livvy watched Imogen hungrily devouring the sight of her grandson, eyes darting from one part of him to the next: head, shoulders, knees, toes. There was something voracious in it, as though Imogen were a character in a fairy tale who would, if Livvy were not careful, gobble Leo whole.

'I asked what you're doing here. Please don't tell me it's just a coincidence.'

Imogen's eyes flicked up to Livvy as though, for a moment, she had forgotten she was there. 'I'm sorry. I didn't mean to startle you. It's just that I know you often come here on Friday mornings—'

'How do you know? Have you been following us?' Even as she spoke, Livvy knew the question was rhetorical. The blue Ford Fiesta skulking past their house. The knock on the door when Dominic wasn't home. Imogen's sudden appearance here now, her clear knowledge of their weekly visits. A cold veil of panic blindsided her momentarily.

'I just thought it might be easier, perhaps, on neutral territory . . .'

There was a moment's hesitation, and then Imogen crouched down slowly, as though her knees were acclimatising to the movement, and stared at Leo as if she had been cast under an ancient spell.

Something clicked inside Livvy, a need to protect her child from this woman who had already wrought such emotional havoc for Dominic. She pulled the buggy away, pushed it behind her, one hand glued to the handlebar even as she turned back to Imogen.

'Can you give Leo some space, please.' Her voice was firm, unequivocal, her hand tightening on the buggy.

'Leo? That's such a beautiful name. Was that your choice or Dominic's?'

Livvy silently cursed herself for having let the name slip. 'It's really not appropriate for you to be here. You must be able to see that.' A voice inside Livvy's head shouted at her for sounding so calm when the truth was that this woman was stalking her – stalking her and Leo – and she needed to get away. She needed to speak to Dominic, decide how best to handle it.

'I'm sorry. I didn't mean to alarm you. I just didn't know what else to do.' In spite of the apology, Imogen's tone was defiant, self-righteous. 'It was one thing, Dominic not coming to see his father in the hospital, but to ignore all my messages about the funeral . . .'

For a second Livvy faltered, the words shaping themselves into meaning inside her head. 'Dominic's father died?'

Imogen eyed her quizzically, and Livvy felt like a creature being scrutinised under the lens of a microscope. 'On Saturday. Didn't he tell you?' She paused, as though to emphasise the obvious answer to her question. 'I left him two voicemails and sent him a text message.'

The words darted in Livvy's ears and she tried to catch them, make sense of them, but it was as if Imogen had spoken in a foreign language.

Her mind rewound to the events of the weekend. The three of them had been to the park, to the swimming pool, to Bristol

Museum to see the Egyptian mummies. It had been a perfect week-end. At no point had Dominic said or done anything to indicate he'd just received the news that his father had died.

Imogen continued to talk, as if determined to fill the widening chasm of Livvy's silence. 'I'm sorry, it just didn't occur to me that Dominic wouldn't have told you. Maybe he was in shock?'

'He must not have known.'

'But that's impossible. Unless he's lost his phone, or had it stolen, perhaps?'

Livvy bristled at Imogen's disingenuity. 'I'm sorry for your loss. But I don't see how that justifies you following me.'

A group of children on a school trip came running towards the goat pen, and Livvy steered the buggy out of their way, moved to the opposite side of the path. When she turned around, Imogen was standing beside her, too close, and Livvy instinctively took a step back.

'The funeral's next Friday. Will you talk to him? Persuade him to come?'

'No, I won't.'

Imogen eyed her, almost pityingly, and Livvy's skin prickled with irritation.

'It was one thing not to tell John and I that he'd got married, or that we have a grandchild. It was another thing not to come and see John in the hospital when he was dying. But to refuse to attend his own father's funeral? Surely even you must see how wrong that is?'

Surely even you . . . ? Livvy gripped the handlebar of the buggy, fingers aching with the pressure. 'I think we're probably done here. Please don't follow us again.' Spinning the buggy around, her pulse raced.

'Wait, please. I know Dominic's got a lot of complicated feelings about his father, and about me, but do you honestly think he should abstain from John's funeral?'

Blood throbbed in Livvy's ears. '*Complicated feelings?* Do you really need to ask why Dominic won't come to his father's funeral? Do you really have no idea how deeply damaged he is by the way you and his father treated him?'

Imogen shook her head with apparent impatience. 'I know Dominic's angry about a lot of things. But John and I were only ever trying to do the right thing, give him some boundaries—'

'I can't listen to any more of this.' Livvy hauled the change bag over her shoulder. 'If Dominic chooses not to reply to your messages, that's his prerogative. You have to stop following us. I don't want you around me or my son.' Flipping the brake on Leo's buggy, she walked away as quickly as she could, only turning to check over her shoulder once she'd exited the farm and left Imogen far behind.

ANNA

LONDON

I sit on the sofa in the living room, hear Stephen's muted voice from behind the closed door into the hallway, apologising for the umpteenth time to the two police officers, reassuring them that it won't happen again. There is something purposefully restrained in his voice, as though he is having to contain his impatience for them to leave.

Eventually I hear the click of the front door, and Stephen re-enters the sitting room, sits down on the sofa beside me, takes hold of my hand. 'What were you thinking, my love? Anything could have happened. Just imagine if that police car hadn't come along when it did.'

His voice is gentle, soothing, and it exacerbates my sense of self-reproach. 'I'm sorry. I just felt so cooped up and I thought if I kept the journey simple, I'd be okay . . .' My explanation tapers off, humiliation burning in my cheeks that I've been brought home by two police officers like a wayward schoolgirl.

Stephen pulls his lips into a strained smile. 'I understand. But your memory's still so fragile. I was frantic when I got home and you weren't here. Please promise me you won't go out on your own again until you're better.'

Guilt claws at my throat. I cannot imagine what this is like for Stephen, finding himself in the role of my carer. 'I promise.' It is not a difficult pledge to make, given my mortification at this afternoon's events.

I glance at the digital display on the DVD player, see that it is not yet five o'clock. 'You're home much earlier than you said.'

Stephen nods. 'I hated the thought of you here all day by yourself. I was concerned about you.' The rest of his sentence hangs in the air, no need to be spoken: Stephen's legitimacy in fretting about me is all too clear.

He leans forward, kisses the top of my head with paternalistic affection, and I wonder whether this is how we always interact or whether he would normally kiss me fully on the lips.

'So what else did you get up to today?' Stephen heads back into the hallway, hangs up the coat he was wearing when I got home, returns to the sofa. The sequence feels both entirely familiar and yet disquietingly foreign, as though we are characters in a play acting out a well-worn scene, but it is our first day of rehearsals and we haven't quite found our rhythm yet.

I think back through the hours since Stephen left, and it feels both unimaginably prosaic and yet eventful at the same time. 'I tried to get into the loft, but it's got a padlock on it.'

Stephen looks at me with alarm. 'What were you doing, trying to get up there? I told you – that ladder's treacherous.'

'I wanted to find the photo albums.'

'But I said I'd get them for you at the weekend. Honestly, my love, you've only just got home from hospital and you've had a serious concussion. You shouldn't be clambering around on ladders. You could have had a blackout, or fallen, and I wouldn't have been here to look after you.'

I think about my awful dizzy spell earlier, decide not to share it with Stephen. I do not need to give him any further cause for concern. 'I won't do it again. But why's it locked?'

Stephen rolls up the sleeves of his shirt, dark hairs bristling on his arms. 'Some friends of ours were burgled a few years ago when they were on holiday and everything valuable in the loft was cleared out. We've kept ours locked ever since.'

I wonder who those friends are, whether I would remember them, decide it is not worth the risk of asking just to discover that I don't.

'How did you get on with the books today?'

Our heads turn in unison to the trio of novels staring accusingly at me from the coffee table as if daring me to lie.

'I found it quite hard to concentrate. I've had a pounding headache all day.'

'Have you been taking your painkillers regularly?'

I nod, thinking about how I have been spacing them out to ensure I still have some left for bedtime, unable to countenance the thought of another fretful night.

'Maybe try with the novels again tomorrow. I honestly think they'd do you good. It's like the doctor said – you've got to try and take charge of your own recovery.' He smiles and I feel like a child being encouraged to eat Brussels sprouts against my will.

'Did the supermarket delivery come this morning?' He gets up, walks towards the kitchen, gestures for me to follow. I notice how neatly his tie is knotted beneath his Adam's apple, wonder if it stays that way all day or whether he periodically refastens it.

'Yes, I put it all away. I hope everything's in the right place.' It had taken me nearly an hour to unpack the shopping, opening one cupboard and then the next to find the right home for the new supplies. I had studied each item in turn, wondered what they revealed about us, as though the goat's cheese, dried porcini mushrooms and miso paste were clues in a riddle I was struggling to solve.

'Great. There should have been a fish pie?'

I nod, go to the fridge, take it out from the top shelf, feel a perverse sense of pride that I can recall such prosaic details.

'Why don't we have an early dinner? I know you didn't sleep well – you must be exhausted – and the fish pie will take a good hour to cook. Do you want to get the oven heated up and maybe make a salad dressing? I've got a few emails to deal with and then we'll have a proper evening together.' He smiles encouragingly before heading out of the kitchen and up the stairs.

The oven is easy to operate, and I find a small china jug in which to make a salad dressing. I manage to remember where I put the olive oil and red wine vinegar that arrived with the shopping earlier, feel a strange sense of achievement that I can recall the ingredients. But then the thought of mustard pops into my head, and something tells me that it is an acquired taste, and I have no idea whether Stephen likes it or not.

Heading upstairs, I hear music coming from our bedroom. As I step inside, Stephen's eyes dart towards the door and he snaps closed the lid of his laptop.

'You made me jump.' Twin furrows line his forehead and then he smiles, wiping his expression clean as if erasing the screen of a child's Etch A Sketch. 'Is everything okay?'

I feel myself falter, like a child being given a responsible task and falling at the first hurdle. 'Yes, I just wasn't sure whether you like mustard in salad dressings.' I hear the note of apology in my voice, wonder how many times we will have to go through this cycle of forgetting and contrition before my memory is restored.

'I do. Thanks for checking.'

As I turn to leave, a different piece of classical music begins to play from Stephen's phone: beautiful, spirited, and yet the sound of it grips me as if hands are tightening around my throat. I feel myself grab hold of the door handle as if all the gravity has been sucked from the atmosphere and I am at risk of spinning into the ether. It is such a powerful, atavistic feeling, as though the music is ingrained in every fibre of my being. Panic knocks at my ribs and I feel as though I cannot breathe, as though there is not enough air in the world to fill my lungs.

'What's wrong?'

My eyes are foggy and I blink to clear my sight, but I cannot seem to pull the world into focus. There is just this music, pressing down on me, squeezing my throat.

'Anna? What's happened?'

I try to find the words to explain how I feel, the inexplicable sense that this music is crushing me, even though I do not recall ever having heard it before. 'What's this music?'

Stephen glances at his phone, then back at me. 'Schubert. The Trout Quintet. Why? You look dreadful.'

The music weaves between my ribs, tightens its fist around my heart. 'Where have I heard it before?'

Stephen cocks his head to one side as though he does not understand the question. And then something alters in his expression and he picks up his phone, turns the music off.

The silence is abrupt, but I can still feel the vibrations of the cello, the hammer of the piano keys, the resonance of the violin, like the phantom sensation of an amputated limb.

I am not aware of him moving, but Stephen is standing beside me, rubbing his fingers gently across my forearm. 'The doctor did say some strange things might trigger emotional responses. They're not all going to mean something, but it must be horribly disorientating. But you are going to get better, you have to believe that.'

I open my mouth to respond but cannot locate the synapses in my brain to find the appropriate words. Even if I could, I'm not sure they would accurately convey my feelings.

Instead, I stand in silence beside Stephen while an echo of the music pulses beneath my skin, refusing to reveal when or where I may have heard it before, or why it has left me feeling so profoundly unnerved.

LIVVY

BRISTOL

'So what's the latest on the promotion? Any updates?'

Livvy's mum, Hazel, sliced a loaf of bread. Next to her, Bea ate quickly, watching the clock until her lunch hour was over. Livvy's dad, Robert, scrolled through the *Times* website on his iPad, while beside Livvy in her parents' back garden, Leo sat in his bouncy chair, sucking on a rice cake.

'No, I was supposed to be having lunch with Christian and Aisha next week, but Christian's diary is manic, so I'm just popping into the office on Monday afternoon.'

'Monday? You know that's our National Trust day? We won't be able to have Leo.'

Livvy speared some salad onto her fork. Since retiring three years ago, her parents had been volunteering two days a week at a local National Trust garden. 'Don't worry – I didn't expect you to. I'll take Leo with me. He was fine last time.'

'But you're definitely going to accept the job?'

Livvy hesitated, thought about her conversation with Dominic the day before last. 'I think so. Dominic's worried that I'll be snowed under and never get any time with Leo, and I can see his point. I'll be a lot busier than I was before.'

'So why doesn't Dominic take a career break to look after Leo when you go back?' There were sharp edges to Bea's words, as though she had honed them to a point before letting them out.

'He earns more than I do. It wouldn't make financial sense.'

'But you're not seriously considering turning it down? You've been waiting for an opportunity like this for years. You have to take it. And anyway, what does Dominic expect you to do – sit around at home going out of your mind with boredom until Leo starts school?'

Bea's voice was combative, and Livvy allowed herself a moment's pause. Her sister's antipathy towards Dominic seemed to have shifted into a new, heightened gear recently. After Bea's birthday dinner, she'd told Livvy she thought it presumptuous and arrogant, Dominic making a toast when some of her friends had known her for almost forty years. When Livvy had defended him, explained he was just trying to be nice, Bea had shaken her head, insisted it had been inappropriate. Livvy hadn't mentioned it to Dominic, didn't want to add fuel to an already combustible situation. But sometimes she wondered whether Dominic was right, whether Bea might be jealous of their relationship; she knew Bea had no desire for a partner or children of her own, but Dominic had pointed out that it might still be hard for her, adjusting to Livvy being married and having less time for Bea than she used to.

'I just need to figure out how it'll work, with childcare and everything. I don't really want to be one of those mums who only sees her child at the weekend.' She could hear the tension in her voice, feel it in the muscles in her throat. It had been over an hour since Livvy had walked away from Dominic's mother at the urban farm, but still a sense of disquiet flickered inside her, like static from a badly tuned radio. The same image kept appearing in her mind: the rapacious expression on Imogen's face when she'd first laid eyes on Leo, as though, if Livvy had turned her back for a moment, Imogen might have grabbed the buggy and disappeared with Leo forever.

'Is everything okay, love? You seem a bit . . . on edge?' Her dad put down his iPad and switched it off.

'I'm fine.'

'Are you sure?'

Livvy nodded. 'Honestly.' She thought about her promise to Dominic not to discuss his familial issues with anyone else. 'It's nothing.'

Bea looked at her through narrowed eyes. 'It's obviously not nothing. Come on, tell us. What's wrong?'

Looking at Bea's expression, Livvy knew her sister wouldn't let it go. And even sitting here now, Livvy couldn't help worrying that she might get home to find her estranged mother-in-law camped out on her doorstep.

Before she knew it, the whole story emerged: the doorstep visit last Friday, the surprise appearance at the urban farm this morning, the awareness that Imogen must have been watching the house, following her, finding out when Dominic would be absent.

'Jesus, that's really creepy. What does Dominic say?' Bea declined their mum's offer of more bread.

'I haven't told him about today's ambush yet. I want to wait until he gets home tonight.'

'But do you think Dominic knows that his father's died and has just kept it to himself?'

Livvy contemplated her mum's question. For the past couple of hours, speculations had raced through her mind as to why Dominic might have chosen not to tell her about his father's death. Perhaps his head was so full of the new job that he simply couldn't process it. Perhaps he hadn't wanted to share it because he'd known she would worry about him being in Sheffield alone. Perhaps the news had overwhelmed him and he'd buried it deep in a corner of his mind until he was ready to excavate it, examine it, reveal to himself how he felt. 'I honestly don't know. Things are so complicated with his parents . . .' Livvy allowed her voice to trail off.

'We don't want to pry, love, but it is quite hard for us to understand. All these difficulties between Dominic and his family – is there really no hope of a reconciliation?' Her dad knelt down, picked up the toy plastic keys Leo had thrown out of reach, handed them back to him.

'I don't think so.' Livvy was aware of a flurry of furtive looks passing across the wrought-iron garden table.

'I do feel very sorry for Dominic. It's such a difficult situation to be in, having no contact with his family. And he's so wonderful with Leo, it's a shame he can't share that with them.' Her mum drank from her glass of water.

Bea let out an audible sigh of frustration. 'Look, obviously you know Dominic much better than we do, but it does seem pretty dysfunctional. What actually happened between Dominic and his parents to make him hate them so much?'

Livvy hesitated. A part of her wished she could confide in her family. The secrecy was oppressive. But Dominic had asked for her discretion and she couldn't betray his trust. 'I can't say. He's asked me not to, and I need to respect that.'

Bea leant back in her chair, folded her arms across her chest. 'So you're being stalked by Dominic's crazy mother, but you're not allowed to tell us the reason why?'

'I'm not exactly being stalked—'

'Well, that's what it sounds like.'

'I was just a bit freaked out. But it's fine. Dominic and I will sort it out.' There was a definitive full stop in Livvy's tone – more brusque than usual – and her mum tactfully changed the subject, asked Bea about the new young vet Bea had taken on at the practice where she was a partner.

As she listened to them talk, Livvy found herself silently cursing Imogen for having arrived unannounced in their lives and for opening a can of worms she knew Dominic would rather keep firmly shut.

ANNA

London

A light breeze brushes my cheeks, the sun warming my scalp. It feels good to be breathing air that has not been circulating inside the same eight hundred square feet of our house, good to be looking at trees, sky and grass rather than whitewashed walls and wooden floors. The park is quiet, too early yet for the lunchtime crowd. For now, it is just retired people, parents with preschool children, and whatever category I fit into.

For the past two days I have kept my promise to Stephen. I have stayed at home, trying to read novels I once loved but now seem unable to enjoy, prepared dinners from cookbooks in which brightly coloured Post-it notes mark the pages of favourite recipes, none of which I recall ever having made before. I have watched the woman in the house behind ours stare at her laptop screen, tap busily at her keyboard, and speculated about what work she is doing. I have wondered when I'll be able to work again, whether it will be the library services to which I'll return or whether I'll have to reinvent myself entirely. I have napped copiously, like a newborn baby, falling asleep for an hour or two in the armchair when I'm supposed to be reading, or taking myself upstairs to bed and slipping gratefully under the duvet.

But today, I couldn't bear being trapped at home any longer. The past two days have felt stifling, the dimensions of every room seeming to narrow with each passing hour.

I didn't leave the house until after Stephen's call this morning: he phones as soon as he gets to the university, again at lunchtime and often in the afternoon. He is not due to phone again until long after I plan to be home.

In the jacket of my pocket is a folded piece of A4 paper and a pencil, and I have diligently mapped my route here – only ten minutes' walk from home, but far enough, I know now, for me to get lost – every street name specified, every landmark noted. I have even written Stephen's mobile number at the top in case history repeats itself and I have to ask a shopkeeper to use their telephone, admit to Stephen that I have broken my promise. But I won't get lost. I need to prove to myself that I can do this, that I can leave the house without supervision or misadventure. I cannot stay cooped up indoors, locked inside a mind that seems determined to keep my past from me. I have to do something to try and unfreeze my memories.

In the six days since the crash – as Stephen and I have woken up together, eaten dinner, talked about our respective days – I have wondered how much this quotidian rhythm resembles our lives before the accident. Whether, since being made redundant, I have counted the hours until Stephen's return, as I do now: the pivotal moment in an otherwise uneventful day. Whether our dinner-time conversations have always been dominated by Stephen's anecdotes about university life. Or whether the tenor of our relationship has changed beyond all recognition. And, if it has, whether it will ever revert to the way it was before.

Yesterday evening, Stephen told me he has been researching amnesia online. He's read that it's best for now that we dwell not on the past but focus on the present, that by anchoring my experiences in the here and now we are more likely to help strengthen my memory. *'Memory recovery isn't something that can be rushed. We just have to be patient and let your brain have time to heal.'*

Last night, after dinner, he suggested we watch one of our favourite films, *The Royal Tenenbaums*, telling me we'd seen it multiple times before. I managed to follow the plot but remembered nothing about it from previous viewings and found its eccentricity too pronounced, too self-conscious. But Stephen kept turning to me, asking with such optimism whether I was enjoying it, that I had smiled and nodded, fabricated the response I knew he wanted.

There is a gust of breeze and my head feels light suddenly, as though my brain has been scooped out and replaced with helium. The sensation is debilitating and I wish I were at home, in familiar surroundings, where I could lie on the sofa or crawl under the duvet and wait until the episode passes.

I close my eyes, consciously regulate my breathing, hoping that a steady supply of oxygen to my brain will recalibrate my feelings. I sense my lungs expand and then contract, fill and then empty, until gradually the light-headedness begins to subside. It feels like a small moment of triumph, to have survived this dizzy spell away from home, and I try to use the knowledge of it to calm the pulse tapping at my wrists reminding me that this kind of episode is precisely why Stephen didn't want me to leave the house alone.

There is a change of weight on the bench and I snap open my eyes, spin my head around, a surge of inexplicable fear flooding my veins.

'God, I'm sorry, I didn't mean to make you jump. Are you okay?'

There is a woman smiling at me, apology in her eyes, and it takes a few seconds for me to recall where I have seen her before. It is the woman from the playground a few days ago, the mother with the little boy wearing the blue tractor jumper. I follow the quick dart of her eyes to the sandpit, where the same little boy – now wearing a bright green sweatshirt – is dragging a plastic digger through the sand.

'Yes, I'm fine.' My voice feels strange in my mouth and I realise that I have spoken to no one other than Stephen and the police officers since leaving the hospital.

We smile at one another and then look away, fall into a silence which may or may not be comfortable, I cannot tell. The woman watches her son, and I watch with her as he scoops piles of sand into his digger, dumps them behind him, creating a hole on one side, a mound on the other.

'He's very sweet. How old is he?' My words take me by surprise, as if they have chosen to leave my lips without prior consultation.

'Just turned three, last month. He certainly has his moments. Have you got kids?'

I shake my head, my chest swelling with a feeling I cannot put a name to.

'It's a lovely park, isn't it?' The woman looks around, checks on her son before turning back to me. 'I'm Zahira.' Her voice is gentle, and she places the flat of her palm on her chest as she introduces herself, her manicured nails crisp against her white t-shirt. She is about the same age as me, perhaps a few years younger, dark hair sitting in sleek, straight lines just below her shoulders. Her eyes are watchful, intelligent, her skin flawless. A thin black pencil line shapes the top of her eyes, a light sheen of blusher across her cheeks. She is objectively beautiful, and next to her I am acutely aware of my own shabbiness: my face free of make-up, pasty with sleeplessness, shadows hanging beneath my eyes like crescent bruises.

'I'm Anna. Anna Bradshaw.' I state my full name as if to affirm my identity and yet there is something uncanny in it, as though I have not yet earned the right to say it out loud. 'It's only the second time I've been here but, yes, I really like it.' Even as I speak, it strikes me as probably untrue. Stephen and I have lived in our house for over a year: I imagine we must have walked through this park many times.

'Mama! Look!'

We both turn our heads to where Zahira's son is pointing to the mound of sand he has created, a twig stuck in the top. 'I made a castle!'

'Well done, little bear. What are you going to build next?'

The boy places a finger on his chin, gazes up at the sky, thinks for a few seconds before responding. 'A choo-choo train!'

Zahira laughs. 'Okay, I'll come and have a look when you're done.' She turns back to me, leans against the arm of the bench. 'So have you not lived around here long?'

I think about her question, realise there are two possible answers: the factual and the experiential. 'I've lived here for over a year, but I had an accident recently and lost my memory so I don't remember anything about it.' It is barely a chapter of my story and yet I feel as though I am standing at the top of a cliff as a strong wind threatens to force me over the edge.

'God, I'm so sorry. That sounds awful. Are you okay?' She glances towards her son, then looks back at me.

I am about to nod, offer a platitudinal response, but then something shifts inside me, and the confusion about all that has happened suddenly feels unwieldy. Before I have time to consider it, the story is spilling from my lips, as though it knows the way and has no need for me to guide it. And even while I am telling this woman about the events of the past six days – about the crash and the concussion, the amnesia and the hospital, Stephen and the house and the life I do not remember – a voice in my head is telling me I am being absurd, unburdening myself to a complete stranger. And yet I do not stop, cannot stop, this need to confide so great that I have no power against it.

When I finish, I feel exhausted, spent. The telling has taken no more than a few minutes and yet I feel as though I have reached the end of a marathon. But there is also a sense of relief, like plunging into the sea on a hot summer's day.

'God, you've really been through the mill. I'm so sorry.'

It's only seeing the story reflected in someone else's eyes that I appreciate just how shocking it is.

'You must feel so . . . unsettled. Are you getting any help?'

Without any warning, tears prick my eyes, and I blink them away. 'The doctor at the hospital has put me on a waiting list for therapy, but he said it could be a while before I get an appointment.' I know it's ridiculous, disclosing all this to a woman I don't even know, and yet I want to keep talking to her.

Zahira rolls her eyes. 'That's so typical. You need help now, not in six months' time. What about the rest of your family? Are they able to rally round?'

The question snags, like a plaster tugging on bare skin. 'I don't know about the rest of my family. I can't remember anything about them.'

'But your husband must have told you?'

I shake my head, do not know how to explain the strangeness of the past few days. Time seems to have taken on a different dimension: some moments it has felt like weeks since I arrived home from the hospital, at others it seems mere hours. I don't know how to convey the fragility of everything around me, as though my connection to the present is a single thread of cotton that could snap at any moment should I test it too hard. And yet Zahira's question niggles at something, like a scab I have been wary of picking.

'Look, I'm not a doctor, but I'd have thought the most important thing for you right now is to be surrounded by family and friends. As much as anything, it must be hard for your husband, dealing with all this on his own. And you must want to know about the other people in your life?'

Zahira's words expose an issue I've been trying to repress for the past six days, but now that she's articulated it, I can no longer delude myself that it doesn't exist. 'I do. I just haven't felt able . . . I need to ask Stephen.'

Glancing down at my watch, I see that it is almost midday and feel a stab of panic. I have been out for over an hour. There is every chance Stephen will ring soon and that I will miss his lunchtime call. 'I'd better get home. I'm not used to being out alone for long stretches of time.' I look across the playground, towards the entrance to the park, silently reassuring myself that I know the way back. I have my map, it will tell me the directions.

'Will you be okay?'

I nod, even as I know that one wrong turn could be disastrous. 'I'll be fine, thanks.'

There is a momentary pause. 'Elyas and I are here most Tuesday and Friday mornings, so if you're at a loose end, we're invariably around.' Zahira smiles with complete openness, and I find myself imagining it: meeting her here twice a week, tentatively beginning a friendship. And then I feel embarrassed by my sense of yearning for it to come to pass.

'That's really kind of you, thanks.' I get up from the bench, say goodbye, begin to walk away. At the gate, I glance back over my shoulder, see Elyas run into Zahira's arms, feel something pull taut in my chest.

Turning right out of the park, I head for home, taking out the piece of paper, following my meticulous instructions: turn left on the main road, walk over the railway bridge, turn left again onto the street with pedestrian-only access. Buoyed by my conversation with Zahira, I know that tonight, when Stephen gets home, I need to ask him about the rest of my family. I'm ready to find out more about who else was in my life before the crash.

LIVVY

BRISTOL

'She *followed* you to the farm? And then asked you to persuade me to go to my dad's funeral?'

Dominic ran his fingers through his hair, picked up his glass of red wine, swigged a large mouthful. On the table in front of them, plates of arrabbiata pasta remained untouched.

'I'm sorry. I probably should have told you as soon as you got home, but you've had so much to deal with lately.'

'It's not your fault. It's my bloody mother. I can't believe she did that to you.' He shook his head, drank another gulp of wine. 'What kind of crazy person harasses their daughter-in-law and grandchild at an urban farm, for god's sake? It's genuinely mad.'

Livvy pushed her plate to one side. 'I guess she was desperate and grief does strange things to people.' She paused, knowing she had to ask the question. 'So did you know – about your dad?' She was aware of gauging her way through the conversation as though walking across a frozen lake, unsure if the ice was thick enough to hold her.

Dominic nodded. 'I'm sorry. I know I should have told you, but I just don't want them in our lives.'

There was ferocity in his voice, and Livvy had never seen him like this before: jaw tensed with bitter resentment, face tightening like a fist. She rubbed the back of his hand, his knuckles rigid beneath her fingers. 'You don't need to apologise. I know what a difficult situation this is for you.' She hesitated, knowing she should mention it, uncertain whether now was the time. 'But in all honesty, your mum's behaviour was pretty strange. It was obviously the first time she'd seen Leo properly, and there was something about the way she looked at him—'

'What do you mean?'

'I don't know how to explain it. There was a kind of single-mindedness about her, as though Leo was the only person in the world and she just had to get close to him. Maybe that's what some grandparents are like. But she seemed . . . fixated on him. I can't really describe it. It was just really unnerving.'

'Right, that's it.' Dominic stood up from the table, strode towards the stairs.

'Where are you going?'

'I'm going to email my mother. She has to be told. I don't want her anywhere near you or Leo.'

'Do you really think that's wise? I thought you said we shouldn't give her the oxygenation of contact.'

Dominic shook his head. 'This has gone far enough. I'm not having her hassling you and Leo like this. It's got to stop.' He didn't wait for a reply before bounding up the stairs, two at a time, in search of his laptop.

At the kitchen table, Livvy looked at the plates of congealing pasta, wondered whether Dominic would want his heated up when he came back down. Glancing at the baby monitor, she watched Leo sleep in his cot, her heart buckling with a desire to protect him, and felt a wave of relief that Dominic was emailing his mother, drawing a line, instructing her not to contact them again.

ANNA

LONDON

Stephen slices the last of his steak in two, forks one piece into his mouth, chews with visible effort. The steak is overcooked, griddled not for the two minutes on either side Stephen had advised but for significantly longer because my thoughts were elsewhere, rehearsing one side of a conversation I know we need to have.

'Aren't you hungry?'

I look down at my plate: the steak barely touched, sautéed potatoes still heaped in a pile, only a few florets of broccoli missing. 'Not really.'

Stephen puts down his knife, reaches for my hand. His thumb glides across the inside of my wrist and that feeling is there again: an abrupt, unfathomable panic. I tell myself to calm down; moments of intimacy – however small – are inevitably going to feel strange with a man I cannot remember. I wrack my brain, try to find the version of myself who fell in love with Stephen eighteen years ago, but I cannot seem to locate her.

'Are you still feeling nauseous?'

I nod, even though it is only a partial truth.

Stephen squeezes my hand before returning to the last of his dinner. I watch him spear the final piece of steak onto his fork and eat it decisively.

In the forty-five minutes since he arrived home – half an hour later than I'd been expecting him – I have silently been practising how best to begin. What question to open with. What details to focus on.

'Have you finished?' Stephen tilts his head towards my plate.

'I think so.'

He pushes back his chair, and something jars inside me: a sense of urgency, a need to know. 'There's something I need to ask you.' The words leave my lips and, once they do, it is as though I have launched a sledge down a snowy hill and know I cannot stop before it reaches the bottom.

'What?'

I take a deep breath. 'Why hasn't anyone come to see me? Any friends or family?' I pause, even as I know I have to continue. 'Why haven't my parents been to visit? It's been almost a week.' Something seems to open up inside me, like a heavy stone being rolled across the entrance to a cave, my desire to know rushing through.

'Have you remembered something about your parents?'

I shake my head. 'I don't remember anything.'

Stephen interlocks his fingers with mine, studies my face with earnest eyes. 'It's still early days, my love. I think it might be overwhelming, trying to remember too much at once.'

His tone is gentle, persuasive, but the urgency persists. 'Please, I really want to know.'

Stephen drops his head, breathes slowly. The seconds seem to lengthen and stretch, and I do not know why my heart is drumming against my ribs.

When he raises his head, Stephen's face is drained of colour, deep grooves lining the edges of his eyes. He sucks in another long breath, clasps both my hands inside his. 'I didn't want to have to tell you. Not yet. I'd hoped I could put it off a bit longer.' He hesitates, and I feel beads of perspiration lining my palms. 'Your parents died in a car crash when you were twenty-one. They've been dead for eighteen years.'

The words hit me as though I have been physically assaulted. I have a sense of falling from a great height, do not know where I will land, what will happen when I do.

'I'm so sorry. I didn't know when I should tell you. I haven't been able to bear the thought of you having to go through all that grief again . . .' His voice is muffled in my ears, as though a pair of conch shells are being held against my head, all other sounds distorted by the swell of a raging sea.

I close my eyes, try to understand what Stephen is saying, but it is like trying to grab hold of air. I cannot make sense of it, do not know what I am supposed to feel. A crater opens up in my chest and I cannot tell whether it is emptying me of all feeling or spilling over with grief.

'I'm so sorry, my love.'

I keep my eyes closed, do not know how to respond.

My parents are dead. I do not remember them dying. I don't remember anything about them at all.

Shock burns behind my ribs: febrile, blistering. I hear myself inhale a deep breath as if gasping for air.

'I didn't know how to tell you. I just wanted to protect you a bit longer.'

I hear the distress in Stephen's voice, wish I could offer him some morsel of reassurance, but I cannot move, cannot speak. My body feels numb.

'After what happened . . . with our crash . . . and your head injury. I thought it might bring it all back. I'm so sorry.'

I feel his fingers wrap around mine, sense him try to impart some love, some condolence, but I do not understand what I am supposed to do with this knowledge.

My parents are dead. I will never see them again.

Whatever scant tethering has kept me tied to the world for the past six days seems to snag and then break, and I cannot tell whether I am floating or falling, waving or drowning, whether there is any feeling beyond a profound, desolate sense of loss.

LIVVY

Bristol

Livvy wheeled Leo's buggy through the office's revolving door and out onto the street. Pulling her phone from her pocket, she typed a WhatsApp message to Aisha.

> *Thank you SO much for that. You are AMAZING. Did I ever tell you that you're the best boss in the world and that I am going to miss you loads? Seriously, I can't thank you enough. Coffee and cake on me before you head off to Namibia. Xxx*

She reread the message, wondered if it was too effusive, then thought back over the meeting she'd just had with Aisha and Christian and pressed her finger down on the send button.

Livvy had walked into the meeting to discuss her potential new role with a sense of disingenuity. Over the past few days, she'd thought about what Dominic had said, had been unable to silence the anxiety that perhaps, in taking the promotion, she'd be short-changing everyone: Leo, Dominic, Christian. But as soon as the meeting had begun, Aisha had opened with a speech about how they knew that stepping up to Policy Director just as she was returning from maternity leave was a challenge, but that they were sure they could make it work with a bit of flexibility. Christian had chimed in, told her how thrilled he was that she was considering the role, had joked that he wouldn't have contemplated a month-long hiatus for anyone else. By the time Livvy left the meeting, she'd felt so invigorated that she half wished she were returning to work sooner.

Pushing the buggy towards the car park, she remembered that the ticket machine wasn't taking cards, delved into her bag for her purse to see if she had any cash. Unzipping the inside pocket, she found a square of paper, neatly folded. Flattening it out, she saw Dominic's meticulous handwriting. *To my beautiful goldfish. Don't forget to call the council about the bin collection. I love you. D xx.*

Her memory jolted. For two weeks, the refuse collectors hadn't taken their rubbish, and she'd been promising Dominic that she'd log it with the council. Cursing herself for having forgotten yet again, she picked up her phone and set a reminder for the following morning, folded the note and put it back in her bag.

There had been an abundance of Dominic's notes left around the house last week: in the freezer next to the ice cream (*Don't be tempted! You'll only be cross with yourself afterwards! xxx*); in the cutlery drawer (*Remember that we go TIP UP in the dishwasher xxx*); in Leo's toy box (*Dear Leo, Please make sure that I am FULL when Daddy gets home. You know he doesn't like clutter all over the sitting room floor xxx*). Sometimes Dominic's notes were a comfort: a sense of his presence even in his absence. But other times – notes reminding her to collect something, send something, pay for something – she wished he'd just send her a reminder on WhatsApp so there was no chance of her overlooking it.

Her phone pinged and she looked at the screen, anticipating a reply from Aisha. Instead, there was a text message from a number she didn't recognise.

> *Hello Livvy. It's Imogen, Dominic's mother. I wanted to apologise again for our encounter last week. I didn't mean to upset you. But I really do need to get hold of Dominic. He's still not replying to any of my messages. I'd be very grateful if you could have a word with him about John's funeral. It's this Friday. I've sent him all the details. Thank you. Imogen*

Livvy whipped her head around, looked left and right, behind her and in front, eyes scouring the people milling by for the face of her mother-in-law. She was aware of her heart rate accelerating, of her hand reaching over the top of the buggy, resting on Leo's shoulder.

She looked back down at the message, her skin bristling with a sudden realisation: she hadn't given Imogen her mobile number. She had no idea where Dominic's mother had got it from.

Rereading the message, she saw the outright lie in it. It was three days since Dominic had emailed his mother, instructing her not to contact them again. And yet here she was, claiming that Dominic had failed to reply to any of her messages.

Taking one last glance around to reassure herself that Imogen wasn't spying on them, Livvy turned back to her phone, saved Imogen's number under an innocuous letter 'I' so that she could screen any further communications, and then pressed a finger down on the delete button, eradicating the message. The decision was there without her consciously having taken it: ignore the message, don't tell Dominic, spare him yet more anger and upset. If both she and Dominic ghosted all Imogen's communications from now on, surely she'd get the message and leave them alone.

Looking inside her purse, she discovered precisely eighty-seven pence, realised she wouldn't be able to pay for parking without withdrawing some cash.

At the cashpoint, she entered her pin to check the balance on the joint account, and a number flashed up on screen that caused Livvy to pause, blink, stare.

It didn't make any sense.

Only last week there had been almost five thousand pounds in their joint account. Now there was little more than two hundred. Confusion darted in Livvy's head as she considered the possibility that somebody had hacked into their account and taken all their money. Dominic had been berating her for months about the inadequacy of her online security, imploring her to change her passwords to something less obvious. A year ago, when they'd got married and Dominic had suggested they move all their separate finances into a single joint account, she'd promised to improve her banking security and yet somehow it had never moved off her To Do list. And now, twelve months later, almost five thousand pounds had inexplicably disappeared.

'Are you gonna be much longer?'

Livvy whipped her head around, saw a man standing behind her in tracksuit bottoms and a hoodie pulled up over his head. Heart pounding, she mumbled an apology, withdrew ten pounds, retrieved her bank card and moved out of the way.

Pulling her mobile from her pocket, she dialled Dominic's number, heard herself groan when it went to voicemail. 'It's me. Can you call me as soon as you get this? Something's happened. Nothing terrible – we're both fine – but . . . well, can you just call me?'

For a few moments she stood on a street corner, staring down at her phone as though, if she looked at it long enough, she could summon Dominic, like a genie from a bottle. But her phone remained stubbornly silent. Her mind raced, trying to devise a meaningful reason why Dominic might have withdrawn that much money, but she knew she was clutching at straws. Dominic was careful with money. There was no imaginable scenario in which he'd have spent almost five thousand pounds in a week.

She thought about phoning the bank, reporting the lost money, asking them to investigate. Glancing at the time, she saw it was almost half past five. Leo was late for his dinner and Dominic would be video-calling soon. And the damage had been done now anyway: the money was gone. All she could do now was go home, wait for Dominic to call, and hope that between them, they could figure out what on earth had happened.

ANNA

LONDON

I wander through the gallery, past pale marble statues of naked figures and floor-to-ceiling windows, the soles of my trainers squeaking against the tiled floor. I walk slowly, trying to take everything in, waiting for something to spark a memory, but my mind is like a blank slab of clay, yet to be moulded into any recognisable shape. Stephen has told me that the sculpture gallery at the V&A is one of my favourite places in London and that I come here regularly. He felt sure it would ignite some memories, even went into work late so he could escort me here for opening time, has left me with typed, bullet-pointed instructions as to how to get home.

I gaze up at a statue of three nude women, their bodies entwined, recognise the name on the plaque – *The Three Graces* by Canova – but there is no recollection of ever having stood beneath it before.

Frustration pangs in my chest. It is a feeling that has punctuated each yawning hour of the past three days, since learning about the death of my parents. Three days in which I seem to have existed in multiple time frames, both real and imagined. I feel as though I am a collection of unrelated fragments, like broken glass that cannot fit together because the shards all come from different sources.

Over the past three days, Stephen has patiently answered my litany of questions about my mum and dad, about their accident, about a childhood I cannot recall. I have learnt that it was the night of my graduation ceremony when my parents, returning late from Manchester University to my childhood home in Gloucester, crashed into a tree on a dark, unlit B-road, both of them dead by the time a passer-by found the smoking crush of their car. I have learnt there was another car involved but that it left the scene, presumed to be culpable but never found. I have discovered that I am an only child, that my parents had me late in life, that I have no extended family. I am nobody's daughter, nobody's sister, nobody's cousin, nobody's niece. It is knowledge that has left me with a feeling of profound incompleteness: as though I am somehow unfinished, just a fraction of a whole.

Stephen has told me how we met soon after my parents' death, how we were friends at first – for months, in fact – my grief too acute to contemplate anything more. How, as I gradually began to emerge from the fog of mourning, our relationship tentatively developed.

Stephen has told me everything I want to know. And yet the story feels distant, hazy, like a mirage in a desert. There are moments when I fear I might only ever exist in the slipstream of Stephen's memories.

At the thought of Stephen, guilt needles my skin. All weekend he has been so unfailingly kind, so unremittingly patient. On Saturday afternoon we watched a concert on BBC iPlayer, a repeat of a Proms performance Stephen told me we'd seen at the Royal Albert Hall almost a decade ago. It was *Tristan and Isolde* by Wagner, one of our favourites he said, and as we rewatched it together, Stephen recalled a moment when I'd been moved to tears in the third act. I sensed Stephen watching me, waiting to see if it would provoke a similar response, and I searched deep within myself for why I had been so affected. But there was only a crushing sense of disappointment when nothing stirred, and I felt grateful to Stephen for not mentioning it again.

Yesterday he drove us to Hampstead Heath, held my hand as we walked up Parliament Hill and looked out over the city skyscape – the Shard, the Gherkin, St Paul's Cathedral – all buildings I recognised but could not recall ever having viewed from that location before. Stephen told me it was one of our favourite walks, that we often went there on Sunday mornings before heading down the hill to the ponds and trudging up Fitzroy Park, into Highgate Village, for a pub lunch and a read of the weekend papers. He asked if I remembered going there on Christmas Day, stroking a brown cocker spaniel puppy that had skittered around my ankles, watching the bathers swimming in the ponds even as frost clung to the branches of trees. I had to shake my head, felt like a schoolchild who has been taught the same thing over and over but still cannot grasp it.

When we got home yesterday afternoon, I mentioned the photo albums in the loft, and Stephen suggested we wait a little while before tackling those. He said I often found it upsetting, looking at photos of my parents, and given everything I'd learnt that week, it might prove overwhelming.

I stop in front of another sculpture – a mother nursing her child – and am aware of something tightening across my chest. The air in the gallery feels oppressive suddenly and I know I need to escape this failed excursion.

Turning around, I hurry through the shop and towards the exit, frustration and disappointment jostling for prominence. I feel a quiet sense of determination that this is not how it will always be for me, this state of in-betweenness: stuck between a past I cannot remember and a future I dare not imagine. There must, I feel certain, be another way to jolt my memories out of hiding.

LIVVY

BRISTOL

Livvy's laptop sat open on the sofa beside her, screen fully illuminated.

Six minutes to seven.

She felt like a job candidate, arriving early for her interview, eager to make a good impression. Her palms were clammy as she thought about the lost five thousand pounds, about the text from Imogen, about how on earth her mother-in-law had got hold of her mobile number. She was still convinced it was best not to tell Dominic about Imogen's message. She suspected that a reaction from Dominic was precisely what Imogen wanted, and Livvy had no intention of playing into her mother-in-law's hands.

Two minutes to seven.

Livvy sipped a glass of water. Five thousand pounds. It was a vertiginous sum of money to have lost.

The Zoom screen opened and there was Dominic, smiling. 'Hey sweetheart.'

Apprehension churned in Livvy's stomach. 'Did you hear my message?'

Dominic looked down at his phone, then back at the computer screen. 'Sorry, I only just saw a missed call from you as I was jumping on here. Is everything okay?'

Livvy took a deep breath. 'Not really. I went to the cashpoint today, and I don't know how it happened, but I think someone must have hacked into our account. There's only a couple of hundred pounds left.' She paused, swallowed. 'I know you've been on at me for ages to change my passwords, but do you think we'll get the money back if we can prove we've been hacked?' The words tripped from her tongue as though they couldn't get out fast enough.

Dominic eyed her quizzically for a moment. 'We haven't been hacked. I withdrew the money.'

The explanation stumbled inside Livvy's head. '*You* took it? Why?'

'I've been doing a bit of an audit of our finances.' He leant back in his chair, placed his hands behind his head as though lazing on a sun lounger. 'Do you know how much money we haemorrhage every month on coffees and cake?'

Livvy shrugged. 'Ten, fifteen pounds?'

Dominic paused like a quiz master on a television show. 'Forty-two pounds, on average. Forty-two pounds on coffees and cake. Do you know that's over five hundred pounds a year? And I hate to say it but most of that's when you're out with your sister or your friends.'

Livvy did some quick mental calculations. 'I know it sounds a lot when you put it like that, but it's only a couple of trips a week to a café. I can't stay cooped up at home every day.'

Dominic pressed at something on his keyboard, seemed distracted for a moment, then turned his attention back to Livvy. 'Sweetheart, you can't keep moaning about the fact that most of your friends have already lost all their baby weight if you're eating forty-two pounds of cake every month.'

'It's not forty-two pounds of *cake*. And anyway, most of my friends don't have husbands working away all week, and they can actually leave the house by themselves to do some exercise.'

'But that's not really the issue, is it? The issue is our regular outgoings. Do you know what our monthly food bill is? Or how much you spend on petrol?'

'Not off the top of my head. But I only fill up the car once a fortnight, if that.'

'But that's my point. How can we keep track of our finances if we don't know how much we spend? I've been going through the last six months' accounts and we can make huge savings just by being a bit more mindful.'

Livvy considered pointing out that she would happily give up responsibility for the weekly food shop, for planning and cooking all their meals, for being the only person who made sure Leo had enough nappies in stock, but she didn't want to have a row on Zoom. 'That still doesn't explain why you've taken five thousand pounds out of the joint account.'

'It was madness having all that money sitting in a current account, earning no interest, just waiting to be frittered away. I've put it in an ISA. And from now on I think we should have a monthly budget for household costs and put the rest into savings.'

The implication of what Dominic was saying spun in Livvy's head. 'You want us to have *a household allowance*? Like it's the nineteen-fifties and I'm a housewife who can't be trusted with money?'

Dominic laughed. 'Don't be so pejorative about housewives.'

'I'm not—'

'It's not about *trust*. It's about us working together to manage our income better.' He wiped a finger along the edge of his keyboard, flicked whatever dust he'd collected onto the floor.

'And you've just decided all this independently, without any discussion?'

'We're discussing it now.'

'No, we're not. You're informing me of a decision you've already taken.'

'If you feel that strongly about it, we can put the five thousand pounds back in the joint account and spend it on cake. I don't understand why you're so angry. I'm just trying to do something good – something practical – for our family.'

'I'm not angry. I'm frustrated. You can't just go making unilateral decisions like that without me.'

Dominic sat forward, elbows on the desk, hands clasped under his chin. When he spoke his voice was softer, gentler. 'I honestly didn't think you'd mind. You hate anything to do with money.'

'No, I don't.'

'Oh, come on, Squidge. The bills would barely get paid if it was left to you.'

'That's rubbish. I managed perfectly well before we got together. Just because I don't have everything organised in anally retentive spreadsheets, doesn't mean I'm incapable.'

Neither of them spoke for a few moments, irritation hot in Livvy's cheeks.

'I honestly didn't imagine for a second you'd be this angry. I really was just trying to do something positive. After all, we'll need a bigger house one day if we have another baby.'

Livvy opened her mouth to reply, discovered that words were reluctant to make an appearance. She and Dominic had never discussed having a second child, and it hadn't occurred to her that he – at nearly fifty – would want another. In truth, she had no desire for more children. She loved Leo fiercely but she'd known by the time she was six months pregnant that one child would be enough for her.

Pulling the laptop onto her lap, she made a conscious decision to change the subject and avoid an argument when Dominic wouldn't be home for another four days. 'Let's not row. Tell me how the meeting with the developers went this morning.'

The screen blinked and then froze, Dominic's face static, eyes closed, mouth wedged open as if sitting in a dentist's chair. Livvy checked her internet connection, saw it was at full strength, waited for Dominic to return.

'For god's . . . bloody . . . shit . . .'

Livvy wiggled her cursor as though it were a magic wand with the power to conjure Dominic back.

'This . . . me . . . unstable . . .'

She waited, swallowing her frustration. There had already been an evening last week when an erratic internet connection had soured their video call halfway through.

'Is that better?' Dominic's face re-emerged fully focused, irritation lining his forehead.

'Perfect.'

'I'm having to sit on the windowsill with the computer on my knees. This bloody office. The Wi-Fi's appalling.'

'I'm sorry you're still there so late. It's annoying you can't call from the flat. At least you'll be home on Friday.'

Dominic shifted position, his face blurring for a second before sharpening back into focus. 'That's what I wanted to tell you before the internet connection went ropey. There's an issue with the plans for one area of the supermarket – not my fault, the architect's. But it means I'm going to have to reconfigure a whole bunch of calculations on top of everything I'm already juggling. There's no way I'm going to get home on Friday night.'

Disappointment curdled in Livvy's stomach. 'You're really going to have to work that late?'

'It's not ideal, I know. But I'd rather get it done here than bring it home with me. I'll head off as soon as I've finished on Saturday morning. I'll be back in time for lunch. We'll still have most of the weekend together.'

Something in Dominic's voice, like an interrupted cadence in a phrase of music, made Livvy ask the question before she was even aware of thinking it. 'Is there something else?'

She watched him readjust the laptop on his knees.

'I was going to tell you at the weekend, but you're too good at picking up when something's wrong.' He paused, took a deep breath. 'It looks like the timeline on this build was a bit optimistic. Talking it through with the team this morning, we think a two-month extension is pretty likely.'

Dates flipped in Livvy's head like departure times on a railway station board. 'But that's after I'm due back at work.'

Dominic raised a pair of defeated eyebrows. 'I know. But what can I do? Projects like this are always at risk of over-running.'

Livvy scrabbled to assemble her thoughts. 'But how are we going to manage my return to work if you're away? I can't do drop-off and pick-up at nursery every day. It'll be impossible.'

Dominic shook his head. 'I don't know. Would it really be the end of the world if you took another couple of months off?'

Irritation prickled Livvy's skin. 'Of course it would. I'd lose the promotion. They're already holding Aisha's job open for a month for me. I can't expect them to wait any longer. Christian can't be without a Policy Director for three months.'

The computer connection stuttered again, the picture freezing and then returning.

'I thought you hadn't definitely decided to take it anyway?'

Livvy frowned. 'What gave you that idea?'

'You did. You said it was still up for discussion.'

'When?'

'When we talked about it on Zoom, the day they offered you the job.'

Livvy wracked her brain, trying to recall the specifics of their previous conversation. 'I don't think I did.'

Dominic shifted the laptop again, the picture pixelating momentarily. 'You did. You said that nothing had been decided yet and it was all still up for discussion.'

'That was about childcare.'

'No, it wasn't. You definitely gave the impression you weren't sold on taking the promotion.'

Before Livvy had a chance to respond, the image on the screen juddered and then stalled, leaving Livvy staring at a static picture of Dominic, forehead furrowed, lips parted, as if cryogenically frozen mid-sentence.

She stared at the screen, waited for Zoom to re-animate, a minute ticking by without any movement. Beside her on the sofa, her phone pinged and she opened WhatsApp, found a message from Dominic.

I don't think the internet is going to be kind to us tonight, sweetheart. I'll call you in the morning. And let's talk about the work stuff when I'm home at the weekend. I'm sorry that delays here make things tricky for you. But surely if Christian and Aisha rate you that highly, they'll consider giving you another two months off? Like I've said before, it's not as if a year's maternity leave is unusual. Anyway, let's talk it through on Saturday. Speak in the morning. I love you. xxx

Livvy snapped closed the laptop, frustration pulsing at her wrists; whatever Dominic's cavalier attitude, she knew that Christian wouldn't keep the job open for another two months, and she was damned if she was going to give it up now.

ANNA

London

It is early in the park. Too early, even, for parents with young children. An elderly man walks a limping black Labrador. Two young women run side by side in black Lycra leggings and fluorescent tops, each with headphones pressed against their ears. A middle-aged woman power-walks past the bandstand, elbows thrusting back and forth as she strides along.

The morning breeze winds its way around my shoulders, slips beneath the open collar of my jacket. I fasten the zip, pull it up to my neck. The sun is making valiant attempts to burn through the clouds but is yet to gather its strength for the day.

Glancing over my shoulder, I scan each of the paths, left and right, but there is no sign of them yet. Looking down at my watch I see that it is not yet nine-thirty, tell myself to be patient. A part of me feels foolish, waiting for a woman I have spoken to only once, a woman who does not even know I am here. I cannot explain this need to talk to her, to tell her what I have learnt. Only that, since finding out about my parents' death last Friday, I have felt a need to confide in someone, as though perhaps only the act of telling another person will enable me to comprehend it fully myself.

When Stephen got home from work last night and asked about my trip to the V&A, I almost fibbed and told him I remembered visiting it before, just to avoid our collective disappointment. But instead, I told him the truth, and he wrapped his arms around me, said he was sorry, reminded me that it's still early days. He urged me not to get too despondent, reassured me that my past would return soon enough. I want to believe he is right and yet, with each passing hour, my faith in my recovery seems to wane.

'Hey.'

I turn around, feel a rush of relief.

Zahira lowers herself onto the bench beside me as Elyas runs straight for the sandpit. Zahira is dressed casually – skinny jeans, a loose-fitting white t-shirt, navy blazer rolled up at the sleeves – but she looks elegant, poised, and there is a sense of calm about her that seeps into me as if by osmosis.

'How have you been?'

It is such an innocuous question and yet I know there are two possible answers: the platitudinal and the truthful.

I tell her all I have learnt over the past few days, watch the emotions shift across her face like clouds across the sky: shock, horror, sadness. It is reassuring, somehow, to see my own emotional journey reflected back at me.

'I can't imagine what you must be going through, finding that out after everything that's happened. How are you feeling?' Zahira rests a hand on my arm, her eyes flitting between my face and her son playing in the sandpit.

'I'm not really sure. Numb, I think. And then I feel guilty because I think I ought to feel something, some sort of grief, but it's like it's out of reach somehow.' I think about the past few days, about my fear that I cannot seem to mourn my parents' death. There is only panic that perhaps I will never remember them.

'I don't think there's any prescribed way to feel when you've been through what you have. You just have to be kind to yourself and get through each day as best you can.'

A phone rings and Zahira reaches into the pocket of her jeans, pulls out her mobile, turns to me apologetically. 'Sorry, I need to take this.' She steps up from the bench, walks a few paces away, eyes still tracking her son.

Elyas plays happily for a minute, clambering up the short wooden ramp to the top of the toddler slide and gliding down. But then he looks towards the bench and his face crumples at the empty space where his mother had been sitting. Fear clouds his expression and I can almost feel his panic thumping in my chest. I dash towards him, crouch down to his level. 'Don't worry, poppet, your mummy's just over there, look.' He follows the line of my finger to where Zahira is waving at him, just a few yards away, and I watch the anxiety melt from his eyes. 'How about we go and sit on the bench, wait for Mummy to finish her call? She won't be long.'

He stares at me with non-committal eyes, studying my face with concentrated intensity. Looking towards his mum, she nods encouragingly and it is reassurance enough. Placing his hand in mine, Elyas lets me lead him towards the bench. Settled on the wooden slats, he looks up at me expectantly as though, now I am here, I might at least entertain him.

'Do you like poems?'

He eyes me suspiciously and I remind myself that he's only three, he probably doesn't know what a poem is. I wrack my brain, try to summon a remnant of children's verse from deep in the recesses of my mind.

'*The Owl and the Pussycat went to sea,*
In a beautiful pea-green boat.'

'My granny has a cat. It's called Pusskins.' Elyas grins and I smile at him, continue.

'*They took some honey, and plenty of money,*
Wrapped up in a five-pound note.'

The rhyming stanzas follow, one after another – the land of the Bong-Trees, the pig in the wood, the turkey on the hill – and I do not know where they have come from, why they have managed to appear now, when I need them. And yet here they are, every line, until the end.

'*They danced by the light of the moon,*
The moon,
The moon,
They danced by the light of the moon.'

'God, did you do all that from memory?' I turn around, find Zahira standing behind the bench. 'I must have read that poem a hundred times and I'd never be able to recite it like that.' She sits down and pulls Elyas onto her lap. Pressing her face to his neck, he giggles as she covers his skin with kisses.

I watch them and something cramps in my chest.

'Elyas loves rhymes, don't you?' She turns to me. 'That's very impressive, knowing it off by heart.'

She squeezes her son tightly, and I look away, the sight of their intimacy like a naked flame threatening to scorch me should I get too close.

'I'm afraid, little bear, we have to get going.' Elyas lets out a plaintive wail. 'I know, I'm sorry – we haven't been here nearly long enough.' Zahira stands up from the bench, reaches for the pushchair. 'Usually we're here for hours, but I need to get some work done. So much for working part-time.' She rolls her eyes, puts Elyas into his buggy, slips his arms through the straps.

'What do you do?'

Zahira grapples with the clasp, clicks it into place. 'I'm a portrait photographer, for magazines and newspapers mostly.' She untwists one of the straps over Elyas's shoulder.

I think about my own idle days, empty for months since being made redundant, and feel a stab of envy that Zahira has so much with which to fill hers. 'That sounds really interesting. So do you photograph famous people?'

Zahira laughs. 'Sometimes.' She lowers her voice conspiratorially. 'They're rarely as interesting as you'd hope. But a lot of my work is human-interest stories – weekend supplements, women's glossies, that kind of thing.' Zahira reaches for the bag tucked beneath the pushchair, pulls out a banana. She peels it, hands it to Elyas before turning back to me. 'We're going to my parents' this Friday, but why don't you give me your mobile number and I can let you know when we'll be here next week.'

I shake my head, knowing even before I speak that my answer doesn't really make sense. 'I don't have a mobile.'

Zahira looks confused. 'But everybody has a mobile.'

I know she is right: I may have lost my personal memories, but I haven't forgotten the existence of modern technology. I feel foolish, suddenly, that I haven't asked Stephen about it before. A phone would have all my contacts in it – friends, former colleagues, previous correspondence. 'I'll ask Stephen about it tonight.'

Zahira presses a foot down on the brake of the pushchair, turns it in the opposite direction. 'Anyway, we'll be here next Tuesday morning – about nine-ish – unless it's pouring with rain. Maybe see you then?'

I tell her I'll be here and watch them leave. Zahira leans forward over the handlebar, chatting to her son, and it is there again, that feeling twisting beneath my ribs, as it has been each time I've seen them together; something unnameable tugging deep inside me.

And then I realise what it is. In all the conversations Stephen and I have had over the past ten days, there has been no mention of children. We have been married twelve years and yet we are childless. As I watch Zahira and Elyas exit through the park gates and on to the street, the sensation billows inside me as though it has a life of its own. I know that this feeling – a yearning, painful and raw – is not a symptom of my head injury. It speaks to something deeper, and I feel sure that there are other things about my life Stephen has chosen not to tell me. What I don't know yet is why.

LIVVY

BRISTOL

Livvy pulled armfuls of dirty washing from the linen basket and piled them onto the floor. She wondered how it was possible for three people to generate so much laundry. In the bedroom next door, Leo was having a mid-morning nap. The night had been restless, Livvy unable to soothe him back to sleep when he'd woken just after four a.m., both of them becoming increasingly fractious as the minutes had marched on. Eventually, a little after six-thirty, Livvy had given up, taken him downstairs, retrieved some toys from the chest beside the fireplace, and played with him in the sitting room, her eyes scratchy and dehydrated from lack of sleep. By ten-thirty, Leo could barely keep awake, and Livvy had put him back in his cot, closed the blackout blind and sung to him until he had fallen asleep.

Piling the clothes into her arms, she carried them down two flights of stairs to the kitchen and stuffed them into the washing machine. The lack of sleep clung to the backs of her eyes and she tried to imagine how she would cope if she were heading into the office today, leading a team of policy advisers, running meetings with NGOs, lobbying politicians. The prospect was exhausting and yet still there was a desire to be there.

Measuring out the laundry liquid and pouring it into the dispenser, she thought about her call yesterday with Aisha, the confirmation that any extension to her maternity leave would rule her out of the promotion. '*You are still okay to come back as planned, aren't you? I managed to persuade Christian he can do without a Policy Director for a month, but there's no way he'll agree to any longer.*' Livvy had backpedalled furiously, told Aisha not to worry, reassured her that she still planned to return as agreed and take on the new role.

Now, twenty-four hours later, the conversation seemed like a moment of madness, or perhaps just hope over reality. She had accepted a job despite having no idea how she would manage childcare for the first two months of it.

Remembering that she needed to take one of Dominic's jackets to the dry cleaner's, she headed upstairs, retrieved it from the wardrobe, carried it into the sitting room. Laying it over the back of the sofa, she slipped a hand inside the pockets to check he'd left nothing inside. She found an empty packet of artisan salted pistachios and felt a spark of irritation that Dominic was buying overpriced snacks while she was avoiding cafés to save money on coffee and cake.

Patting the inside breast pocket, she felt something rustle, reached inside, pulled out a small square of white paper. Turning it over, she saw it was a car park ticket, price and date printed in thick black letters. She was about to crumple it into a ball ready for the bin when the location caught her eye: Waterloo Station Car Park.

The four words jarred in her head like a dissonant musical chord. Picking up her phone, she opened Google Maps, tapped in the location, watched it hone in on a blue pin. She waited as the surrounding buildings revealed themselves: the Royal Festival Hall, the Hayward Gallery, St Thomas' Hospital. The curve of the River Thames, a quintet of bridges over the water.

London.

Opening her internet browser, she googled the name, wondered if perhaps there were two Waterloo stations: another, less famous incarnation somewhere on the outskirts of Sheffield. But Google only offered page after page about the London landmark.

Turning back to the ticket, she double-checked the date and opened the calendar on her phone. It was last Friday, when Dominic was still in Sheffield. The time on the pay-and-display ticket told her it had been bought at 14.23 and had expired three hours later.

The numbers danced in front of Livvy's eyes, refusing to slot into any comprehensible narrative.

Opening WhatsApp, she scrolled back to the previous Friday, eyes scanning the correspondence between her and Dominic. There was no mention of a trip to London, just prosaic messages about his estimated arrival time home.

It didn't make any sense. Dominic had no reason to be in London. And she had no recollection of him mentioning a trip there.

My beautiful goldfish. Dominic's familiar epithet rang in her ears and irritation bristled her skin. She knew Dominic was only being playful, but sometimes it stung, like the prick of a thorn not deep enough to draw blood but sharp enough to wound. And yet now she couldn't help but wonder if he'd mentioned a trip to London and she'd simply forgotten, or perhaps hadn't been paying attention: there were plenty of days when they spoke and she had half an eye on Leo.

Looking at the ticket again, she told herself there must be some logical explanation. Dominic would be home in two days; she would ask him then.

The house phone rang and Livvy scrabbled to answer it, didn't want it to wake Leo when he was so in need of sleep.

'Hello?'

'Is that Livvy?'

Livvy felt a hint of recognition, hoped she was wrong. 'Who's calling?'

There was a pause, the silence heavy with anticipation. 'It's Imogen. Dominic's mother.'

Livvy heard herself inhale a deep rush of air.

'Please don't hang up. I know I shouldn't have followed you last week, but I was desperate. It's the funeral tomorrow and I just wondered—'

'I've already said I can't help you with that.' Livvy tried to keep her voice steady.

There was another pause, and Livvy could almost hear a dilemma being evaluated on the other end of the line.

'I wanted to ask if you might meet with me. There are things I think we should talk about.'

Livvy felt her body stiffen. 'What things?'

'I can't say. Not over the phone. They're too . . . delicate. Please will you meet me, just once? If you don't want to see me again after that, I promise I'll leave you alone.'

Thoughts scrabbled for clarity in Livvy's brain.

'It doesn't have to be for long.'

From upstairs, Leo cried out, and Livvy glanced down at her watch, realised with a heavy heart that he'd managed only a single sleep cycle.

'Will you think about it? Just one meeting.'

Leo began to squall and Livvy felt an urgency to get to him. 'I'm sorry, I have to go.'

'Of course, I can hear Leo, poor mite. You go.'

Livvy replaced the receiver, raced upstairs to collect Leo. Lifting him from his cot, Imogen's words echoed in her ears – *There are things I think we should talk about . . . Not over the phone. They're too delicate* – and however much she tried to tell herself that Imogen was just trying to bait her, the words burrowed under her skin, niggling at her, refusing to let her go.

ANNA

LONDON

'Are you going to have your usual?'

Stephen looks at me over the top of his menu, and I am aware of a now-familiar sense of failure flickering in my chest like a faulty light bulb. 'What do I usually have?'

There is a moment's hesitation before Stephen places his menu flat on the table, reaches across the polished marble tabletop, strokes the back of my hand.

'I'm sorry. That was tactless of me. You usually have the grilled chicken salad.'

My eyes return to the menu and I read the description of it, think it sounds rather bland. 'What are you having?'

'Same as always – pasta with meatballs.'

I find it on the menu, turn back to Stephen. 'That sounds nice. I think I'll have the same.'

Stephen raises an eyebrow, smiles. 'Really? Usually you won't go near pasta. You say it's the devil incarnate for women approaching forty.'

I look back down at the menu, try to connect to the version of myself who would happily relinquish nice food for the sake of a few extra calories. 'No, it's fine. I'll have the salad.'

'Are you sure?' Stephen turns his head, raises a hand, catches the eye of a waitress and orders for us both.

It was Stephen's idea for us to come out for dinner tonight. Nothing fancy, he said, just the local branch of a chain restaurant within walking distance of home. '*We've been there so often, it might help jog something.*' There was a note of quiet encouragement in his voice, and as we'd walked into the brightly lit restaurant, I had felt his eyes on my face, was aware of the charge of expectation between us, waiting for a glimmer of recognition that didn't arrive. I'd fixed a smile on my face even as I could sense the disappointment passing between us like an electrical current.

As we wait for our food to arrive, I wonder what it was like before, when we came out for dinner: whether we talked non-stop, gossiped about people we knew, discussed politics and world affairs. Whether we speculated about the lives of other diners, held hands romantically across the table. Whether we made each other laugh. Or whether, like now, we sat in slightly awkward silence, feeling conspicuous for our lack of conversation.

I look around the restaurant, in search of something – a smell, a sound, a sight, a word – to give some insight into our marriage as it was before, but nothing materialises.

At a nearby table, two men are scrolling and tapping on their phones, and it reminds me of my conversation with Zahira. 'Where's my mobile phone?'

Stephen looks up from the wine list he is studying even though the glass in front of him is still half full. 'What?'

'My mobile phone. I must have had one, before the crash. I wondered where it is.'

Stephen slots the wine list back into its plastic stand. 'It got broken in the accident. We need to get you a new one.'

'But what if there are people trying to contact me? Friends and . . . other people.' I don't know who I mean, cannot recall the name or face of anyone specific who may be trying to get in touch.

'They can always call the house phone, or me. I suspect the only calls you'll be missing are people trying to sell you PPE.' He rolls his eyes as if I am having a lucky escape.

I think about Zahira in the park today, about her surprise when I said I didn't have a phone. 'When can we get me a new one?'

'I can order one tomorrow. It'll probably take a few days to arrive. But what's the rush? You've always got the house phone.'

I think about my walks to the park, about my fear that I might not be able to find my way home even with my handwritten map. 'It would make me feel safer if I had one. At least if I go out I could call you if anything happened.'

Stephen eyes me with concern. 'You promised you wouldn't go out without me.'

I feel myself hesitate. I haven't told Stephen about my trips to the park last Friday and today, or about my conversations with Zahira. It seemed better not to. But now I've made two successful trips, I feel more confident in telling him the truth. 'I went to the park, but it was fine. I made a map on my way there, and I found my way home without any problems.'

Stephen looks startled. 'Oh, my love, I wish you hadn't. What if you'd got lost again? I know it must be tedious, being at home all day. But going out by yourself . . . It's such a risk when you're still recovering.'

He stops abruptly as the waitress places our food in front of us. I look at the grilled chicken strips arranged on a bed of leaves, glance enviously at the steaming plate of pasta and meatballs Stephen has ordered. We both remain silent as the waitress heaps spoonfuls of Parmesan onto Stephen's food, watch as it begins to melt, and I thank the waitress as she leaves.

'If you do go out, just please don't stray too far from home.' Stephen takes in a long, deep breath. 'We love living in London but . . . it's not always a safe city if you haven't got your wits about you.'

A phone pings and Stephen picks up the mobile lying face down on the table, looks at it, puts it back again. He hesitates before reaching into the pocket of his suit jacket and taking out a second phone, one I haven't seen before, its transparent cover stained with the clear impression of fingerprints. He glances at me before swiping a finger across its screen, reading a message.

'Why have you got two phones?'

He looks up at me, distracted. 'It's my work phone. I should have left it at home. I'm sorry.' He sighs, slips it back into his pocket.

'What's wrong?'

Stephen shakes his head. 'Nothing.'

'It doesn't seem like nothing.'

He hesitates, rests his fork against the edge of his plate. 'I suppose I'm going to have to tell you at some point. I've got to go away this weekend, to an academic conference. I know it's appalling timing. I told my Head of Department it wasn't fair to expect me to go but she's . . . well, she's not the most sympathetic of women.'

The words sink in, panic churning in my stomach. The thought of an entire weekend at home alone when I will have already spent all week by myself presses down on my chest.

'I'm really sorry. It's just one night – just Saturday to Sunday. You'll be okay. I'll phone every few hours, and I'll make sure you've got a fridge full of food. If we keep you busy with books and movies the time will fly by.'

I hear the supreme effort in his voice to reassure me, and I know it is not his fault, my dread at being left alone overnight. I understand that his entire life – his whole career – cannot be put on hold just because I can't remember anything beyond the last ten days. I force my lips into a smile, swallow against the narrowing in my throat. 'It's fine.'

'It's not fine. It's infuriating. But next week I'll do my best to get home early every day so we can go for a walk before dinner.'

I find myself nodding even as the prospect of yet more lonely days yawns before me like a series of uncertain question marks.

He reaches out a hand, places it on mine. 'I really am sorry. I don't have to go away for work very often. If I could get out of it, I would. But Veronica – my boss – she's such a . . .' His face stiffens like a jammed door, and then he lets out a long stream of air, rearranges his features into something more benign. 'It's just really unfortunate timing. I know how vulnerable you are at the moment, and I hate the thought of leaving you. But it's only a couple of days. I'll get back as early as I can on Sunday.'

I try to feel the reassurance in Stephen's explanation, but there is something else on my mind, a question that has been haunting me all day. It whispers in my ear and I cannot ignore it. 'Why don't we have any children?'

Stephen's fork halts in mid-air, hovering as if uncertain whether to continue its journey or retreat back to the plate. The white noise of other diners is loud in my ears.

He lowers his fork, stares down at his pasta for what seems an inordinate length of time. When he finally raises his head, I see it immediately: the apology in his eyes even before he begins to speak. 'We tried, really hard, but it just never happened for us.'

I hear his words, wait for them to accrue some meaning, but they are like hard pebbles sinking into quicksand: gone before my fingers can grab hold of them.

I am aware of picking up a tumbler of water, taking a sip, the cool liquid slipping down my throat. I am aware of the waitress gliding past, plates balanced along her arm, of the couple sitting behind Stephen, laughing. I am aware of all these things and yet there is a sense that I am somewhere outside myself, unable to inhabit my body. 'Why couldn't we? What was wrong?' My voice is small, shrunken, as though it fears what may greet it if it ventures beyond the shadows.

Stephen shakes his head. 'We don't know. The hospital did endless tests, but they never identified what the problem was. We just couldn't seem to conceive.'

'What about IVF? Did we try that?' I hear myself clutching at straws, my hope that there may yet be a stone unturned.

'We had two rounds on the NHS. That was as many as we were entitled to.'

'What about going privately? Did we try that?'

Stephen's eyes crease at the edges. 'We felt—' He stops abruptly, looks down, fiddles with the button on the cuff of his sleeve. 'We felt we'd done enough. We'd already been trying for five years when we had the first round of IVF. And when that didn't work . . .' He wavers and I do not fill the silence. 'It had been hard. On both of us. You, especially. It had made you . . . You'd found it very difficult, emotionally. After everything that had happened with your parents, you felt you needed a child of your own. It was a tough few years. But in the end, we just had to accept that it wasn't meant to be.' He stops speaking, as if he knows he could go on explaining forever but that no outpouring of words could ever fill the void.

Something seems to fracture inside me: regret, sorrow, despair. I think of Zahira and Elyas in the park, feel that same burning sensation I did the very first time I saw them, and I understand that it is not a new longing. It has been there for years: a feeling that something within me is missing and may never be found.

'I'm so sorry, my love. I'd give anything to be able to say things were different. I can only imagine how hard it is, having to relearn all these things about our life. I hate seeing you so upset.'

I feel Stephen's hand on mine, feel the warmth of his touch, but it is as though I am not really present, as though my mind has wandered elsewhere, trailing after something I must have craved for so long and learnt would never be mine.

LIVVY

BRISTOL

'What do you fancy? My treat. I'm having a blueberry muffin.'

Bea looked at Livvy, and Livvy looked at the selection of cakes in the café's glass cabinet.

You can't keep moaning about the fact that most of your friends have already lost all their baby weight if you're eating forty-two pounds of cake every month.

Shaking her head, Livvy pulled off the thin cotton blanket from where it was tucked around Leo in his pushchair. 'Nothing for me. I'll just have a decaf latte with skimmed milk.'

Bea held Livvy's gaze for a heartbeat longer than necessary, and it was Livvy who looked away first.

'You get us a table, I'll bring it over.'

Livvy navigated the buggy through the narrow avenue of tables, found space by the window. Lifting Leo onto her lap, she took the teething ring from its sterilised pouch, handed it to him. Glancing at her phone screen, she clocked the time: quarter to ten. Almost three hours until Dominic was due back from Sheffield.

'So has the promotion been formally signed off now?' Bea sat down opposite Livvy, handed her a coffee.

Livvy picked up the teaspoon, stirred her drink even though she no longer took sugar. 'Aisha and Christian think it is, but I can't really see how I can make it work.'

'Why not?'

Livvy took a tissue from her pocket, wiped some dribble from Leo's chin. 'Dominic's project is overrunning by a couple of months at least. He won't be back when I'm due to start. I can't see how I'll manage all the drop-offs and pick-ups at nursery just doing my old job, let alone starting a new one. I think I might have to delay going back until Dominic's home for good. Which means giving up the promotion.' She tried to keep the resentment from her voice but could hear it seeping through.

'But that's ridiculous. Dominic can't expect you to give it up. Why can't he finish his contract on time? He's freelance – he can get another job. You could be doing that Policy Director job for years.'

They were all questions Livvy had asked repeatedly since Monday, her conversations with Dominic circular, repetitive. 'Dominic says there's no way he can get out of his contract early – he's got to see it through to the end.'

'So you're just expected to relinquish the promotion you've been working towards your whole career? That's absurd. Has Dominic got no understanding of how important this is to you?'

Livvy reached into her bag, pulled out a pot of nectarine she'd sliced earlier, handed a piece to Leo. In her mind, she tried to separate Bea's hostility towards Dominic from the validity of the points she was making, but it was impossible to delineate a clear, unwavering line between the two. 'I'm angry about it, obviously. But if Dominic's insistent he can't finish his contract early, I don't see what I can do.'

'But it's completely unreasonable. What does Dominic want – for you to be a stay-at-home wife for the rest of your life?' Derision dripped from Bea's voice, and Livvy watched her sister take in a deep breath, try to restrain her annoyance. 'Are you sure you can't make it work? It's only a couple of months.'

Livvy wondered how many times she had played through the various scenarios in her mind. It was like an impossible mathematical proof, resisting any neat solution. 'I talked it over with Mum yesterday. I could drop Leo off at nursery every morning but there's no way I can be there at six every evening to collect him. Mum and Dad have offered to do three days a week – pick Leo up, take him back to mine, give him dinner and get him ready for bed. But they can't do the other two because of their National Trust stuff, and I wouldn't expect them to give that up.'

There was a moment's pause, and then Bea looked across the table at Leo, then at Livvy. 'I'll do it.'

'Do what?'

'Collect Leo the other two evenings. Take him home, give him his dinner.' The way Bea said it – so matter-of-fact – it was as though the offer wasn't huge, generous, above and beyond.

'I can't ask you to do that—'

'You're not asking. I'm offering.'

Possibilities skittered through Livvy's mind like marbles on cobblestones. 'But what about your job? Early evenings are one of your busiest times at the practice.'

Bea waved a hand dismissively in the air. 'What's the point of being a partner if I can't be flexible with my hours once in a while? The other partners are forever taking time off to go to their kids' school plays or sports days or some other child-related thing they can't possibly miss. Why shouldn't I do the same for my nephew? Honestly, it'll be fine.'

Livvy began to recalibrate her expectations. 'Are you sure?'

'Absolutely. It's only for a couple of months.'

Livvy reached across the table, took hold of Bea's hand. 'Has anyone ever told you you're the best sister in the world?'

Bea laughed. 'Well, if they haven't, it's probably about time they started.' She squeezed Livvy's fingers. 'But seriously, there's no way I'm letting you miss out on that promotion just because Dominic's putting his own career first. And anyway, it'll be nice for me to spend a bit more time with Leo. You know how much I love him.' Stretching out an arm, she tickled Leo's tummy. 'So that's all sorted then?'

'Yep. I'll just talk it over with Dominic, check he's happy.'

Bea's eyes narrowed at the edges. 'Why do you need to check with Dominic?'

Livvy handed another piece of nectarine to Leo, tried to inject some levity into her voice. 'Well, he is Leo's dad. I wouldn't want him making plans that affected Leo without talking to me.'

'You mean, other than him extending his contract by two months, putting your promotion and Leo's childcare in jeopardy, you mean?'

Livvy took a sip of coffee, allowed herself a moment's pause, balancing the tightrope between her divided loyalties. 'I don't think that's entirely fair. We're two parents, trying our best to juggle two careers and a young baby. It's not easy.'

There was a moment's silence. 'Is that all?'

Something in Bea's voice made Livvy hesitate. 'What do you mean?'

'Is everything okay with you and Dominic? Outside of the work stuff?'

'Of course, everything's fine.'

Bea studied Livvy's face intently. 'It's just that, if it isn't, you know you can talk to me. Whatever's going on – with work, or with Dominic – I'm always here for you, you know that.' Bea had tried to keep her voice neutral, but her articulation of Dominic's name was chiselled at the edges.

Livvy thought about the first time she'd introduced Bea to Dominic – over dinner at Livvy's old flat, three weeks after they'd met – and how she'd known, before she'd even served the main course, that Bea wasn't impressed. Her sister had been polite, but Livvy had been able to tell from Bea's quizzical expression that there was something about Dominic she instinctively disliked. And although Dominic had tried to be his usual, charming self, something had been off beam in him that evening too, as though he were going through the motions of ingratiating himself with Bea, but his heart wasn't in it. Every encounter between the three of them since had been a variation on the same theme and now, eighteen months later, Livvy generally tried to keep her sister and her husband compartmentalised in separate areas of her life. 'Look, I know you're not Dominic's biggest fan, but I honestly think you'd like him if you gave him more of a chance.'

'I don't *dislike* Dominic. I just don't really feel I know him. I know he's charming and confident and amiable. But I don't really have any sense of what's beneath all of that.'

Livvy laughed, but it sounded forced, strained. 'Has it ever occurred to you that perhaps that's it – that he really is just charming and amiable? Perhaps he's just a nice man who really wants to get on with you and can sense that you don't really like him?'

Bea rolled her eyes. 'I'm never *not nice* to him. I just think . . . he seems to have some very fixed ideas about things, and when those things affect you and your promotion, I get annoyed on your behalf.'

Livvy thought about how the rhythm of her relationship with Bea had been altered by her marriage, as though it were a piece of music in which Livvy had moved into a different time signature and Bea was still playing to the old meter. 'You don't need to feel annoyed on my behalf. But it really would mean a lot to me if you two could get on.'

Leo cried out as he picked up the nectarine pot, found it empty. Livvy grabbed her phone to check the time, wondering if she could risk giving him a rice cake without spoiling his lunch, and found a message from Dominic. Opening it, she was greeted by a photo of their empty sitting room.

Great homecoming. I get up at the crack of dawn to drive back early and surprise you, and you're not even here. Where are you??

Shoving the empty nectarine pot back into the change bag, she tapped out a quick reply.

Sorry – just popped out. Back v soon! Xx

She turned to Bea. 'I'm really sorry, I'll have to go. Dominic's got home early.'

Bea shrugged. 'Why does that mean you have to rush off? I'm sure he'll cope on his own for half an hour.'

Livvy began strapping Leo into his buggy, knocking the chair of the person next to her and apologising for her clumsiness. 'We haven't seen each other all week – it can't be much fun getting home to an empty house. I just wish he'd told me he was going to be early.'

'What, so you could have cancelled me altogether rather than shooting off after ten minutes?'

Bea's tone caused a flush of heat to creep around Livvy's neck. She looked away, swung the change bag over the handlebar of the pushchair, shoved her cardigan into the well underneath. 'I didn't mean it like that. It's just, after we've been apart all week, it would be nice if I'm there when he gets home.'

There was a beat of silence. 'Fine. But I'll see you on Tuesday night – dinner at yours? I should be able to get away by half seven.' Bea rested a hand on Livvy's arm. 'And don't forget what I said. If there's anything wrong – or anything you want to talk about – you know where I am.'

Livvy nodded, hugged her sister, thanked her again for saving her promotion. Angling the buggy out of the café, she waved through the window and sprinted for home, checking her phone and wondering why Dominic was yet to reply.

ANNA

LONDON

The house is unnervingly quiet. Logically, I know it is no quieter than on any other day. But the knowledge that Stephen will not be here for the next thirty-six hours seems to exacerbate the silence.

I glance down at my watch: just gone half past nine. On a weekday, Stephen would not be home for another ten or eleven hours. And yet today, knowing that he is two hundred miles away and will not be back until tomorrow evening, time seems to have stretched, each minute lengthened like a piece of plasticine rolled into a narrow line, so thin it is on the verge of breaking.

In the corner of the room, the telephone sits silently in its cradle. It is only a few minutes since I finished speaking to Stephen. He seemed harried, said the traffic had been appalling even though he'd left at first light. He wasn't able to speak for long, needed to register for the conference, locate some of the academics from other universities he'd arranged to meet. He just wanted to hear my voice, check I was okay, reassure me I would be fine. He promised to phone again later, reminded me about the bag of stir-fry in the fridge for my lunch that only needs a few minutes' cooking in the wok.

A light comes on in the house behind ours and a woman enters, a child in her arms. The little girl is about a year old, wearing a pale yellow dress. As the woman leans over her laptop screen, the child places a palm on the woman's cheek, leans her head against her neck, and there is such intimacy in the gesture, such instinctive trust and love, that I have to turn away, sit in the armchair with its back to the window, force myself not to look.

In the few days since Stephen told me about our failed attempts to have a child, I have been unable to think about much else. Thoughts of parenthood – the death of my parents, my own inability to conceive – have developed a gravitational pull, drawing me back, again and again, to a sense of impotent grief.

I have imagined what it must have been like, month after month, to have hoped and prayed for my period not to come, have imagined the sorrow that must have accompanied every stomach cramp heralding its imminent arrival. I have tried – and failed – to remember those two rounds of IVF, tried to envisage the cautious optimism and the crushing disappointment. I have wondered whether those turbulent swings from hope to despair put a strain on our marriage or whether they brought us closer. I have questioned whether my acceptance of our childlessness is the whole story or whether there is a private grief I keep stored in a corner of my heart, like a pair of knitted baby booties, bought with hope but never worn, wrapped in tissue paper and kept out of sight, to be looked at only in moments of quiet contemplation.

The doorbell chimes and my whole body flinches. There is nobody I am expecting, no reason for anyone to visit. Unease creeps across my skin and I think about the head injury leaflets that I have read countless times now, their words so familiar I can recall them verbatim: *Nervousness and anxiety are common symptoms after a head injury. Patients can experience irrational fears and oversensitivity to light and noise.*

Peering out of the window, I try to see who's there, but my eyeline cannot achieve the right angle. Entering the hall, I slip the security chain into position, pull down the Yale lock, open the door the few inches that the chain will allow.

On the other side is a man in his early twenties, wearing loose denim jeans and an unironed white t-shirt. He looks at me expectantly, but when I say nothing, he is the first to speak.

'I'm here to mend the leaking tap.'

It is a statement made with conviction, but sweat prickles the skin at the base of my spine.

'Can I come in?'

My throat feels hot and when I speak there is a tremor in my voice, like unintended vibrato. 'Who sent you?'

'The letting agent.'

My head spins, too much information to absorb. 'What letting agent?'

The man on the doorstep sighs, glances down at his watch. 'The person you pay your rent to.'

He looks at me as if I am mad, or stupid, and for a moment I wonder if perhaps I am both.

'Do you want to let me in?'

I hear the impatience in his voice, spot the toolbox in his hand. It is true that the bathroom tap has been leaking for the past few days, true that Stephen said he would organise somebody to fix it. But he did not warn me they were coming today. And, more importantly, he has never mentioned our house being rented. I have assumed that we own it, and the revelation that we don't leaves me feeling as though I am standing on shifting sands.

Pulling the chain out of the chrome bar, I open the door, let the man in.

'Bathroom tap, isn't it? Upstairs?'

I nod. 'Just at the top, straight ahead.'

The man leaps up the stairs, two at a time, and I hover below in the hallway, tell myself that it is okay: he is meant to be here, Stephen must have arranged it. And yet, having this stranger in the house has knocked something out of kilter, like a collision of asteroids, shifting them onto a different orbit.

A few minutes pass and I cannot help myself, call up the stairs. 'Is everything alright?'

'Fine. Just a faulty valve. Won't take a minute to fix.'

Relief fills my lungs and I tell myself it is okay, he will be gone soon. I find myself craving the silence and solitude that only a few moments ago I had found oppressive.

The telephone rings, thrusting its way into the quiet, and I run to answer it, assume it will be Stephen.

'Hello?'

'Can I speak to Anna Bradshaw, please?' It is a woman's voice: educated, softly spoken, the faint hint of an East European accent.

'Yes, speaking.'

'My name's Carla Stanislaw. I'm a therapist with the West London Wellbeing Service. You've been referred for a course of therapy after your recent accident. I'd like to make an appointment for you, if that's okay.'

It takes me a moment to get my bearings. In the emotional disarray of the past two weeks, I have forgotten about the consultant's referral.

'Anna?'

'Yes, sorry, of course. That would be great, thanks.'

She offers me some dates and times, and I tell her I am always free, am grateful when she does not laugh as if I have told a joke. We agree on an appointment for next Friday, and I'm relieved it is in the afternoon, that I will not have to miss Zahira in the park in the morning.

Writing the details of the appointment on the notepad by the phone, I say goodbye and replace the handset in its cradle. Footsteps thud down the stairs, and by the time I reach the hallway, the plumber is already standing by the front door, one hand on the latch.

'All done. Any more problems just give the agent a ring.'

He smiles a little cautiously before opening the door and letting himself out. My belated thank-you trails behind him.

Heading into the kitchen, I pour a glass of water, check the time, take a couple of tablets in the ongoing battle against the pain clawing at my temples.

Leaning against the kitchen sink, I try to recollect any mention of our house being rented. But I don't remember Stephen and I discussing the ownership of it at all. It is simply an assumption I have made.

Thinking of all the boxes in the spare room, I recall Stephen's explanation on the day I came home from hospital: '*Every weekend we promise ourselves that we'll finally tackle all this and every weekend we somehow manage to find something more interesting to do.*' The empty weekend stretches before me like a weary sigh, and it occurs to me that I could make myself useful while Stephen's away. I can begin to unpack all those boxes and perhaps, in the process, I may find something that will restore a fragment of my past to me.

LIVVY

BRISTOL

Livvy's fingers fumbled with the key, unable to find the precise angle required for it to turn, cursing under her breath as it jammed in the lock. All the way home she'd kept checking her phone, but still nothing from Dominic.

With a satisfied click the key swivelled in the barrel and Livvy tipped the buggy onto its back wheels, steered it through the narrow doorway. The hall door was shut – she always left it open to avoid a tight manoeuvre – and she sucked in her tummy as she squeezed past the buggy, one leg suspended in the air as if performing an ungainly arabesque, and pushed open the door.

Wheeling the buggy into the sitting room, she found Dominic in the armchair at the far end of the room.

'I'm so sorry we weren't here when you got home. Why didn't you tell me you were coming so early?' Unstrapping Leo from the buggy, she picked him up, settled him into his activity chair.

'I wanted to surprise you. I just assumed you'd be here.' Dominic's voice was low, unemotional, but there was something uneven in it, like a misaligned paving stone that might trip Livvy up if she didn't watch her step.

'I'm sorry.' It was only now that she noticed the bouquet of flowers – pink freesias, orange gerberas, red berries – lying on the floor beside him, cellophane crumpled, a handful of petals scattering the floor. Dominic usually favoured white flowers, said he found bright ones gauche. 'You bought me flowers. They're beautiful. Thank you.' She picked them up, put them on the coffee table, pulled up the pale grey footstool next to Dominic. 'So did you get all your work done?'

There was an almost imperceptible nod of his head. 'I stayed up until midnight finishing it so I could get on the road first thing this morning.'

'I'm really sorry.'

Dominic's Adam's apple rose and fell. 'Where were you, anyway?'

'I was just . . .' Livvy hesitated, wondered whether a little white lie would be better in the circumstances, before settling on the truth. 'With Bea. For a quick coffee – her treat. I even declined the offer of cake.' She laughed, but it sounded thin, reedy, like air escaping from the pinched neck of a balloon.

Dominic said nothing for a few seconds, his gaze fixed on something out of the window. When he finally turned back to her, his voice was flat, muted, a hinterland between emotions. 'Yet again, your family comes first.'

The comment was disorientating, as though she and Dominic were travelling through an unfamiliar landscape and he had changed their route without telling her. 'What do you mean?'

Dominic shook his head. 'Don't you think it would be nice, just occasionally, for our marriage to be your priority, rather than you always putting your parents and your sister first?'

Livvy paused, knowing the topography of this conversation was littered with mines. In the early months of their relationship, Dominic had seemed to revel in the warmth of her family;

he'd been charming and funny, and her parents had adored him from the outset. It had seemed to Livvy that he'd embraced the opportunity to be part of a functional, loving family. But more recently she'd been aware of snatches of resentment creeping in, moments when Livvy's closeness to her family seemed to emphasise Dominic's estrangement from his. And after the events of the past fortnight – his mother's reappearance, his father's death – those occurrences seem to have been exacerbated further. 'I don't think that's really fair.'

'But you're *always* with them. The amount of time you spend with them, it's like you're still a child.'

The accusation stung, not because it was true but because it was unfair. Repressing her frustration, she reminded herself that yesterday had been his father's funeral, that even though Dominic hadn't attended, it would still have provoked difficult feelings for him. She softened her voice, placed a hand on his knee. 'I rarely see them at weekends because I know . . . I understand it can be difficult for you. But they're my family. Of course I want to spend time with them.'

There was a heartbeat of silence. 'I thought Leo and I were your family.'

Livvy faltered, as though she had stepped on what she thought was solid ground only for it to shift beneath her. 'You're all my family. You and them.'

'But your parents and your sister come first?' He stared at Livvy as if challenging her to a duel.

'No, of course not. You know that you and Leo come first. Please, let's not ruin the day when you've only just got home. I've been really looking forward to seeing you.'

'So much so that you weren't even here when I got back.'

Livvy allowed herself a breath. 'I've said I'm sorry. I'd never have gone out if I'd known you were coming so early.' Taking hold of his hand, she kissed the back of it, felt Dominic shift in his seat, sensed the tension between them begin to dissolve.

'I'm sorry. It was just such a disappointment to get home and find an empty house.' He half smiled and Livvy felt as though she were emptying her lungs for the first time since arriving home. 'Anyway, what were you and your sister gossiping about today?'

Livvy ignored the arch tone, kept her voice breezy. 'I was just telling her about all the work stuff.'

'Oh, great. And what pearls of wisdom did Bea have to offer?'

'She was actually really helpful—'

'I'll bet she was. Instructing you to go back to work and get Leo settled into childcare as soon as possible?'

'It wasn't like that—'

Dominic squeezed her shoulder. 'I'm only teasing. But seriously, do you think Bea has any clue about your life, or your priorities? She can't possibly understand how you feel about going back to work. She's not a mother.'

'I think that's a bit unfair—'

'Is it? I like Bea, you know I do. I just hate the way she makes you doubt yourself sometimes. Think about all the times she's tried to push you into decisions that would be right for her but aren't right for you. If you'd listened to her advice, Leo wouldn't be here now.'

Instinctively, Livvy reached across to Leo, smoothed her hand gently along his forehead, remembered the morning she'd told Bea she was pregnant. Bea had cautioned Livvy to think through her options before sharing the news with Dominic. There had been nothing sinister in her sister's advice: she was simply trying to ensure that Livvy knew her own mind before bringing Dominic into the equation. And yet, ever since Livvy had told Dominic the story of that morning, in Dominic's version of events, Bea had practically dragged Livvy to the doors of an abortion clinic and thrust her inside.

'Bea wasn't making me doubt anything. She was being amazing. She's offered to collect Leo from childcare two days a week, and Mum and Dad can do the other three, so between them they can cover your share of nursery pick-ups until you're back from Sheffield. It means I can take the promotion without any impact on Leo. They're all doing us a massive favour.' She could hear the defiance in her voice, wished there were no need to defend one part of her family against another.

Dominic said nothing, fidgeted in his chair as though he could not, all of a sudden, get comfortable, and Livvy felt compelled to fill the silence. 'I know you've got some worries about me going back to work when Leo's so little, but he really will be fine, and this promotion's important to me.'

Dominic looked down at Leo, then back up at Livvy. 'It's not that. It's the reason I really wanted you here when I got home. I've got a confession to make.'

ANNA

London

It is early afternoon by the time I am walking briskly along tree-lined streets towards the park. I'd wanted to get out earlier, but I knew Stephen would be phoning at lunchtime and I didn't want to miss his call. He ended up phoning later than expected, said a conference session had overrun and he didn't have long before the next. He sounded pressed for time, and I spoke quickly, told him about my conversation with the therapist, and he said it was great news, a step in the right direction. I asked about our house being rented and there were a few moments of awkward misunderstanding before he apologised, said he hadn't thought to clarify before. He explained that we'd sold our home last year, but the house we were purchasing had fallen through at the last minute. We'd moved into rented accommodation and were now looking to buy slightly further out of town, where we could get more space for our money. Hearing Stephen's explanation, it suddenly made sense why so much of our furniture seems ill-fitting in this house.

Arriving at the gate to the park, I see Zahira and Elyas immediately, experience a wave of relief that they are here, on a Saturday afternoon. As I head towards the playground, Zahira turns, sees me, smiles and waves. It is such a small gesture and yet I feel like a new pupil on the first day of school who has unexpectedly been taken under the wing of the most popular girl in the year.

When I reach Zahira, she is pushing Elyas in the toddler swing, just as she was the first time I saw her. 'I hoped we might see you today. How are things?'

I stand beside her, watch her push. 'Okay, thanks. Stephen's away at a conference for the weekend and he won't be back till tomorrow night, so I thought it would be good to get out of the house.' I am gabbling slightly and I stop myself before explanations run away with me.

'He's gone away? So soon after your accident?'

I hear the surprise in her voice. 'It's a work thing. An academic conference. He tried to get out of it but he couldn't. I'll be fine.'

Elyas removes his hands from the safety bar, lifts his arms into the air.

'Hands back on the bar, sweetie.'

Elyas obeys immediately, begins singing a song about two little dickie birds sitting on a wall, and even though I do not explicitly remember it, it seems to resonate with something in me. It is as though I have been transported to a different time, a different place, but I do not know where or when. And yet the more I try to pull it into focus, the hazier it becomes, as though a small, invisible hand is tugging on my arm, trying to show me something, but my legs are refusing to move, not allowing me to discover what it might be.

'I tried befriending you on social media, but you're impossible to find. Do you have a different username or something?'

I shake my head. 'I'm not sure.'

Zahira stops the swing for a moment, reiterates to Elyas that he needs to hold on tight. 'I looked everywhere – Instagram, Twitter, Facebook. Maybe you don't do social media?'

I scour my brain, searching for a snippet of memory to help answer Zahira's question. There seems to be something on the periphery of my vision, like a floater gliding across the edge of my eye, but each attempt to focus on it slides it further away from me. 'I just don't know. I'm sorry.'

Zahira shrugs. 'It's just quite unusual in this day and age. Not that I'm saying it's a bad thing. There've been times since I split up from Elyas's dad when I really wished I didn't have access to quite so many details about his life.'

It is the first time Zahira has mentioned Elyas's father, and I find myself stepping tentatively into the space left by her reference. 'So you're not still together?'

Zahira waves a hand in the air. 'God, no. I realised he wasn't *the one* when he missed Elyas's birth because he was in a hotel room with his mistress.'

There is a matter-of-factness to the way Zahira says it, but the bitterness beneath is sharp, distinct.

'I'm so sorry. That must have been awful.'

Zahira stops the swing, zips up Elyas's jacket against the breeze, begins pushing him again. 'It was pretty hard at the time. He gave me all the usual rubbish: said it meant nothing, that he'd just felt overwhelmed at the thought of becoming a parent, that he'd found the pregnancy difficult. *He'd* found the pregnancy difficult! I discovered the affair had been going on for six months and that was that. He moved out and I became a single mum.'

Elyas demands to be pushed higher and Zahira complies. I watch, thinking about how different her story is from the one I'd imagined. I saw an impeccably dressed woman, a devoted mother, a successful photographer, and made assumptions about the rest of her life based on nothing more than appearances.

'So is he involved in Elyas's life now?' I feel my cheeks redden, wonder if it is too personal a question, but Zahira doesn't miss a beat before replying.

'He usually has him every other weekend, though he's not entirely reliable on that front. But he's always on time with maintenance payments, and given some of the horror stories you hear, I guess I should be grateful for that.' Stepping back from the swing, she undoes the loose bun at the nape of her neck, reties her hair with nimble fingers. 'My parents always warned me: be careful who you have kids with. Mortgages, joint bank accounts, marriages – you can extricate yourself from all of it. But have a child with someone and you're linked to them for the rest of your life.'

Elyas calls out for her to stop, and Zahira halts the swing, lifts him out, and we both follow as he runs over to the slide. He waits his turn before climbing up, sitting proudly at the top like a king surveying his domain, and glides down.

Watching Elyas, the conversation with Stephen from earlier in the week replays in my head. We have not talked since about our inability to have children. It seemed so definitive that to discuss it further would feel like picking a scab. From what Stephen told me, we have done our best to make peace with our childlessness, have accepted that parenthood will not be a part of our lives. But watching Elyas now, I sense a deep uterine tug, cannot help but imagine that perhaps my acceptance was only ever skin-deep. Perhaps I simply became adept at masking my grief.

'I'm afraid I've got to go in a minute. I've got some friends coming for dinner tonight and for some inexplicable reason I've decided to do an Ottolenghi recipe that requires about a thousand different ingredients.'

She laughs, and an image slips into my head: a dinner party, candlelight, food, wine, friendship. And then a guillotine slices across my thoughts and I wonder whether the image was a memory or simply a fantasy.

Zahira calls to Elyas, tells him he can have three more slides and then it's time to go. She turns to me, hesitates. 'Would you like to come back for a cup of tea? My flat's only a couple of streets away. You'll have to watch me chopping herbs, but it'd be nice to have the company.'

Something glides across my skin and I do not know whether it is appreciation or caution. *We love living in London, but it's not always a safe city if you haven't got your wits about you.* Stephen's vigilance reverberates in my head, in a tug of war with the desire for friendship.

I glance down at my watch, see that I have been out for over an hour already. 'I'd love to, but I don't think I can. Stephen might phone soon and he'll worry if I'm not at home.'

There is a fleeting quizzical expression on Zahira's face. 'Didn't you find your mobile?'

I shake my head. 'It was broken in the accident.'

'But that was two weeks ago? Couldn't you have got a new one by now?' There is an inflection of curiosity in her voice, as though I am a puzzle in need of solving but have given her only the sparsest of clues.

'Stephen's ordering me one. He said it'll take a few days to arrive.'

'Won't he just assume you're out and phone back later?'

Again, the possibility skims before me like a kingfisher over a lake, but something pulls me back. 'I don't want him to worry.'

Zahira eyes me as though reading something etched on my skin. 'That's a shame. Another time, maybe?'

I nod, try to project myself into a future where I am sitting in Zahira's kitchen, free from uncertainty as to whether it's the right decision.

'Will you be okay on your own this weekend?' Zahira doesn't wait for a response as she delves into the dove-grey leather handbag slung over her shoulder. She retrieves a pen and an old shop receipt, writes on the back of it. 'That's my number. Just in case you need it.'

I take it from her, gratitude swelling in my chest. 'Thank you.'

'No worries. Call if you're at a loose end. And see you Tuesday morning?'

I nod and she turns around, collects Elyas from the bottom of the slide, allows him one last turn before picking him up and strapping him into his pushchair.

'See you next week. *Wave goodbye, Elyas.*' He grins, waves, and the sight of his miniature fingers stirs something in me that clutches my heart in its grip. I force my lips into a smile, wave back, tears smarting my eyes.

Turning in the opposite direction, I begin making my way home, an image affixing itself in my mind: a little boy's hand, wrapped around my gently pulsing heart, refusing to let go.

LIVVY

BRISTOL

Livvy was aware of her heart rate accelerating.

In front of her, Dominic sat in the armchair, his expression blank, unreadable.

Possibilities tumbled through Livvy's mind like Alice down the rabbit hole, too quick for her to grab hold of.

Dominic reclined in his chair, stretched his legs out in front of him. 'I've got a new job.'

It was so unexpected that for a moment Livvy struggled to reply. 'A new job? I didn't know you were even looking. Your Sheffield contract doesn't finish for ages.'

Dominic shook his head, grinned as though he were in possession of the world's most delicious secret. 'It's not for when Sheffield finishes. It's starting in seven weeks.'

'Seven weeks? But what about Sheffield? You said you couldn't possibly leave before the build's finished.'

Dominic waved a hand dismissively in the air. 'They'll survive. And Sheffield's only a temporary contract. This new job's permanent.'

Frustration blazed in Livvy's cheeks. 'So when I needed you to finish the Sheffield contract on time so I could take my promotion, your contract was absolutely unbreakable. But now you've got a new job, you're going to terminate it early?' The question was sharp in her mouth, like the finely tuned point of an arrowhead.

Dominic leant forward, took hold of Livvy's hands. 'Sweetheart, there was no way I could have broken that contract if I was still going to be self-employed. My name would have been mud, and I'd never have got another job. I'm only doing it now because this new role is permanent. You know I'd never deliberately stand in the way of your career. But my hands were tied then.'

For a few seconds, Livvy could find no adequate response. Their conversations over the past fortnight – about the promotion, about her return to work, about Dominic's Sheffield contract – flitted in her head like the wings of a hummingbird, too fast for her to focus. 'So if you're coming back from Sheffield early, we won't need any help with childcare from my parents or Bea?'

Dominic sat up straight, crossed one leg over the other at the knee, the hem of his trousers riding up over his ankle. 'Ah, well, that's where the second part of the confession comes in.' He smiled, in the way a child who's just found a secret stash of chocolate might smile. 'The new job's in London.' There was a note of triumph in his voice, as though he'd presented her with a winning lottery ticket.

The implication of Dominic's news flailed in Livvy's head. 'You're going to commute to London?'

Dominic laughed extravagantly. 'Of course not. It's a permanent job. We'll have to move there.'

The words took a few moments to settle, like the first flakes of snow on hard winter ground. 'Move to London? All of us?' Even as she said it, it sounded foolish, implausible.

'It'll be great – a new adventure.'

Livvy stood up from the stool, moved to the sofa, folded her arms across her chest. 'But I don't want to move to London. My life's here.'

Dominic picked up a glass of water from the bookshelf. 'I know it'll be a big change, but it's exciting, isn't it? I think it could be really good for us.'

'But what about my job? Have you forgotten about my promotion?' The question sounded surreal, as though she had found herself in a piece of absurdist theatre and couldn't follow the plot.

'Sweetheart, this could be great for your career too. There are loads more think tanks and lobbying groups in London, and they're much more influential than the ones here. This could be a great move for both of us.'

'But I don't want a different job. I want the one I've been offered. Did you not think to discuss this with me before you applied for a job on the other side of the country?'

Dominic rolled his eyes. 'It's a hundred miles away. It's not as if I'm proposing we emigrate to Australia. It's literally a few hours' drive down the M4.' There was a hint of impatience in his voice. 'Honestly? I thought my application was such a long shot there wasn't any point even mentioning it.'

Livvy tried to order the chaos of her thoughts. 'It may only be a hundred miles, but I've got no interest in living in London. I love living in Bristol. My family's here. My friends. My job. I don't want to leave.'

'For god's sake, Livvy, do you think it's normal for a grown woman with a family of her own to be living in the pocket of her parents still?'

'I'm not—'

'Yes, you are. I think it'll do us good to have a bit of space from them.' Dominic rubbed a hand around the back of his neck, shook his head with frustration.

161

'But I thought you wanted to buy a bigger house, I thought that was the point of your new budgeting system. If we move to London, we'd be living somewhere half the size of this.'

'Who said I wanted a bigger house?'

'You did. When we were talking about money—'

'This isn't about the size of house we're living in. This is about you being too scared to try anything new. Would it kill you to venture outside your comfort zone once in a while?'

The accusation hummed in her ears, but she tried to stay focused on the issue at hand. 'So you're just expecting me to give up the promotion? Without so much as a discussion?'

'I'm discussing it with you now. Jesus, Livvy, there *are* jobs outside Bristol. With all your experience, you'd have a much better career in London. I'm not suggesting this move just for my benefit. This would be good for both of us. Why do you have to be so unadventurous?'

The criticism stung, an echo of her final row with Tom, when he'd accused her of exactly the same thing. 'I'm not. You just spring this on me and expect me to agree—'

'For god's sake! You could see how excited I was. I've been looking forward to telling you ever since I found out. I thought you'd be happy. I thought you'd see this as an opportunity for us to do something new together. And yet all you can do is be negative. All you can do is moan about having to move away from your bloody family.' He slammed the glass on the edge of the bookshelf, the bottom shattering beneath the pressure, water splashing over his hand, the shelf, the floor.

Leo jerked his head up from where he was playing in his bouncy chair, a moment's silence as his eyes darted from Livvy to Dominic and back again. And then his face crumpled, howls of shock reaching from his throat, tears spilling over the edges of his eyes.

Heart drumming against her ribs, Livvy bent down, scooped Leo into her arms, began to walk away.

'Where are you going?'

Livvy didn't answer, pressed Leo to her chest, started walking up the stairs.

'Livvy, we haven't finished talking.'

She stopped, turned around, looked over the banister to where Dominic was glaring at her. 'Leo's upset, in case you hadn't noticed.'

'*I'm* upset.'

For a moment, Livvy was speechless. 'I think Leo probably needs me more.' Without waiting for a response, she climbed the stairs, went into their bedroom, closed the door behind her. With Leo still tight in her arms, she sat down on the bed, breathed in the smell of her son, and tried to work out what on earth had happened over the previous fifteen minutes.

The door opened. Livvy didn't look up from where she was playing with Leo on the bed. She sensed Dominic come in, sit down beside her.

'I'm sorry I sprang it on you like that. I do understand it must have been a shock. I was just so happy and I wanted to surprise you.' He inhaled a deep breath, let it out slowly. 'Everything I do is for you and Leo. You must know that. I honestly thought you'd be excited. I didn't mean to get angry. I was just disappointed by your reaction.'

Livvy said nothing, could not find a way to unravel her feelings.

'I genuinely thought you'd be over the moon. It's such a great opportunity. I didn't imagine for a second that you wouldn't want to share in it.'

'It's not completely straightforward though, is it?'

'I know. But I still thought you'd be happy for me.' Dominic hesitated, twisted his platinum wedding ring around his finger. 'Sometimes I worry that perhaps we don't want the same things.'

A knot of disquiet coiled in Livvy's stomach. 'What do you mean? You can't spring something like this on me and then be annoyed because I don't immediately jump for joy. I do have my own career to think about. That's not unreasonable of me.'

There was a brief hiatus, like the seconds before a magician pulls a rabbit from a hat.

'There's something else I haven't told you. I had the final interview last Friday, but I honestly didn't expect to be offered the job . . .'

Last Friday. Livvy thought of the parking ticket for Waterloo station in Dominic's jacket pocket, felt it slot into place like a piece of a jigsaw puzzle.

' . . . and then they phoned on Thursday afternoon and offered it to me.' He held up his hands in mock surrender. 'I know, I should have told you straight away, but I really wanted to talk about it in person.' He spoke quickly, his voice animated, so different from the anger and frustration just a few minutes before. 'Anyway, my first thought was you, and how a move to London might affect your career.' He paused, glanced down to where Leo was rattling a wooden shape sorter. 'So I thought I'd test the water for you. I emailed your CV to a couple of the big think tanks, just to enquire about possible opportunities.'

'You did *what*?' Incredulity flooded Livvy's cheeks. 'You sent emails, pretending to be me? From my account?'

Dominic offered a guilty half-smile. 'I have been telling you for months not to have the same password for everything.' He pulled a face, like little boy who'd been discovered with his hand in the cookie jar. 'But listen – both of them got back to me straight away, suggesting you go in for a meeting as soon as we're settled in London. Honestly, sweetheart, they both sounded really keen. This could be an incredible opportunity for you.'

Livvy tried to absorb what Dominic was telling her, but his words were like scuttling ants, refusing to stay still.

'Please don't be angry. I do appreciate it would be a big move for you, and I thought if you knew there were fantastic career opportunities for you too, it might make the decision easier.'

He smiled at her with such intense focus it reminded her of their early dates, when he would listen earnestly to everything she had to say.

'Which think tanks did you contact?'

Dominic told her and Livvy couldn't contain her surprise. 'But they're two of the most influential think tanks in the country. And they really sounded interested?'

Dominic grinned. 'I'll show you their replies. I hid them in a folder in Gmail so you wouldn't see them. But, yes – one of them said they were looking to expand the team and thought they might have a role you'd be interested in within the next few months.' He ran his fingers gently along the ridge of Livvy's spine. 'I really wouldn't be suggesting this move if I didn't think it would be good for us both.'

Livvy tried to cohere her thoughts. 'It's just a lot to get my head around.'

'I know. But your promotion . . . there's always the worry when you're promoted internally that you're never really viewed properly in the new role. There's an argument that a fresh start at this point in your career would actually be better for you.'

Livvy considered what Dominic was saying, knew in part that he was right.

'So will you think about it? Properly, I mean?'

Livvy looked down at Leo, prised his toy rabbit gently from his mouth. Turning back to Dominic, she found herself nodding. 'Let's talk about it over the weekend.'

Dominic smiled, wide and grateful. 'I don't want to put any pressure on you, but this really is my dream job. And I'm convinced there'll be great opportunities for you too.'

From Dominic's back pocket came the familiar trill of his mobile phone. He pulled it out, stared at the screen, frowned. Standing up from the bed, he strode towards the door.

'What is it?'

'Work. I'd better take it. Won't be long.'

She listened as Dominic ran down the stairs, heard him take the second flight into the basement kitchen.

Sitting on the bed with Leo, the events of the past half-hour recapitulated in Livvy's head. She thought about London – about leaving her family, moving to another city, working for a different organisation – and was unable to decipher whether the feeling flitting in her chest was that of anxiety or excitement.

ANNA

LONDON

The late-afternoon sky is a dense pewter, as though a thick blanket has been wrapped around the earth, blocking out the sun.

Turning away from the window, I look at the stacked boxes in front of me. Yesterday afternoon I began opening some but found nothing of interest: old duvet covers, a tattered leather holdall, some ornaments which didn't seem to match our decor.

Opening the blades of a pair of scissors, I slice along the brown packing tape of a sealed box. Inside is some spare bedding, vacuum packed in transparent bags, wrinkled and stiff. I wonder if sometimes we have people to stay overnight, whether we make up a bed for them on the sofa downstairs. I try to imagine who those guests might be, but no faces or names spring to mind. Closing the lid, I write its contents on the top in thick black marker pen, move the box to one side.

The next box holds a large desk fan and I glance out of the window, the sky ashen and unmoving, try to picture a day hot enough to need it. The third box contains a pair of frosted glass lamps minus their bulbs and an ornate table candelabra in distressed silver. I put them to one side: the sitting room needs extra light and the candelabra would look nice on the kitchen table.

Pulling open the next container, I'm greeted by a pile of clothes, neatly folded. The first item is a yellow blouse in broderie anglaise. Pinching the shoulders between forefinger and thumb, I hold it up in front of me. The blouse is thin cotton, delicate enough to require a vest or t-shirt to be worn underneath. A faint residue of deodorant under the arms suggests it has been worn many times, and yet even as I hold it, I cannot imagine a version of myself who might have dressed in it. It seems too feminine, too *yellow* to be something I may have worn. Looking at the grey-marl jogging bottoms and loose-fitting t-shirt I'm wearing now, it is hard to reconcile the person I am today with the woman who once chose to wear a top like this. Searching through the box further, I find silk blouses, smart fitted blazers, scoop-necked cardigans in a variety of colours. At the bottom are three pairs of elegant, slim-legged trousers in black, grey and navy which I assume I once wore to work. Checking the labels, I notice they're a size smaller than the clothes I'm wearing now, suspect it is the tedium of unemployment that has caused me to put on weight.

Placing the clothes back neatly – I cannot imagine having any use for them in the immediate future – I turn to the next box, cut the tape, open the lid.

Inside is an assortment of paraphernalia. Small, brightly coloured pouches of jewellery jostle for space with handbags, purses, sunglasses. I root around, find a creased chiffon scarf the colour of merlot, a cosmetics bag dusted with pink blusher, an empty credit card holder in bright cerulean.

At the very bottom, tucked beside a hairbrush, is a slim cardboard wallet. I prise it out, ease open the flap, extract its contents. And as I look at what it contains, my heart stutters in my chest.

It is a pack of photographs. Colour photographs. A couple of dozen, maybe more.

I stare at the first one and my head begins to spin.

I look at the next, and then the next, make my way through the entire collection. They are all variations on a theme, all iterations of the same tableau.

There is me, centre frame in each one: a different, happier version of me. No dark rings under my eyes, no bleached skin, no haunted expression.

And in every photo, a baby is nestled in my arms. A newborn baby dressed in a white cotton babygrow, a hat cradling its head. The same baby gracing every photo, a different pose each time: cheek pressed against my clavicle; eyes staring up at me; mouth open in a wide gummy yawn.

And in every photo, I am looking not into the lens of the camera but down at the baby in my arms with an unmistakable expression on my face.

I am looking at the baby with love.

I study the photographs and I know immediately what they are. I know it with a level of clarity beyond words, beyond language. It is as though a metal grille has been lifted on my thoughts and I understand something clearly for the first time since the accident.

This baby is mine.

I hear myself say it out loud, and the words sound both preposterous and indefatigably true. My heart is racing and I tear my eyes from the photographs, wonder if I am going mad, whether this is some form of delusional wish fulfilment. Whether the after-effects of the concussion are making me believe things that cannot be real.

I think about the distress in Stephen's voice when he told me about our unsuccessful attempts at IVF. I think about the grief and longing I felt, about how real it seemed, as though it were not just something I was being told but something that existed within me on a deep, visceral level.

I close my eyes, tell myself I must be mistaken. There is no reason Stephen would lie about our infertility. This must be someone else's baby, a close friend's perhaps, and the reason I am looking at it with such love is because it was a painful reminder of what I knew would never be mine.

But then I open my eyes, look again at the photographs, feel it deep inside me, powerful and profound: the absolute certainty that this baby belongs to me.

Nausea rises into my throat and I run into the bathroom, crouch over the toilet bowl, retch, but nothing comes. Just a churning in my stomach, a sense that I do not know if it is me or the world spinning out of control.

I look down at the photographs, the baby lying in my arms, the rapturous expression on my face, and I know I am not wrong.

A thought creeps into my head, so diabolical that for a moment I cannot bear to see it. But it keeps pushing, shoving, until it has forced its way to the front of my mind.

If this baby is mine, then where is it now?

LIVVY

BRISTOL

'That's a lovely necklace. I don't think I've seen it before. Is it new?'

Livvy instinctively brought a hand to her neck, felt the three delicate rose-gold discs on the end of the chain. 'Dominic gave it to me on Saturday.'

'It's not a special occasion, is it?' Her mum frowned as if rustling through a filing cabinet in her mind, checking she hadn't forgotten any significant dates. On the floor beside them, Livvy's dad played with Leo, rolling a red metal fire engine across the carpet.

'No, he just surprised me with it.'

'What a thoughtful thing to do. It's beautiful.'

Livvy fingered the necklace, wondered if there was anything in her expression to betray the story behind it.

After they'd made up on Saturday morning, Dominic had handed her a small purple box tied with lilac ribbon. Opening it, Livvy had found the necklace inside with its three gold discs. '*One for each of us,*' Dominic had said. '*Our perfect family. And space to add another if we ever need to.*' Instructing her to lift her hair, he had secured the chain at the nape of her neck, kissed the spot where the clasp lay against her skin. '*I'm sorry things got heated earlier. I saw this in a shop a few days ago and thought of you.'* With his hands on her shoulders, he'd turned her around, kissed her again. It had been such a deviation from his earlier anger that Livvy had felt as though, during their row, she had been visited by an interloper, like Loki shapeshifting into different guises, and only now had the real Dominic returned.

Over the course of the weekend, they had talked endlessly about the possible move to London. Hunched over their laptops, Dominic had shown her emails from the think tanks inviting her in for meetings when she was settled in London, and Livvy had not been able to deny the excitement she felt at the prospect of being employed by one of them. It was not the same as when Tom had shown her endless photographs of Thai beaches and Tibetan monasteries, expecting her to match his enthusiasm for backpacking in their mid-thirties. What Dominic was showing her were great professional opportunities.

Later, Dominic had opened links to flats and houses in London they could feasibly afford. He told her he'd already made enquiries with letting agents in Bristol for their current house and they'd assured him it would be easy to rent out. He'd given her more information about his job, about the interview process, about how invigorated he felt: *'You know I've always been much more interested in the ideas – the philosophy – of construction than the practical reality. This will be so much more intellectually stimulating for me. I need a fresh challenge and this is perfect.'* His words had almost outrun his tongue as he'd listed all the ways in which it would be better to bring up Leo in London: more museums and galleries, greater diversity, better schools. It was as though, in Dominic's mind, the decision had already been made, the wealth of opportunities spread out before them like roads paved with gold.

After Leo had gone to bed on Sunday night, she and Dominic had sat on the sofa, Dominic with a glass of red wine, Livvy with a slimline tonic. '*So, what do you think? Can I make the call tomorrow and tell them I'm accepting the job?*' Livvy had thought about all she would be relinquishing – familiarity, security, proximity to family and friends, her job – and had almost told him that she couldn't, it was too much to ask. But then his words from the previous morning had rung in her ears – *Why do you have to be so unadventurous?* – and it had felt like a depressingly repetitive soundtrack: first Tom, now Dominic. She had contemplated all the reasons it would be good to go, not just for her and Dominic but for Leo too. And before she had time to doubt herself, she had been nodding, agreeing, and Dominic had been flinging his arms around her, thanking her, telling her it was going to be the best move they ever made.

When he had left for Sheffield early yesterday morning – '*Just think, sweetheart, only another seven weeks of this and then no more commuting. Just the three of us, together, in London*' – she had closed the door behind his disappearing car and felt as though the weekend had been like looking through the window of a speeding train, picking out a handful of landmarks while the rest of the scene hurtled by in a blur so that she wasn't sure exactly where she had been, which locations she'd passed through, what she had seen.

'Actually, I do have some news.' Livvy steeled herself. 'Dominic's got a new job.'

Her mum's expression widened into a broad smile. 'That's wonderful. So no more traipsing back and forth to Sheffield?'

Livvy hesitated, the right words reluctant to appear. 'The job's in London. We're moving to London.'

'London?' Her mum said it as though it were the name of a newly discovered planet.

'When did all this happen?' Her dad clambered to his knees, sank into the floral-patterned armchair that her parents had owned since Livvy was a child.

'He told me on Saturday. It's a fantastic opportunity for him. I've never seen him so excited about work before.' She tried to inject a shot of optimism into her voice, feared it may have fallen short.

'But what about you and Leo? What about your promotion?' The skin across her mum's forehead creased into deep pleats.

Livvy paused, reminded herself of all the positive reasons for the move. 'There are plenty of think tanks in London. A couple of them have already expressed an interest. I'll have a lot more career opportunities there.'

'But it's so far away.'

Livvy was aware of a compression in her throat. 'It's only a hundred miles down the M4. Less than three hours by car. Half that by train.' She could feel Dominic's words parroting from her lips, had the sensation of being a ventriloquist's dummy.

'But how do you feel about this, love? Do you actually want to go?' Her dad's voice was calm, but Livvy could hear his unease.

'Of course. It'll be great for us to have an adventure together. And it'll do me good to get out of my comfort zone.' She smiled as widely as she could, hoped her parents would focus on the words she was saying rather than any ambivalence in her tone.

'But we'll hardly ever see you.' Her mum's voice wavered and it took all Livvy's self-control to keep the muscles in her cheeks fixed in a taut smile.

'Of course you will. You can come to London as often as you want. And it'll be easy for Leo and me to hop on a train to visit. We'll be back and forth all the time.' Even as she said it, Livvy wondered how true it might be, particularly once she was working again.

'It's just so . . . unexpected. And I don't care what you say. To me it's a long way away.' Her mum's eyes drifted down to where Leo was rolling the red fire engine along the carpet in half-moon rotations.

174

Guilt pooled in Livvy's throat. She thought about her mum's joy when she'd first told her she was pregnant: how, in that moment, she had understood that until then, her parents had all but relinquished any hope of becoming grandparents. She thought about the hours they had spent with Leo since he'd been born: two, three times a week. And now she was taking him away from them. 'We'll still see loads of you. I wouldn't want Leo growing up without you in his life. You know how much I value your relationship with him.'

A calendar flicked through Livvy's head as she calculated how often, realistically, her parents might see Leo once they'd moved to London. There was no use pretending it would be the same as it was now.

'What about childcare? It'll be prohibitively expensive in London.' Her dad fiddled with the cuff of his jumper, pulled at a loose thread, pushed it back under his sleeve.

'I've got to find a job first.' Livvy laughed, but it sounded forced, as though it were being dragged involuntarily from her throat.

'It's just that Dad and I . . .' Her mum glanced at Livvy's dad, a silent communication passing between them. 'We were going to suggest that when you went back to work, we'd have Leo a couple of days a week. Not just the nursery pick-ups you asked about. I mean, two whole days. It would have helped out on the financial front and we'd have loved to have had him . . .' Her mum's sentence floated away, as if she were watching a bubble drift through the air, waiting for it to pop.

Livvy fiddled with the chain around her neck, a parallel future playing out in her mind: staying in Bristol, taking the promotion, leaving Leo with her parents twice a week. Entrusting her son to people she loved.

She breathed deeply, held the disappointment tight in her chest. 'That would have been amazing, Mum. It's a really generous offer, and Leo would have loved it. But like I say, we'll still see loads of you.'

A look of concern darted between her parents like a pair of swifts passing in the air.

'So when's all this going to happen?'

Livvy refilled her lungs. 'In seven weeks.'

'Seven weeks?'

'And you're sure you're happy about this? I know you want to be supportive of Dominic, but you do have to think about yourself too. It's not just your job you'll be leaving behind. It's all your friends, your family. It'll be such a wrench.' Her mum's tone hovered somewhere between distress and anxiety.

For a moment, Livvy considered telling her parents the truth: that of course she was nervous about all she'd be leaving behind. But looking at their fretful expressions, she reminded herself that the decision could not be undone: Dominic had handed his notice in to his Sheffield employers yesterday morning. To confess any ambivalence now would only mean burdening them with misgivings it was impossible to resolve. 'Honestly, I'm fine about it. More than fine. It's going to be great.'

There were a few moments' silence, the air in her parents' sitting room stale suddenly, as though they had been gathered there for a year, not an hour, recycling one another's exhaled breaths.

'Has there been any more contact from Dominic's mother?' There was something uneven in her mum's voice, as though an attempt at neutrality had been tipped off balance.

Livvy thought about the text message and the phone call that she was yet to share with Dominic. 'No, not since she turned up at the farm.' The lie slipped from her tongue, and Livvy reassured herself it wasn't really a lie, more a benign fib to protect the integrity of her promise to Dominic not to discuss his family with anyone else.

'It's just . . . Dad and I were thinking. Maybe you should meet her. It seems such a shame, none of you having any contact with Dominic's family.'

Livvy shook her head. 'Absolutely not.'

'But she must feel dreadful. She's just lost her husband, she's estranged from her son, she has no contact with her only grandchild. Imagine if that was me or Dad.'

'But you or Dad wouldn't be in that position in the first place. There's a good reason why Dominic doesn't want to see her.'

'Well, maybe if you explained things to us a bit more, we might understand.' Her dad smiled encouragingly.

Livvy hesitated, thought about her promise to Dominic, weighed it up against her parents' concern. 'I can't – it's not fair on Dominic. But his dad was . . . quite abusive. And his mum did nothing to protect him. I can't go into details, but you just have to trust me: he's right not to want contact with her.'

Her mum glanced at her dad, then back at Livvy. 'But now that his dad's passed away, maybe it would be a good moment to reconcile with his mum? Obviously we don't know exactly what happened, but if Dominic's father was abusive to him, isn't it possible that his mother was a victim too?' There was something elliptical in her mum's words, as though half her thoughts had been erased before she spoke, leaving only faint indentations on the page.

She just stood there, like a rod of iron, and wouldn't tell me anything.

Livvy thought about the harrowing events Dominic had described, about his mother's complicity and her failure to keep him safe. 'That's not the impression I've got. But anyway, it's Dominic's family, so it's up to him whether or not he has contact with her. It's not my decision to make.'

Her dad drank the last of his tea, patted Livvy's leg. 'Well, you have to do what you think is best. It just seems terribly sad, that's all.'

On the floor next to Livvy, Leo picked up the metal fire engine, threw it across the floor, and she bent down, picked it up. 'I think this one's getting a bit restless. Shall we take him to the park?'

Gently pulling Leo's arms through the sleeves of his coat, Livvy was aware of an ambient, unnameable anxiety flickering behind her ribs. Strapping Leo into his pushchair, she tried to ignore it, hoping that if she looked the other way for long enough it would somehow manage to fix itself.

ANNA

LONDON

It is dark outside by the time I hear the metallic slice of the key in the lock. I have not noticed the light fading, have been oblivious to the gradual dimming of the sky, night devouring day, leaving only shadows behind.

Stephen walks into the sitting room, snaps on the light, startles to find me sitting in an armchair, legs curled beneath me, palms tucked between my thighs.

'God, you made me jump. Why are you sitting in the dark?'

'You're late.' My voice is flat, as though it has been turned through a mangle, all the emotion wrung out of it.

'No, I told you this morning there was a late addition to the programme – a seminar I wanted to attend. You haven't been sitting there waiting, have you?'

I shake my head, ignore the concern in his voice. I cannot recall him telling me he was going to be delayed but so much has happened since, it is possible there has not been enough room in my head for it all.

Bending down to kiss me, Stephen's stubble bristles against my cheek, and I feel myself recoil.

'Is everything alright?'

I open my lips to speak, but all the moisture has evaporated and there is a small sticking sound as I unpeel my tongue from the roof of my mouth.

'Anna? What's wrong?'

He is crouching in front of me and I can feel the heat of his gaze on my skin, but I cannot lift my head to look at him. The enormity of what I have to ask him is like a tsunami rushing towards us and I cannot imagine that we will not both be drowned.

'Anna? You're scaring me. What's happened?'

There is a moment's hesitation, and I wonder if my imagination has been playing tricks on me, whether I am inventing stories in lieu of memory. Whether my earlier certainty was nothing more than a fantasy, conjuring into being what I wish to be true.

And then my bare toes make contact with the cardboard wallet tucked next to the cushion: the photographs I have been studying all afternoon. They flick through my mind as though on an old-fashioned overhead projector, one after the other, presenting themselves as all the evidence I need.

Slipping one hand into the slim gap next to the cushion, I retrieve the pack of photographs, pull them out, hand them to Stephen.

Colour leaches from Stephen's face. 'Where did you get these?'

I see it immediately in his eyes, hear it in his voice; the confirmation that there is a story to be told. Something he has not yet divulged and which he has no desire to tell me now.

'Anna. Where did you get these?' There is an edge to his voice: serrated, precise.

'They were in a box. In the spare room.' I pause, summoning the courage. 'It's my baby, isn't it?' Five short words and yet now they are out in the open, they take on a life of their own, and I know I can never fetch them back.

For a few seconds Stephen doesn't move, doesn't speak, as though my question has frozen time. And then he lifts himself from his knees, sits on the edge of the armchair next to mine, buries his head in his hands.

The suspension is stifling and I feel as if I am being suffocated by it, waiting to learn whatever the truth might be. Impatience tautens every muscle in my body and I reach out, grab hold of his sleeve. 'Just tell me.'

Stephen looks up, tears pooling in his eyes. The room seems to be holding its breath and I do not know what I am hoping he'll say.

'I'm so sorry.' He speaks softly and I wait for him to say more, anxiety wrapping itself around my throat, stealing my words. 'We had a child. But he died.'

Time seems to bend and stretch. Stephen reaches out, takes hold of my hand, and I can see it on top of mine but I cannot feel it, am no longer aware of myself, as though my mind and body have been separated, and I am nothing more than a chaos of disordered thoughts. 'When?' I hear the sound of my voice but am not conscious of having articulated the question.

'Two years ago.'

Two years ago. I try to make sense of the time frame but it is abstract, inscrutable. 'What was his name?' Words find their way through my lips but I do not know where they have come from, how they dare make their way into the world.

Stephen pauses, swallows, looks down to where his hands are clasping mine. 'Henry. We called him Henry.'

There is a flicker of something, like the faint light from a distant star, and for a brief moment I am aware of something on the periphery of my memory: a baby in my arms, the light snuffle of breaths, a profound, all-consuming love.

I try to unlock the memory, paint detail where there is just a muted outline, but it is too far away and I cannot make it more distinct. 'How old was he?'

'Four months.'

A crater opens up in my chest. And then my grief seems to spill over, and I start to cry, cannot stop, dare not stop, because if I stop the world will be quiet again, and I will have to face the enormity of what has happened. 'Why didn't you tell me? You should have told me.' The words burn in my throat, splutter through hot tears.

I'm aware of Stephen wrapping his arms around me, enfolding my body in his, clasping me tight. He holds on to me, my shoulders shuddering as he rocks me back and forth, whispering the same words over and over: 'I'm sorry, my love. I'm so, so sorry.'

LIVVY

BRISTOL

Livvy carried the last of the shopping bags inside the house, secured Leo in his activity chair, turning it on so that the lights flashed. She watched as he began pushing buttons with chubby, uncoordinated fingers.

'I'll just put the shopping away, angel. I won't be long.'

Heading down to the basement kitchen, she unpacked the week's food. Her phone pinged and she fished it out from the bottom of her handbag. Opening Gmail, she found a message from Aisha.

Hi Livvy

I've spoken to HR and everything's sorted – there's no need to return any of your maternity pay. Like Christian said, we're just really sorry to see you go.

We'd love to arrange a proper send-off. Would you like to pop into the office one afternoon for team prosecco and cake? Or we could do a meal one evening if childcare isn't an issue? Just let me know what suits. And let's make sure you and I grab a coffee before we both head off. I know you've already got some irons in the fire, but I've put out some feelers with friends in London, so I should have some leads in the next week or so.

Speak soon,

Aisha x

It had been over two weeks since she'd agreed to move to London, and yet even now when she thought about it, there was a sense of unreality to it. But tenants had been found for their house, a deposit paid, a moving date set. Livvy had handed in her resignation at work, sent her CV to other environmental lobby groups in London, received more encouraging responses. Dominic had been investigating areas in London where they might rent, and Livvy had suggested leaving Leo with her parents one Saturday so they could house-hunt together. But Dominic had insisted he wanted to do it alone: '*I'm the one who's precipitated this move, I'm the one who should do all the legwork to make it happen.*'

Putting the last of the shopping in the fridge, she heard a knock at the front door. Running up the basement stairs, she passed Leo in the sitting room, reassured him she'd be back in a second.

Opening the door, a stone sank deep into the pit of Livvy's stomach. 'What are you doing here?'

Less than two feet away, Imogen stood on the garden path, holding out a small square box. 'I wondered if you could give this to Dominic?'

The box hovered in the air, Livvy's hands remaining firmly by her sides. 'What is it?'

'It's John's watch. He wanted Dominic to have it.'

184

Livvy looked down at the box, then back up at Imogen, felt as though she had opened the door on a different version of reality. 'I don't think that's appropriate.'

'Please. I would have posted it, but I was worried it might get lost. John so wanted Dominic to have it.'

Imogen's voice was replete with emotion, and Livvy felt as though she were negotiating her way through a hall of mirrors, each image more distorted than the last.

'I can't take it from you. I'm sorry.'

Imogen stared at her as though Livvy had spoken in tongues. 'But you have to. John wanted Dominic to have it.'

'I don't think Dominic will want it.' The words felt harsh in Livvy's mouth, but she didn't know what else to say to make Imogen understand.

Imogen dropped her arm by her side. 'I know John and Dominic didn't always see eye to eye, but I never imagined he'd still be so angry, even after John's death.' Imogen swallowed hard, and Livvy could see she was on the brink of tears.

Stifling her frustration, Livvy smoothed out the edges in her voice. 'It's very difficult for Dominic, as I'm sure you can understand, after all that's happened.'

There was a fractional nod of Imogen's head. 'I know he's resentful about a lot of things, but I wish he could have forgiven John at the end. It all just feels so . . . unnecessary.'

A wave of disbelief destabilised Livvy for a moment. She wondered if Imogen's naivety was a symptom of grief, but then she recalled everything Dominic had told her and suspected his mother had always been this way. 'I don't think that was ever going to happen.'

From inside the house, Leo cried out, sharp and urgent.

'Is Leo okay?' Imogen's forehead creased into a concerned frown.

Livvy didn't reply, ran back inside to check on her son, discovered he had simply dropped his toy caterpillar on the floor.

When she turned around, Imogen was standing just behind her, eyes fixed on Leo.

Something inside Livvy snapped. 'You need to leave.'

Imogen didn't move.

'Imogen, you have to leave.'

Livvy's voice was firm, resolute, but still Imogen didn't move. Scenes flashed through Livvy's mind like a speeded-up film: having to manhandle her septuagenarian mother-in-law out of the house, having to call the police if she refused to go, having to explain to Dominic why she'd neglected to tell him about the text and the phone call. 'Imogen, you shouldn't be in here.' She kept her voice low, steady, in spite of her racing pulse.

'He looks so much like Dominic.' Imogen spoke in a quiet voice, as though hypnotised.

Livvy glanced down to where Leo was pressing light-up buttons on his activity chair, oblivious to the stranger in their midst and to the tension she had brought with her into the room.

'Can I hold him?'

Livvy stared at her, incredulous. 'No. You need to leave.' She placed a hand on Imogen's arm, tried to steer her towards the door, but Imogen flinched as though Livvy's fingertips were made of fire.

'Please let me hold him, just for a moment.' She looked at Livvy with something close to desperation.

Panic knocked against Livvy's ribs, her thoughts groping in the dark for a solution. 'Not today. But how about I talk to Dominic, see if maybe we can work something out?' The deceit felt spiky on her tongue.

'Will you really?'

Livvy sensed a glimmer of opportunity, nodded, returned her hand to Imogen's arm. 'But now I have to make Leo's dinner. I really do need to get on.' She steered Imogen towards the door, felt the older woman's resistance begin to wane.

They got as far as the hallway before Imogen stopped, looked back over her shoulder. 'He really is beautiful. And he does look uncannily like Dominic at that age.' She spoke as if in a trance, and Livvy had to press her hand further into Imogen's blue blazer, shepherd her out through the open front door.

It wasn't until Imogen was standing on the path that Livvy finally dared let go of the breath she'd been holding.

'Perhaps, when I come back, I could bring some photos of Dominic as a baby, and you'll be able to see the resemblance for yourself.'

Livvy managed to pull her lips into an approximation of a smile, a silent voice in her head telling her to agree, say whatever was necessary to get this woman away from her house.

Imogen looked at her, trusting, expectant. 'I really would like a chance to get to know my grandson. He's the only one I've got.' She paused for a moment, gazing at Livvy intently. 'Is Dominic good to you?'

The question swerved through the air, landed in Livvy's head with a thud, so unexpected that she didn't know what to say.

'I only ask because Dominic hasn't really had . . . as far as we knew . . . there hadn't been anyone serious before. It was just a shock to find out he'd got married and become a father.'

Livvy felt the muscles across her shoulders tense, made a conscious effort to restrain her impatience. 'To be fair, you've been estranged from Dominic for a long time. It's hardly surprising that you don't know what's going on in his life.'

Imogen gave a small shake of the head. 'Don't get me wrong. I'm delighted if he's happy and settled. It was just . . . a surprise. He hasn't always found relationships easy. But if he's . . . if he genuinely makes you happy . . . ?'

Livvy bristled at Imogen's invasiveness. 'I really do need to go.'

'But you'll talk to Dominic, about me seeing Leo?'

Livvy nodded, the lie tight in her chest.

She closed the door, stood still for a few seconds, hand on the Yale lock as though a part of her feared Imogen might yet try to force her way inside.

The smell of Imogen's perfume lingered in the hallway, cloying in her throat, sweet and sickly.

She waited for a minute and then another, before finally taking her hand from the lock, slipping the metal chain across, tiptoeing into the sitting room and creeping towards the front window. Peeking through the edge of the shutters, she heard herself exhale when she found the front path empty.

Turning to Leo, she lifted him out of his activity seat and into her arms, tried to calm her sprinting heart.

In four weeks' time, they would be in London, at an address where Imogen would not be able to find them. All Livvy had to do was to keep her mother-in-law at bay for another month, and then she would never be able to turn up on their doorstep again.

ANNA

LONDON

I do not know how long we have been sitting in silence in the semi-darkness, the only light a tangerine glow from the street lamps filtering through the window.

'Why didn't you tell me?' The flesh around my eyes is taut, salt from my tears tightening my skin.

Next to me, Stephen shakes his head with short, jarring movements. 'I couldn't do it to you. Not when I'd already had to tell you about your parents. You were already so heartbroken . . .' Anguish burrows into the crevices at the edges of his eyes.

'But everything you said . . . about the infertility, about IVF? Why make all that up?'

He wipes his palms on the thighs of his charcoal-grey trousers. 'I don't know. I just panicked. When you asked why we didn't have children . . . I couldn't bring myself to tell you the truth.'

I open my mouth to say something – to weep, to grieve, to tell him he should never have kept something so fundamental from me – but nothing comes. Every part of me feels anaesthetised.

'I know it was wrong, but I didn't know what to do for the best. Those deaths – your parents and Henry – they happened over fifteen years apart. But if I'd told you the truth when you asked me on Tuesday, you'd have been grieving them all in a matter of days. I couldn't do it to you. It would have been too cruel.' He knits his fingers, presses them tightly together. 'I couldn't bear watching you go through all that again—'

He stops abruptly, and even though I am scared of the answer, I cannot stop myself asking the question. 'What were you going to say?'

Stephen breathes slowly. 'Henry's death . . . it almost destroyed you. It almost destroyed both of us.' He pauses, swallows, takes another deep breath. 'In the past few months there's been a glimmer of hope that you were starting to feel better. Not recovered – I know neither of us can ever fully recover. But better than you had been. I was worried it would set you back months in the grieving process. I hated the idea of you mourning all over again, from the beginning, just when things were starting to improve. You're already dealing with so much.' He cups a hand over the cap of my knee and I do not shift away, even though it feels alien, unfamiliar.

Neither of us speaks for a few moments. There are so many questions circulating in my head I do not know where one ends and another begins.

'There's something else I haven't been honest with you about.'

The air stills, like the hush of birds before a storm.

'You didn't get made redundant a year ago.' His eyes dart towards my face and then away again. 'After Henry died, you took extended compassionate leave and then decided not to go back. You haven't worked since.' He glances at me once more, so brief I would have missed it had I blinked. 'I'm sorry. I just couldn't bear to dredge it all up for you again. I knew I'd have to tell you at some point, but I just wanted to protect you a bit longer.'

I try to compute this new information, to locate the neural pathways along which it needs to travel to become part of my history, but it is like trying to navigate my way through a maze without a ball of string to guide me home.

'It's why we're a bit isolated. You haven't wanted to see much of friends for the past couple of years. We've lost touch with quite a few people.' He pauses, and I sense him balancing on a wire, assessing whether he can make it to the other side without falling. 'We've just tried to support each other through it.'

I think about the silent house phone, the lack of friends paying visits, the absence of a social life, and suddenly the insularity of our marriage makes sense: the contracted lives we must have been leading since the death of our son. I imagine what the past two years must have been like, wonder how we have managed to survive with our sanity intact. 'How old would he be now?' The question springs from my lips without any warning.

Stephen closes his eyes slowly, then opens them again. Time feels thick, as if we are traipsing through dense fog. 'Almost two and a half. Twenty-eight months.'

My breath catches in my throat and something inside me seems to come undone.

There is another question, one I know must be asked, but courage stutters in my chest and I have to breathe deeply against the fear. 'How did he die?'

My words hang heavy in the air like a cumulus cloud before the first deluge of rain. Outside, the street lamp flickers, plunging us into a split second of darkness.

'He had meningitis.'

I wait for Stephen to say more, but he looks down at his hands, kneads his knuckles as if grinding them into submission.

Thoughts swirl in my head, each eager to be noticed. 'What happened? Most children recover from meningitis, don't they?'

Again, Stephen darts a swift glance at me as though there is danger in holding my gaze. 'He deteriorated very quickly, overnight. You weren't to know.'

'What do you mean, I wasn't to know?'

Stephen's eyes widen. 'I mean we weren't to know. Neither of us could have done anything. He'd had a fever. He'd been tired and irritable and off his food, just for a day. He didn't have a rash or anything when you put him down for the night.'

I try to imagine it – my baby, hot, tired, irritable – but cannot unlock the memory. 'And then what happened?'

Stephen blows a stream of air out through a small circle in his lips. 'When you woke up in the morning . . . he was already dead.'

His words are hazy, as though I am viewing them through extreme desert temperatures. 'But he was only four months old. Surely he needed a night feed?'

'No. He was tired and poorly. You wanted to let him rest. You did what you thought was for the best.'

I am struggling to absorb it all, but I need to know more. 'What happened in the morning, when we found him?'

Stephen avoids my gaze, and it is there, writ large in his evasion: a chapter of the story he is reluctant to share.

'What is it? What aren't you telling me?'

He looks at me and I see it in his expression as clearly as if it were tattooed on his skin: the pre-emptive apology for what he is about to say. 'I wasn't there. I was away for work that night. I wasn't there to help you.'

The words tilt in my head, unable to find their balance. 'So it was all my fault?'

'Of course not. It was my fault for not being there. You told me before I left that he wasn't well and I still went away. I should have stayed.'

'But that doesn't change the fact that I didn't check on him all night. What kind of a mother doesn't check on their baby when he's sick?'

Stephen takes hold of my hand. 'You wanted to let him rest. You thought that's what he needed. He had a temperature and was a bit off-colour, that's all. No parent would have sat vigil by their child's bedside all night just for that. And anyway, you were exhausted. You hadn't slept properly for weeks by then.'

'So I was too tired to check on my own baby?'

Stephen squeezes my hand. 'That's not what happened. We went through all this with the doctors at the time. You weren't to know how quickly he'd deteriorate. It wasn't your fault. Millions of parents would have done exactly the same as you.'

'But some wouldn't. Some would have been able to save their child.' The truth roars in my ears.

I shut my eyes, think of the little boy in the photographs – *my* little boy – and guilt clutches my heart in its fist.

I think of him lying in a cot beside my bed, becoming weaker and weaker through the night, as I slept through his suffering.

I imagine waking up in the morning, finding his lifeless body, knowing instinctively what had happened before the paramedics arrived.

I think about the brevity of his existence, suspended in time at four months old, a sliver of a life that will never be fully lived.

My throat burns as sobs claw their way from my chest.

'I'm sorry, my love. This is why I didn't want to tell you. I knew you'd have to grieve all over again.' Stephen envelops me in his arms, and I do not resist. 'It wasn't your fault. You have to believe that. It was a horrific, unspeakable tragedy.' He holds me tight as though he is aware that I am drifting away, into my own world of pain. 'We'll get through this. I promise you.'

I hear his words, but I cannot believe them, cannot conceive that there is life beyond such a loss.

I am aware of deep lacerations scoring my heart, inscribing on it the name of the son whom I will now never get the chance to know. The little boy I was supposed to protect but whom I failed so egregiously that I know I will never be able to forgive myself.

LIVVY

BRISTOL

'Do you really need to keep all these photo albums? You've got enough here to fill a small museum.'

Livvy looked across their basement office to where Dominic was rifling through a cardboard box she'd brought from her old flat. 'It's only one box. Of course I want to keep them.'

'You keep saying that about everything.' He smiled. 'Honestly, I had no idea you were such a hoarder.' He picked up an album with a faded blue hessian cover, opened it at random, flicked through a few pages where the plastic film was peeling away from the page, photos slipping out of place. Peering at one and then another, he turned the album towards Livvy, eyebrows raised. 'I mean, do we really need to keep all these photos of your ex-boyfriends?'

Livvy looked at the pictures, taken during her university years – at parties, in the halls of residence, in pubs – her arms around the shoulders of various young men whose names she'd long since forgotten. She laughed. 'Trust me, none of those were ever my boyfriend. Those photos are twenty years old. I don't think you've got any competition.'

Dominic snapped the album shut and slid it back in the box.

Livvy turned back to the old CDs she was sorting through – *(What's the Story) Morning Glory?*, *Different Class*, *Parklife* – and thought about her conversation with Bea a fortnight ago, when she'd told her they were leaving Bristol. She'd anticipated resistance from her sister but not outright hostility. '*I really don't think you should go. You'll be separated from everybody you know. Just because Dominic hates all his family and doesn't have any friends doesn't mean you should have to be cut off from yours. And what about* your *career? Are you supposed to give up your promotion, just like that?*'

'What about all these books?' Dominic held up a couple of tattered paperbacks, Elizabeth Taylor in one hand, Elizabeth Jane Howard in the other.

'They're some of my favourites. I can't get rid of those.'

Dominic turned them over, scrutinised their jackets. 'Come on, they're a bit trashy. We don't need to keep them, do we?'

Livvy took one from him, thumbed through it. 'They're not trashy. They're modern classics.'

Dominic raised a sceptical eyebrow. 'Well, we can't take everything with us – there won't be room. And you can't care about them that much if they've been stuffed in a box for the past fourteen months.'

Livvy decided not to remind him that it wasn't her decision for her books to have been stashed away all this time. When she'd first moved in and unpacked some of her best-loved novels – Elizabeth Taylor, Elizabeth Jane Howard, Agatha Christie, Patricia Highsmith – Dominic had looked at his bookshelves, already full, and turned to her apologetically: '*I'm not sure there's going to be room for these in the sitting room. Do you mind if we store them in the office for now? We'll find some space after you've settled in.*' Somehow, the space had never been found.

'Are you happy for me to throw these out?' Dominic held up a pair of framed Frida Kahlo prints that had once graced the walls of Livvy's flat.

'No, I really like those. I know there was never room for them here, but maybe there will be in our new place.'

Dominic looked at one picture and then the other. 'You don't think they're a bit . . . studenty?'

'How is Frida Kahlo *studenty*?'

Dominic stretched across the pile of boxes, kissed Livvy on the lips. 'Sweetheart, we're not going to be able to take everything with us. We have to be a bit ruthless.' As if to prove his point, he opened a box, lifted out four old cushions yellowing with age and tossed them on the pile for the dump. 'Maybe your parents could store some of this for you until we're settled?'

Livvy took the pictures, placed them with her books and photo albums, knew her parents would be happy to put them in their loft. 'I wish you'd let me help with the house hunt. It's not as if I don't have time on my hands. I could at least do some of the internet research.'

'I've already told you, I don't want you to be bothered with all that. I've got a couple of great options – trust me.'

'It just feels a bit weird, the thought of moving into a new home that I haven't been involved in choosing.'

Dominic stood up, rubbed his knees where he'd been crouched on the hard floor. 'I'm just trying to do something nice. Please don't make me feel bad for it.'

'I'm not. I'd just like to have a say.'

Dominic placed a hand on her shoulder. 'It's only our temporary home. Once we've got our bearings, we'll move somewhere permanent, and of course we'll look for that together. I just really love the idea of finding us a place to live and surprising you with it on the day we move. Let me do that for you, please?'

Livvy hesitated. 'Honestly? I'd rather be involved but if it's that important to you—'

'It really is.' He bent down, kissed the top of her head. 'Right, I need the bathroom. Back in a sec.'

As Dominic closed the door behind him, Livvy opened one of the boxes she'd brought from her flat, found her teenage diaries inside, closed it again quickly and marked it for her parents' attic.

On the far side of the room was a tall, wooden cupboard Livvy had never had cause to look in before. Opening the doors, she found a stack of cardboard boxes fastened with ageing Sellotape. Lifting them out, she pulled at the lid of one, the tape brittle beneath her fingers.

When she looked inside, it took a few moments for her to understand what she was seeing. She extracted the first item, then another, put them on the desk beside her.

It was a pair of Airfix models – one Spitfire, one Tiger Moth – each of them painstakingly constructed and diligently painted, not a single brushstroke out of place. And yet the presence of them here made no sense. Dominic had told her that all his childhood possessions – Airfix models included – had been thrown away the day his parents cleared out his bedroom when he was twelve.

Delving back into the box, she found three more Airfix planes, tried to fit their existence into the story she'd been told.

'What have you got there?'

Livvy turned around, startled, saw Dominic standing in the doorway.

'I just found these. Aren't they Airfix models?'

Dominic looked at them, then back at Livvy. 'Yes. Where did you find them?'

Livvy gestured behind her. 'In that cupboard. I thought you said your parents threw them all away?'

Dominic shook his head. 'They threw away pretty much all my belongings but not these.'

Something was askew in Livvy's mind, as though her memory was operating in two different time zones. 'Really? I was sure you'd mentioned Airfix models.'

Dominic shook his head, negotiated his way towards her through the maze of boxes, took the models she was holding out of her hands. 'These were the only things they didn't manage to find. They'd been in a box at the back of my wardrobe and I've kept them ever since.' He studied them for a moment before putting them back carefully with the others. 'I think we could probably do with a break. Do you want a cup of tea?'

Livvy nodded, followed him out into the kitchen, watched as he made them both tea.

'You know what I've been thinking?' He sat down at right angles to her at the kitchen table, placed their mugs on coasters.

'What?'

He eyed her thoughtfully, and Livvy experienced the same feeling she'd had in the early days of their courtship: the intensity of his attention. 'Given we're having a fresh start, what do you think about getting your hair cut short? I think it would really suit you.'

Without even considering her response, Livvy shook her head. 'God, no. I've always had long hair. I'd feel weird without it.' She fingered a strand, twiddled it around her finger.

Dominic reached out, untangled the hair. 'It would stop you doing that for a start.' He looked at her, unblinking. 'I honestly think it would look great on you. You've got such a beautiful face, why hide it beneath all that hair?'

Livvy baulked at the question. Her hair had been long ever since childhood. The thought of cutting it short was anathema to her, like suggesting she cut off a finger, or a toe, or a pound of flesh. 'I like my hair long. I always have. It feels . . . I don't know. Comforting.'

'But maybe that's a good reason to get it cut? Wouldn't you like something a bit more – I don't know – grown-up?'

Heat flushed Livvy's cheeks. 'How is long hair *not grown-up*? Plenty of adult women have long hair.' She could hear the defensiveness in her voice, felt annoyed with Dominic for provoking it in her.

'There's no need to get irritable. I just think short hair would look great on you. I'm paying you a compliment. Not all women could get away with it.'

He smiled, but Livvy looked away, sipped her too-hot tea, scalded the roof of her mouth. Her eyes grazed the clock on the oven. 'God, I hadn't realised it was so late. I'd better go and collect Leo from Mum and Dad's.'

Dominic pushed back his chair and rose to his feet. 'Don't worry, I'll go.'

'Really?'

'Honestly, I'm happy to. You've been taking care of Leo all week. You look shattered. Why don't you have a nice long bath?' He bent forward, kissed her on the lips. 'Shall we watch a film tonight? The new Wes Anderson's on Amazon Prime.'

Livvy nodded, even though she often found Wes Anderson's films pretentious. But Dominic loved them and she knew he'd missed this one at the cinema when Leo was born.

'I'll see you in about forty-five minutes. I doubt I'll get away without stopping for a cup of tea.' He smiled, kissed her again, turned to leave.

Livvy waited until she heard the click of the front door. Retrieving her mobile phone from a shelf on the dresser, she found a WhatsApp message from Bea, the first two lines of which were visible without needing to unlock the screen.

> *I'm at Mum and Dad's, playing with Leo. See you later when you pick him up.*

Opening the message, she read the rest.

We're having a whale of a time. Your son is ADORABLE.
xxx

Livvy stared at the message, speculations drifting through her mind like wisps of smoke, evaporating before she had a chance to study them properly. For a long time, she sat at the kitchen table, gazing alternately at her phone and then at the stairs, trying to decide whether the hint of doubt was legitimate or not.

Shaking her head as if to tip the suspicion out, she tapped out a reply to her sister.

Ah, sorry! Dominic's coming to collect him. I'm having a
rare half-hour alone. Glad you all had fun. xxx

Making her way up the stairs to run a bath, she pushed the unwelcome thoughts into the furthest recess of her mind and closed a door on them.

ANNA

LONDON

Zahira stares at me, visibly shaken, and I don't know what to say to fill the void. It is still too new, too raw, for me to have found the words to ameliorate somebody else's shock.

'I'm so sorry. I can't imagine how you must feel. It's such a terrible thing to learn, after everything you've already been through.' Zahira shakes her head, as though she cannot get the story to settle. She calls out to Elyas to be careful as he clambers up a wooden slope to the peaked-roof playhouse, and he pauses for a second, stares across the playground, before continuing his journey.

Watching him, my grief feels unwieldy. Elyas is only eight months older than Henry would have been had he lived. The knowledge of it seems too cruel to exist in any fair, kind, just world. And yet I know it is true.

It is two days since I discovered I had once been a mother. For the past forty-eight hours, I have felt as though I am existing in two parallel worlds: the real, present world of grief, guilt and self-reproach. And an imaginary world in which Henry is still alive, in which he'll soon be two and a half, in which we come to the park together every day, his hand in mine as we collect leaves, spot green parakeets, splash through puddles in brightly coloured wellingtons. A world in which his words are joining forces in the creation of sentences, in which he has favourite books, favourite toys, favourite games. A world in which my little boy is alive and thriving and I am free to love him as any mother should.

For the past two nights, I have lain awake, Stephen sleeping soundly beside me, wondering how I will ever forgive myself for failing to check on Henry that final night. Stephen may have forgiven me – or, at least, is doing a valiant job of feigning forgiveness – but it is more than I deserve.

Since first catching sight of Zahira and Elyas in the park a fortnight ago, I have been aware of an ache deep in my heart, and I didn't understand where it had come from. But now I know who it's for and I cannot absolve myself for ever having forgotten. Because what kind of a mother forgets her grief at the loss of her child?

'Why didn't he tell you before?'

Zahira's question punctures my thoughts, and I remember Stephen's crumpled features as we sat on the sofa, anguish writ large on his face. 'He thought it would be too much for me, after finding out about my parents.' I do not tell her that I fear he was right, that there are moments when I do not know how to bear this trio of losses. I feel strangled by grief, as though it is sucking all the air from my lungs until there is nothing left but a pair of spent balloons.

'I'm so sorry, Anna. I can't imagine what this must be like for you, or what you must be going through.'

Neither of us speaks for a few minutes. Looking around the playground at the collection of pre-schoolers, I wonder if it is a form of perverse self-punishment coming here: a stark, brutal reminder of all I have lost.

Zahira calls over to Elyas, reminds him to share the playhouse with two little girls trying to get through the door. She watches as he steps back and allows them inside. 'I don't want to interfere, but I do think it's important that your husband's honest with you about your past. I understand how difficult it must have been, having to tell you such painful things. But there must be a whole life of yours that you don't yet know about. Wouldn't it be better to find out?'

Zahira's voice is gently persuasive and yet her words cause my pulse to race. 'I think I'm scared that whatever I find out will be bad. And what if Stephen tells me everything and I still don't remember? Where do I go after that? Maybe it means I'll never remember anything for myself.'

Zahira rests a hand gently on mine. 'I understand. I know it's not the same but there were times after I found out about my ex-husband's affair when I thought every new piece of information might destroy me. But however hard it was at the time, it was really important for me to face it head-on. I don't think I'd have recovered if I hadn't.' She pauses, checks on Elyas, turns back to me. 'Maybe you're right, maybe finding out more about your past won't be the silver bullet you want it to be. But isn't it better at least to try?'

It is a rhetorical question and I let it revolve in my head.

'Believe me, there've been plenty of moments when I wished I'd managed to turn a blind eye to Joe's affair. It would have been so much easier in some ways to stay married to him, to stick together as a family.' Zahira pauses as Elyas runs towards her, holds out a wet hand, wipes it on his sweatshirt before she has a chance to find a tissue. She sends him back to the playhouse, continues speaking. 'But I would have been living a lie and I'm pretty sure it wouldn't have made me happy. I can't tell you how much courage it took for me to call time on my marriage when I had a newborn baby. But sometimes being scared of something is precisely the reason you need to do it. Seriously, what's the worst that can happen if you ask Stephen to tell you more? At least you'll have a better picture of what your life looked like before the accident, even if it is second-hand.'

I try to absorb what Zahira is saying. 'I know you're probably right. It's just a lot to think about.'

'It must be so hard. And I do understand why your husband found it difficult to tell you about Henry. But I'm not sure I understand the rationale in telling you so little about the rest of your life.' She pauses, and it is as if I can hear her searching through a thesaurus in her mind, choosing her words carefully. 'It's almost like he doesn't want you to remember.'

I shake my head. 'Of course he does. I think he just wants to protect me from things he knows I'll find upsetting.'

'But he can't protect you forever. And how will you ever have a full picture of your life unless he tells you everything – the good and the bad? You have a right to know it all – not just what Stephen chooses to tell you.'

I turn Zahira's reasoning over in my mind, trying to unpack how I feel about it. Part of me knows she is right – at some point I will have to learn everything – but remembering my devastation on Sunday night, I understand Stephen's reluctance to have told me sooner.

Elyas runs up to Zahira, announces that he is starving. Zahira feeds him half a banana before he zooms across the playground, clambers onto one end of a low-swung see-saw, bounces gently up and down.

'By the way, I meant to ask – did your new mobile phone arrive?'

I shake my head. 'To be honest, with everything that's happened, I haven't even thought to ask.'

Zahira pulls her grey leather bag onto her lap, roots around inside, brings out a black mobile phone and matching charger. 'You're welcome to have this. It's just an old one of mine. I've put a new SIM card in and twenty pounds of credit on it, just in case you need it.' She holds out the phone to me and there is something slightly off beam in her voice: the deliberate effort to sound casual.

'That's really kind, but I can't take it. It's too much.'

'Course you can. I'm never going to use it again. It's ancient and it doesn't even have Wi-Fi, so there's no maps or internet, but at least you'll have a phone for emergencies.'

The phone hovers in the space between us, and I look down at it, unsure what to do next. I have not told Stephen about my meetings with Zahira, cannot think how I would explain to him that a woman I've never mentioned has given me a mobile phone.

'Honestly, take it. I've put my number in the contacts so you can call me any time. And I've taped the number of the phone on the back in case you need to give it to anyone else. It's just until you get a phone of your own.' There is a gentle insistence in Zahira's voice, like a parent encouraging a child to step into the playground on the first day of school.

My hand outstretches, as if of its own volition, and I watch myself take hold of the phone and the charger, slip them into my jacket pocket, hear myself express thanks. And yet, as Zahira gets up from the bench to check on Elyas, I feel it digging into my ribs and wonder how on earth I will explain its presence in our house to Stephen.

LIVVY

BRISTOL

Livvy sat in front of the mirror, watching the expressions shift across her face like clouds fluctuating in the changing light: apprehension, uncertainty, a tight smile of reassurance. She wondered what someone else would observe, looking at her: whether they would find a woman embracing change, or if they would see straight through her, the fault line of indecision clearly visible, like writing through a stick of rock.

'Are you ready?'

Livvy glanced up at the woman standing behind her, pulled her lips into a smile. She told herself to stop being ridiculous. This wasn't a life-changing decision. It was superficial, really, in the grand scheme of things.

Behind her, the hairdresser took hold of Livvy's newly washed hair, ran a brush from the roots to the ends. There was something soothing in the movement, ritualistic almost, as if they were two women from an ancient tribe performing a traditional rite of passage.

'You're so lucky having hair this thick. Mine's always been thin – nothing much you can do with it. But yours is gorgeous.' The hairdresser smoothed a palm along Livvy's hair, tucked it behind her ears. 'What made you decide to cut it short?'

The question veered from one side of Livvy's mind to the other, no clear path to an answer.

It had been almost three weeks since she had sat at right angles to Dominic at the kitchen table, irritated by his suggestion that she cut her hair. And yet, over the course of that weekend, he had pointed to actresses on television and models in Sunday supplements, advocating hairstyles he thought would suit her. '*What's the worst that could happen? If you cut it and you don't like it, it'll always grow back. It's only hair, after all.*'

Since then, there had been a stream of WhatsApp messages in a similar vein: photos of beautiful actresses with angular bobs accentuating razor-sharp cheekbones; articles about women who felt liberated by a change in hairstyle; upbeat GIFs about seizing the day. Dominic had made the point that shorter hair would look more professional. '*When you go for those meetings in London, you want to look the part, don't you?*' She had begun to feel foolish, her resistance like a childish affectation. She had studied the photos he'd sent her, begun to wonder if perhaps he was right, it was time for a change. Perhaps she did need something a bit more sophisticated.

After she'd booked the appointment, she'd told no one, not even Dominic, in case she lost her nerve at the eleventh hour. She had fibbed to Bea when she'd dropped Leo with her sister earlier, told her she just needed to run some errands.

'It was just time for a change.' The half-truth to the hairdresser emerged with ease, and Livvy folded her fingers together, tucked them in her lap.

The hairdresser swapped the brush for a comb, drew a line along the centre of Livvy's scalp, the plastic teeth scraping her skin.

'And you want it exactly like that?' The hairdresser gestured towards the photo on Livvy's phone, propped up against the mirror. It was a picture Dominic had sent her of an actress Livvy had never heard of, her hair cut in a stylish bob, a slight wave at the ends where it met her jawline.

Livvy looked at the photo, remembered Dominic's accompanying message: *This would look fantastic on you!* She noted the actress's pristine skin, scarlet lips, the sheen across her angled cheekbones. Her blonde hair, accentuated with expensive highlights, so different from Livvy's own auburn hair. Livvy tried to picture the style framing her face, but it felt like putting on someone else's clothes, knowing they didn't quite fit, like a child playing with a dressing-up box.

'Are you okay?' The hairdresser crouched down beside her, their eyes meeting in the mirror. 'You don't have to go through with it if you've changed your mind. Honestly, it happens all the time. It's a big thing, changing your appearance. I could just give you a quick trim. I won't charge you for the restyle.'

The possibility swung before Livvy like a hypnotist's pendulum. She could just get a trim. Nobody ever need know she'd even made the appointment. There was nothing forcing her to proceed.

Wouldn't you like something a bit more – I don't know – grown-up?

Dominic's words echoed in her ears, and before she had time to change her mind, she watched herself nod with the full vigour of certainty. 'I'm fine. I was just having a momentary wobble. Honestly, I want a change.'

The hairdresser stood up, moved behind Livvy's chair.

Livvy watched as the stylist performed one last comb-through. And then the hairdresser separated a section at the back of Livvy's head, held it between two fingers, and Livvy could feel the air against the nape of her neck, could sense how short her hair was going to be. She heard the decisive, irreversible snip of two metal blades coming together, saw the hairdresser take the severed ten-inch lock, watched it fall to the ground.

It's only hair, after all.

Dominic's words repeated in her head like a mantra. She told herself to stop being ridiculous, that it was absurd getting so over-wrought about something so superficial. She was a grown woman. She was having a restyle. There was no justification for this sense of loss.

It was only hair, after all.

ANNA

LONDON

I glance up at the large white analogue clock on the kitchen wall, the hands inching towards a quarter to nine. On the stove beside me, a pot of chilli con carne bubbles gently on the lowest heat, congealing where it has been simmering for over an hour. Touching my fingers lightly to the kettle, the metal is still warm where I boiled it at eight o'clock in preparation to cook the rice when Stephen arrived.

The second hand ticks conspicuously in the silence.

Trying to ignore the flit of panic in my chest, I remind myself that Stephen is often home later than expected, that he does not have a regular nine-to-five job, cannot clock off at a fixed time every day. He tries to avoid bringing work home, will often stay late at the university to finish marking essays or plan the next day's lectures and seminars. It is not unusual for him to be delayed.

And yet, in spite of knowing this, the thought lurches in my mind as to what would happen if Stephen didn't come home. If he never came home. If he disappeared, without a trace, leaving me here by myself. I realise how little I know about our day-to-day life, how incapable I would be of surviving on my own. I have no job, no money, no access to money. I do not know from whom we rent our house, to whom we pay our bills. I have no friends, no family, no wider network on whom I could rely. It is Stephen who knows everything. Stephen who looks after everything. Stephen who looks after me. Without him, I would be lost. He is all I have in the world.

The sound of a key in the lock makes me jump and I jerk away from the kitchen counter, open the kitchen door, and there is Stephen, striding across the sitting room towards me, smiling. And yet, even as relief washes over me, the butterflies in my stomach do not come to rest.

'Hello, you. Everything okay?' He kisses me lightly on the lips and I try not to flinch. I cannot allow my body to keep treating Stephen like a stranger. 'You're shaking. What's wrong?'

I swallow against the anxiety clutching my throat. 'Nothing. I was just worried – about you being late.' I have tried to keep the alarm from my voice, but I can hear it, swimming against the tide.

Stephen eyes me quizzically. 'I told you I'd be late tonight. There were departmental drinks – just some warm white wine and a few peanuts – but I couldn't not make an appearance. I got away as soon as I could.'

I scour my memory for any mention of work drinks, find nothing but empty drawers where the information should be. 'Sorry. I didn't remember.'

Stephen cups a hand to the side of my face. 'It's me who should apologise. I should have written it down for you. The last thing I want is you worrying unnecessarily. God, you're trembling.' He takes my hands in his, rubs them as one would a child's after they've been out in the snow. 'You know it's just the head injury making you anxious like this? You wouldn't usually get so worried if I was late home.'

He pulls my body to his, encircles his arms around me. I try to believe that I have not always been like this: anxious, agitated, uncertain.

Stephen releases me from his arms. 'You need to be kind to yourself, my love. You're still so fragile emotionally. It's understandable that your feelings are all over the place.' He turns his head, looks down at the pan of simmering chilli. 'Dinner smells delicious.' Unbuttoning the cuffs of his shirt, he rolls up his sleeves. 'Anyway, tell me what you've been up to today.'

I flick the kettle on, pick up a plastic spoon, stir the now viscous sauce. 'Nothing much. Just reading, cooking. Nothing very exciting.' The lie tastes bitter on my tongue and I wonder if it is audible in my voice, wonder why I do not feel able to tell him about my meetings in the park with Zahira and Elyas.

'It's just that when I called this morning there was no answer. I was worried.'

Heat floods my cheeks and I wish he'd mentioned it earlier, when we spoke at lunchtime, when my guilt would not have been so visible. 'I just popped out for a walk.'

'Where to?'

'Just around the block. Don't worry – I know my route well now.'

I wait for Stephen to say something, but there is a stillness between us. I think about the mobile phone Zahira gave me, crammed inside a pair of balled-up socks at the back of my underwear drawer, the charger tucked in a shoebox at the bottom of the wardrobe. I wish I had never hidden them. I should have left them out on the kitchen table for Stephen to see, explained where I got them from. But now it is too late: I have tied my deceit in a knot between us and cannot easily unpick it.

'I'll make sure I'm home earlier tomorrow and we can get out for a walk together before dinner.' He slips an arm around my

213

waist, his breath warm on my neck. 'I know it must be boring being home alone all day, but once your memory returns, maybe you can think about looking for a job? We just need to be patient while you get better.'

I nod, my muscles tensing automatically in response to his touch, wonder whether either of us can actually envisage a time when my memory will be sufficiently restored for me to start job-hunting.

Stephen leans his back against the work surface, thrusts his hands into the pockets of his navy chinos. 'I don't know if this is a good time to tell you, but I've got to go away again this weekend, just for a night. I'm really sorry.'

My eyes dart towards him, anxiety creeping between my ribs.

'It's only Friday night. I'll be back on Saturday evening. There's a conference in Southampton I just can't miss. I'll make it up to you on Sunday, I promise. If the weather's good, maybe we could drive to the coast.'

I sense him watching me, waiting for me to respond. But the thought of another night by myself tightens around my chest like a vice, and I can only nod, pull my cheeks into a poor semblance of a smile.

'Perhaps we could go to West Wittering. We've always loved that beach and if we get up early we can have a nice walk before the crowds descend.' There is buoyancy in his tone and I cannot tell whether it is instinctive or deliberate. But I do not remember any beaches, do not feel it is a decision in which I can be an active participant.

There must be a whole life of yours that you don't yet know about. Wouldn't it be better to find out? I hear Zahira's voice in my head and know she is right: I cannot be trapped inside my amnesia forever.

'Stephen . . . I've been thinking – about everything I don't remember. I think it might be helpful for me to know more about my life before the accident.'

Stephen places a hand on my arm, strokes a thumb across the flesh above the crook of my elbow. 'There's no rush, is there? It's still early days.'

'But I think it might help me.' There is urgency in my tone: now that I have asked, I realise how keenly I want to know.

'Part of me is inclined to agree with you, but I think we should probably follow the doctors' advice.'

'Why, what did they say?'

Stephen's thumb continues to caress my skin. 'That we shouldn't flood you with too many memories too quickly. That it would be easy for you to get overwhelmed and you might have difficulty processing day-to-day information if we did that.'

I rummage through my short-term memory, rewind it to my time in hospital. But there were so many conversations with different doctors that I cannot locate the one Stephen is referring to.

'You're doing so well, I think we might be silly to jeopardise it. And you've already had so much to contend with. It's only just over a fortnight since the crash, after all.'

I try to deconstruct the passage of time over the past couple of weeks, but each day has stretched inexorably before me, one hour bleeding into the next, time warping until I have lost any sense of where one day ends and another begins.

Stephen pulls me back into his arms, rests his head on top of mine. 'I can only imagine how difficult this must be for you, my love. But we'll get there. Your memory will come back eventually.'

He kisses my head, and I try to take solace in his encouragement, while somewhere inside me, a little girl stands lost in a forest, no clue how to find her way out.

LIVVY

BRISTOL

Livvy stood on the doorstep of the Georgian townhouse where her sister owned the first-floor flat and wrapped a hand around the back of her bare neck. She felt exposed, shorn, as though she had stepped into the hairdresser's one version of herself and stepped out someone different, someone she didn't quite recognise.

For the duration of the haircut, Livvy had stared at her own reflection, observing the transformation taking place. She had watched as the hairdresser pivoted around her, scissor blades moving quickly, snipping at the line of her jaw. When, finally, the cutting and blow-drying had ended, Livvy had looked at herself in the mirror, the effect disorienting, as though she were staring at a portrait of herself in which the painter had taken liberties with her appearance.

There was no denying that the hairdresser had performed a meticulous facsimile. Apart from the difference in colour, her hair looked exactly like the woman's in the photograph. And yet, even as she gazed at herself, Livvy could not assess whether it was a style that actually suited her.

Livvy pressed a finger to the brass doorbell of her sister's flat. The intercom crackled and then there was Bea's voice, checking it was Livvy, buzzing her in.

Climbing the stairs, Livvy was aware of a gentle thrumming in her chest.

Bea's front door was already open when Livvy reached the landing. Bea stood in the doorway with Leo in her arms, and Livvy saw it immediately: shock spreading across her sister's face like marbling ink in water.

'What have you done to your hair?'

'I've had it cut.'

'I can see that. But . . . why?'

Livvy forced a shrug from her shoulders. 'I just thought it was time for a change.'

Bea stood back from the doorway and ushered Livvy inside. As she passed, Livvy took Leo from her sister's arms, kissed the top of his head, carried him through to the sitting room where floor-to-ceiling windows flooded the room with afternoon sunshine. Sitting down on the pale blue sofa with Leo on her lap, Livvy felt Bea's eyes hot on her face.

'Why didn't you tell me that's where you were going?'

'I didn't want you to talk me out of it.' Leo wriggled out of Livvy's lap and she put him down on the thick sheepskin rug that Bea rolled out whenever Leo came to visit, placed cushions around him lest he topple to one side.

'This was Dominic's idea, wasn't it?'

'Of course not. I just wanted to try something different.'

'So Dominic had nothing to do with it? He didn't even suggest it?'

Heat seeped into Livvy's cheeks. 'For goodness' sake, I've had the same hairstyle for thirty years. I just thought it was time for a change.' She could feel Bea's eyes on her, felt naked beneath her sister's scrutiny.

'There seems to be a lot of change going on in your life at the moment.'

Livvy held out a plastic figurine to Leo, watched him drop it into his yellow toy truck. 'That's a good thing, isn't it? I don't want to be someone who gets stuck in a rut.'

'Sure. But it seems that you're taking on quite a lot at the moment: the move, giving up your job, your appearance—'

'It's only a haircut.'

Bea paused. 'It's not just the haircut though, is it? You hardly spend time with anyone except Dominic and Leo these days.'

'What's wrong with that? They're my family.'

'But that doesn't mean you have to stop seeing everyone else in your life.'

'I'm not. Stop exaggerating.'

'I'm not criticising you. I'm worried about you.' Bea took in a deep breath. 'I wasn't sure when to tell you this, but I've been doing a bit of digging.' She hesitated. 'I spoke to one of Dominic's ex-girlfriends.'

Livvy felt blindsided. 'What?'

Bea sat down on the edge of the armchair, leant forward, fingers interlaced, like a teacher in a classroom about to tell a carpet-time story. 'I googled some of the places he's worked before. And then I emailed some of the people he used to work with.'

The explanation floundered in Livvy's head. 'Please tell me you're joking.'

'I just felt . . . Everything between you and Dominic happened so quickly, and we barely know anything about him—'

'What are you talking about? I know everything about him.'

'Do you?' Bea looked at her, and it was as if the two of them were teetering on a tightrope, arms outstretched, waiting to see if

218

one of them might fall. 'What do you know about an ex-girlfriend of his called Daisy?'

'He doesn't have an ex-girlfriend called Daisy.'

Bea raised her eyebrows, the air charged with friction. 'He does. They broke up six weeks before you met him at that conference.'

A cold trickle of air tiptoed along Livvy's spine. 'That's rubbish. Dominic had been single for over a year when we met.'

On the rug beside them, Leo bashed a wooden stick against a toy xylophone.

'Not according to Daisy. She worked with him on a house extension, in Bishopston. Did you know about that project?'

Livvy nodded. 'It was the job he'd just finished when we met. But that doesn't mean—'

'Just hear me out.' Bea held up her palms, face out, and it reminded Livvy of Imogen performing the same gesture the first time she'd turned up on Livvy's doorstep eight weeks ago. 'Daisy was one of the architects on the project. They started dating, and she really liked him. She thought he was charming, sophisticated, different from other men she'd met. *Attentive* was the word she used. "*He always made me feel like the most important person in the room.*" Sounds familiar, doesn't it?'

Livvy was aware of her heart beginning to drum. 'So? Are you criticising Dominic for being attentive? For god's sake, Bea, I know you've never liked him, but this is extreme—'

'I haven't finished.' Bea's voice – usually so calm and diplomatic – was dogged, determined. 'Daisy said that a few weeks after they started dating, things got a bit weird.'

'In what way?' The question sprang from Livvy's lips in spite of herself.

'She said it got very intense, very quickly.' Bea trained her eyes on Livvy's face, and Livvy looked away, handed Leo a plastic horse he couldn't reach. 'Within a fortnight Dominic had told her he loved her, and Daisy felt it was all moving too fast, that she couldn't keep pace with the strength of his feelings. She said that for a while she just got swept up in it all. A part of her felt guilty that she didn't feel as strongly as Dominic did, when on paper he seemed to be perfect. So she just went along with it, and assumed her feelings would eventually catch up with his. But she said she just couldn't silence a niggle in the back of her head.'

Impatience pinched Livvy's skin. 'Why are you telling me this? So Dominic had a girlfriend and he was more keen than she was. What's the big deal?'

Bea's shoulders rose and fell. 'She said he started getting quite possessive with her. Wanted to spend every night with her, didn't like her going out with her friends—'

'That's totally normal at the beginning of a relationship. That's why it's called the honeymoon period—'

'Six weeks after they met, he asked her to marry him.'

The words were like a sledgehammer across Livvy's thoughts. 'That's absurd. There's no way Dominic wouldn't have told me.'

'Maybe he didn't tell you because Daisy said no. She told him it had all got too heavy, and she broke up with him.'

Livvy shook her head. 'Dominic wears his heart on his sleeve. He would have told me if he'd proposed to someone else. There's no reason for him to lie about it.'

Bea softened her voice. 'Maybe the reason he didn't tell you was because when Daisy broke up with him, he didn't take it very well. She said he wouldn't leave her alone. Kept calling her, sending her messages, turning up at her flat at all hours of the day and night.'

Livvy closed her eyes, tried to visualise what Bea was telling her, but it was like a scene that had found itself in the wrong story. 'Dominic wouldn't do that. He's not like that.'

Bea paused, swallowed, breathed slowly. 'She went to the police. She tried to get a restraining order against him. But it hadn't been going on long enough, and there weren't any obvious threats to her safety. But she felt stalked. That was the word she used. *Stalked.* She was scared and overwhelmed. She ended up moving back in with her parents for six months.'

'Her parents?'

Bea eyed her for a moment, as if toying with a silent dilemma. 'She was twenty-four when it happened.'

'Twenty-four? This is absolute rubbish. There's no way Dominic would have dated a twenty-four-year-old. That's practically half his age.' Livvy reached for a strand of hair to twist around her finger, discovered it was missing. 'Why are you doing this? You find some random woman on the internet, and she makes up a bunch of stories about Dominic, and you choose to believe them? You're my sister, you're supposed to support me.'

'That's exactly what I am doing.'

'What, by telling me a bunch of lies?'

'They're not lies, Livvy. I met her. I've seen it all with my own eyes.'

A silence fell on the room, like the pregnant seconds between a flash of lightning and a clap of thunder.

'What do you mean?'

'I met her for coffee. Yesterday morning. She showed me photos of her and Dominic together. They were all dated on her iPhone – there was no way she could have been lying. And there were dozens of messages – texts, WhatsApps, emails – all from his number and his email address. She wasn't making it up.'

Livvy grabbed Leo's change bag from the floor, began stuffing his toys inside.

'What are you doing?'

'What do you think I'm doing?'

'Livvy, please—'

Livvy spun around, anger throbbing in her cheeks. 'You play amateur detective and think you've found some dirt on Dominic – who, let's be honest, you haven't liked since day one – and you expect me to stay and listen to it?'

'For god's sake, Livvy, he told Daisy he was adopted.'

Livvy stopped abruptly, as though in a game of Musical Statues. 'That's ridiculous. Why on earth would he say that?'

'I don't know. But that's what he told her. He said he was adopted as a baby, and when he tried to find his birth parents, they didn't want to meet him. He told her his adoptive parents felt so hurt that his relationship with them had broken down. Daisy said it made her feel sorry for him, but after things got weird between them, she wondered if it was even true.'

The story lurched inside Livvy's head.

'Something about Dominic doesn't add up, Livvy. He never told you about Daisy. He's told you completely different stories about his parents. And there's a pattern to the way he dated you both, love-bombing you, reeling you in. Can't you see that something's just not right?' Bea paused, as if rehearsing what to say next. 'I'm worried about you. It's like you've lost all sense of yourself, as though you just go along with whatever Dominic wants. Do you really think that's what a marriage should look like?'

Livvy gripped the handle of Leo's change bag tight in her fist. 'I can't believe you're doing this. I know you've never liked him, but this is actually crazy. You say this woman felt stalked by Dominic? What do you think *you're* doing, tracking down his ex-girlfriends, talking to his ex-colleagues? Can't you see how crazy *you're* being?' She grabbed Leo's sippy cup, thrust it in the bag, ignored the spray of water that dripped onto the rug. 'Why are you the only one who can't see how good Dominic is for me? Mum's always said our relationship is like something out of a fairy tale. Why can't you just be happy for me?'

Bea eyed her sadly. 'Because that's what bothers me. Fairy tales don't actually exist.'

Livvy threw her hands into the air in exasperation. 'Dominic can't win, can he? One minute you're accusing him of lying to me. The next you're saying our relationship is too good to be true. Make your mind up.'

They held each other's gaze for a few seconds, the conversation pounding at Livvy's temples.

'I don't want to fight with you, Livvy. I just wish you could take a step back and see what's really going on.'

'What, because you have more insight into my marriage than I do? Do you have any idea how arrogant that sounds? You haven't had a boyfriend for twenty years and yet you expect me to take relationship advice from you?' Livvy stood up and slung the bag over her shoulder. Lifting Leo into her arms, she headed for the door.

'Please don't go. Not like this. I'm just trying to look out for you.' Bea rushed after her, handed Livvy the cloth book she'd left on the rug.

Livvy took it without meeting Bea's eyes, shoved it in the bag. 'I don't need looking out for. And I certainly don't need you going behind my back, snooping into Dominic's past. Stop trying to sabotage my life.'

'I'm not—'

'Really? Well, you're doing a pretty good job of acting like it.' She shifted Leo to the opposite hip, her son heavy in her arms. 'I need to get Leo home.' She turned, walked towards the front door, felt her sister close behind.

'Livvy, please—'

'Thanks for looking after him this afternoon.' Livvy's hand trembled on the front-door lock. Opening it, she stepped through without looking back.

'Livvy, I'm sorry. I didn't mean to upset you, I'm just worried about you . . .'

Bea's voice followed her down the stairs, chasing after her, trying to haul her back, but Livvy kept walking, into the wide expanse of communal hallway, out through the front door and into the street, heart thudding with fury all the way.

ANNA

LONDON

Stephen leans against the kitchen counter. 'By the way, there was a message on the answerphone from the therapist – Carla, is it? She's had to cancel your appointment on Friday but said she'll be in touch with another date soon.'

Disappointment cramps in my chest. 'Why?'

'She didn't say. Just that she'd be in touch. It's hardly surprising, given how services are being cut. To be honest, I was amazed you got a referral so quickly in the first place.'

His words are like treacle in my ears. It is only now that the promise of therapy is taken away from me that I realise how much I was relying on it. 'Why did she tell you? Why didn't she tell me?' I hear the panic in my voice, wish I could contain it.

Stephen frowns. 'She did. She left a message on the answerphone.'

Confusion darts in my head like a fish trapped in a barrel. 'But you've only just got home. How have you heard it already?'

'I can access it remotely. I often check it during the day, see if there's anything important. I don't want you worrying about messages from the landlord or anything like that.' He looks perplexed by my questions. 'What's the matter?'

The kettle boils and I pour steaming water into the saucepan, cover the rice. I do not know how to answer, cannot find the words to articulate the depth of my disappointment. I feel like a deep-sea diver, submerged beneath gallons of ocean water, the prospect of the therapy appointment my oxygen tank, keeping me breathing.

'Anna?'

I swallow hard, stir the rice around the pan to prevent it sticking. 'I'm fine.'

There is an expectant pause. 'I'm sure you'll get another appointment soon.'

I nod, even though we have no way of knowing if it is true.

We are interrupted by the shrill ringing of Stephen's mobile. Pulling it from his trouser pocket, he stares at the screen, mutters under his breath. He glances up at me, cheeks stretching into an apologetic smile. 'It's work, I'd better take it.' There is a sliver of hesitation, like the flit of a shadow through the window of a night train. 'I won't be a minute.'

He hurries from the room, phone still ringing, and I hear his feet bounding up the stairs. I am aware of stilling my movements, waiting, listening. There is a muffled greeting before the scrape of wood against carpet and the rest of the conversation disappears behind our closed bedroom door.

I reduce the heat beneath the rice, think about the cancelled session with the therapist, and feel a sudden urge to take back some control over my life.

Hurrying into the sitting room, I head for the side table where the phone lives, the white notepad next to it, and notice immediately that the piece of paper I'm looking for is missing. I flick through the notepad, thinking perhaps it has become detached from its gummy binding, but only empty pages stare back at me.

My heart begins to race as I search under the phone's cradle, crouch down on my hands and knees to see if it has somehow slipped to the floor like a helicopter seed from a sycamore tree. But there is nothing. No scrap of paper containing the name and telephone number for an appointment that has begun to feel like a lifeline out of my amnesia.

'What are you doing?'

I jerk my head around to find Stephen standing over me, frowning. 'The therapist's number. The piece of paper I'd written it on. I can't find it. Have you seen it?'

He shakes his head. 'Why do you need it?'

'I just want it.'

'Why?'

'I just do.' There is frenzy in my voice and it does not sound like me, or at least not the me I have come to know over the past two weeks. 'You must have taken it, thrown it away.' I resume my search, under the bookshelves, behind the television. I have to find that scrap of paper, need to know I can phone the therapist, that the lifebuoy she has thrown me is not out of reach.

I sense Stephen behind me, feel a hand on my shoulder. 'Anna, come on. Why don't we have dinner? It smells amazing.' His voice is patient, placatory, but I do not want mollification. I want that piece of paper.

'You *must* have thrown it away. It was here, only a few days ago. It was attached to the top of the pad. I *saw* it.' I return to the notepad, run my fingers across it, feel the indentations of my pen marks. I tear the top sheet off, hold it up to the light to prove to myself that it was once there, try to decipher the alphanumerics, but the marks are too faint.

Stephen places his hands on my arms, lifts me to my feet. 'Look at me, Anna. *Look at me*. I haven't touched the notepad. The piece of paper must have got lost somehow.' He speaks in slow, deliberate tones, enunciating each word carefully, a micropause between each one, as though attempting to pacify a recalcitrant child. 'Maybe you threw it away by accident. But you don't need it. The therapist said she'd call back to rearrange your appointment. There's nothing to get upset about.'

He pulls me into his arms, and a part of me wants to resist, wants to search for that piece of paper until I have found it. But Stephen holds me close, runs his fingers through my hair, and I am overcome by a bewildering sense of uncertainty.

'Shall we have dinner? I think the rice is probably ready by now.' There is light-heartedness in Stephen's voice, and I extricate myself from his arms, try to return his smile. But as I follow Stephen into the kitchen, I glance over my shoulder to where the name and telephone number of the therapist should be. I know that I did not move that piece of paper, that I would not have thrown it away. It was too important for me to be so careless. And yet now it is gone, and I will just have to hope that Carla calls me back and that she does not leave it too long.

LIVVY
BRISTOL

Livvy opened the door to her wardrobe, surveyed the jumble of shoeboxes stacked at the bottom. From downstairs she could hear the faint murmur of music, something classical, Radio 3 no doubt. Dominic was down there, packing his books in preparation for the move next weekend. Checking the time, she figured she had a couple of hours before Leo was likely to wake from his post-lunch nap.

Turning around, she caught sight of herself in the mirror, experienced a moment's discombobulation. Her hand shot to the back of her neck, made contact with her bare skin, and she readjusted her expectations, reminded herself that this was her reflection now: the short bob, the swept fringe, the wispy ends she would probably never have time to blow-dry the way the hairdresser had done. It was almost twenty-four hours since she'd had her hair cut and still the sight of her own reflection took her by surprise.

When Dominic had returned from Sheffield the previous evening, the expression on his face had morphed from shock to delight. He had turned her around, his hands on her shoulders, examining her from every angle, as though she were a delicately carved statue on a plinth in a museum. He'd taken copious photos of her on his phone, shown them to her, beaming: '*I told you it would suit you.*' In the hours since, she had caught him looking at her when he thought she wouldn't notice, a curious expression on his face she couldn't quite decipher.

Her phone buzzed and she picked it up, found a message from Bea, opened it even as a knot pulled taut in her stomach.

> *I really am sorry that I went behind your back. I know how angry it's made you, and I do understand why. But you must believe me when I say that I was doing it with the best of intentions. I'm not trying to sabotage your marriage. I'm just trying to make sure you're okay. I love you. Please call me. Xxx*

Livvy exited WhatsApp, tossed her phone on the bed. There had been a constant stream of messages from Bea since their row yesterday afternoon, each one a variation on the same theme: Bea was sorry, she hadn't meant to overstep the mark, please could Livvy forgive her. But Livvy couldn't forgive. It was as though Bea had marched into the middle of Livvy's marriage, grenade in hand, removed the pin and been disappointed to discover that it hadn't detonated.

She hadn't told Dominic the real reason for her falling out with Bea. She'd said Bea hadn't been supportive of her haircut, that she was upset Livvy had cancelled their plans a few times lately. But she'd said nothing to him about Daisy, or about Bea's egregious invasion into Dominic's privacy. And yet still Dominic had leapt to Livvy's defence: '*I know she's your sister, and I love your loyalty to her, but she's never really going to understand your life. She's never going to understand what it's like to have a partner and a child. If Bea really loves you – if she really cares about your happiness – she'll let you manage your life however you choose, even if that means she gets to see you less.*' Aware of all the messages arriving from Bea yesterday evening, Dominic had suggested Livvy ignore them for now, take a step back, let the dust settle. Reconvene with Bea when they'd both had time to calm down.

Picking up a stack of shoeboxes from the bottom of the wardrobe, Livvy carried them to the bed, let them slide from her arms onto the duvet. Lifting the lid of one, she found a neat pile of letters, familiar meticulous writing on the envelopes. Choosing one from near the bottom of the pile, she prised out the single piece of thick, cream A5 paper.

Darling Livvy

You may think me old-fashioned writing to you when an email or text would be quicker. But I wanted to tell you that the last three weeks have been incredible. I've loved every moment we've spent together: you're beautiful and funny and kind and I have, quite simply, never met anyone like you.

Perhaps it's too early to tell you this, but I'm going to say it anyway.

I love you.

I can't wait to see you tonight.

Dominic xx

Rifling through the rest of the letters, she remembered how, in the early months of their relationship, they'd written to each other daily, even when spending every evening together. Their correspondence had stopped when Livvy first moved in, but since Dominic had been away in Sheffield, she'd been writing him a letter every week and slipping it into his suitcase before he left on Monday mornings. Just short notes, telling him how much she loved him and how much she would miss him, but somehow they made her feel more connected to him in his absence.

Within a fortnight Dominic had told her he loved her . . . He always made her feel like the most important person in the room . . . Sounds familiar, doesn't it?

Bea's story about Daisy hissed in Livvy's ears, and she tried to silence it, reassured herself that it wasn't the same. Daisy clearly hadn't been ready for a relationship, and Dominic couldn't be held accountable for another woman's immaturity. If Dominic had chosen not to tell Livvy about it, he must have his reasons. And starting one relationship soon after finishing another wasn't exactly a crime.

Her phone pinged again, and Livvy was aware of something twisting in her stomach as she braced herself for another missive from Bea. But when she picked up her phone and saw the identity of the messenger, a cold sheen of dread skimmed over her skin.

Glancing over her shoulder through the open bedroom door, she strained her ears, heard Dominic whistling to a piece of music. Turning back to her phone, she opened the message.

> *I wondered if you'd had a chance to talk to Dominic yet about us meeting up? I honestly don't want to cause any trouble. I just want to see you and Leo, and ideally Dominic too, if he's ready. I'd be so grateful if you might meet up with me.*

It was Imogen's first communication in more than three weeks. Livvy had dared to imagine that perhaps she'd given up. She reread the message, wondering what to do for the best.

'God, it looks like a bomb site in here.'

Livvy whipped her head around, found Dominic standing in the doorway, casting a critical eye over the room. Heart drumming in her chest, she gripped her phone, finger groping for the activation button to turn the screen dark.

'Have you only managed to fill three bags?' He gestured out to the hallway, where a trio of bin liners were heaped together like children huddled close on a cold winter's day. 'There must be more to get rid of than that?'

Livvy stared at Dominic, tried to muster some words for a reply, found that none would come to her aid.

'Are you okay?'

The truth skittered through Livvy's mind in search of a secure hiding place. 'I'm fine. Just lots to do.'

Dominic studied her face, took hold of her hand, led her to the edge of the bed. As he sat down beside her, Livvy willed her phone not to ping with another message from Imogen.

'What's wrong? Come on, you know I can always tell when something's up.'

It was true. Sometimes Livvy thought Dominic had a direct line into her mind, could read her thoughts and feelings the way other people read the pages of a book.

For a moment she contemplated telling him the truth: Imogen's text, the phone call at home, the second doorstep visit. The bequest of John's watch, the request for access to Leo. But then she looked at Dominic, thought about all he'd had to contend with in recent weeks, and knew she couldn't do it to him. Once they were in London, where Imogen could no longer turn up unannounced, she would tell him then. She needed time to think about how best to broach it, how to explain why she had concealed Imogen's communications from him. Now was not the time. 'The row with Bea. I haven't been entirely honest with you. We didn't just argue about my hair.' The words tumbled out before she had a chance to assess whether this story really was the lesser of two evils.

Dominic's eyes tapered at the edges. 'Okay. So what did you row about?' He placed his hand on top of hers, beneath which lay the mobile phone containing a message Livvy desperately didn't want him to see.

Panic flitted in Livvy's chest. 'She found one of your ex-girl-friends online and made contact with her. She actually went to meet her. It's crazy, I know. I'm so sorry. It's such a huge invasion of your privacy. That's why we fell out.' The explanation spilled from her lips.

'What ex-girlfriend?'

'Some woman called Daisy. I'm sorry. I honestly don't know what possessed her. I'm furious with her. She keeps apologising – she knows it was completely out of order.'

Dominic fell still, silent, and Livvy was aware of the air thickening around them.

'What did Bea tell you?' His voice was low, masquerading calm, but the words were braided with hostility.

'It doesn't matter. It was all a load of rubbish.'

'It matters to me. Tell me.'

'It's not important. I shouldn't have said anything.'

'It's not important? Your sister starts snooping into my life and I'm not supposed to care what she said? For god's sake, just tell me.' Dominic's expression hardened as though set in clay.

Livvy tried to swallow, found that her mouth was dry. 'It's all nonsense. There was some ridiculous story about your relationship getting a bit intense, and this woman getting spooked and calling it off.' Livvy hesitated, unsure whether to say the rest. But then she stole a glance at Dominic's face and felt an uncanny certainty that if she held anything back, he would know. 'She told Bea that you kept trying to contact her after it was over and she ended up going to the police.' She paused, unable to silence the question now that the can of worms had been opened. 'None of that happened, did it?'

Dominic stared at her, unblinking, and Livvy had to look away, the heat of his gaze too intense.

'Do you really need to ask me that?'

'No, of course not, I just . . . Did you ever go out with this Daisy woman? You've never mentioned her.'

Dominic hunched forward, elbows on thighs, hands clenched in fists. 'You lied to me. You told me you and Bea had rowed about your hair.'

'I know, I'm sorry. I didn't want to upset you.'

Dominic shook his head with small, jarring movements. 'So what were you going to do? Sulk with your sister for a bit and then make up? Pretend it never happened? Have me play nice with her when you know what she's been doing behind my back?'

'No, of course not—'

'What then? What were you planning to do?'

There seemed to be no space in Livvy's head to formulate an answer. She placed a hand on Dominic's bare forearm. 'I don't know. I'm sorry.'

He reached out, grabbed hold of her wrist, fingers pressing into her flesh. 'What kind of an idiot do you take me for?'

Beneath his grip, the bones in Livvy's wrist smarted, the pain hot, sharp. 'Let go. You're hurting me.'

He tightened his hold on her, brought his face towards hers, the heat of his breath angry against her skin. '*I'm* hurting you? Your sister acts like some crazy stalker and you don't even have the decency to tell me? And now *I'm* the one in the wrong?'

His hand clenched harder around her wrist, and she heard herself emit an involuntary yelp, tears pricking her eyes. 'Please, Dominic, stop.'

He gripped tighter, their eyes locking, her skin burning beneath his grasp. 'Your fucking family. I don't know why I bother.' He threw her arm to one side, the corner of her wrist bone colliding with the edge of the wooden bed frame, a sharp pain shooting up her arm.

The house reverberated as he stormed out of the room and down the stairs.

And then the front door slammed, the sash windows rattled in their frames, and from the bedroom next door, Leo let out a piteous cry.

ANNA

LONDON

My key is already slotted in the front-door lock when I hear the phone ringing inside the house. My fingers fumble as I try to turn the key, its grooves jamming, refusing to rotate, while inside, the phone continues to trill. I think of Stephen on the other end of the line, worrying where I am, and I wonder if this is not the first time he has rung in the ninety minutes I have been gone, hoping to see Zahira and Elyas in the park only to find they weren't there. Loosening my grip on the key, I wiggle it from left to right, watch it slide finally to the side, the Yale lock clicking open behind it.

Pushing the door closed and running into the sitting room, I pick up the phone, hear the breathlessness in my voice. 'Hello?'

'Could I speak to Anna Bradshaw, please?'

It is a female voice, and the fact that it is not Stephen causes me to pause momentarily before replying. 'Yes, speaking.'

'This is Carla Stanislaw, from the West London Wellbeing Service. We spoke last week about you having some therapy sessions to help with your amnesia.'

'Yes, of course, I remember.' Relief washes over me as I glance down at the empty notepad next to the phone, its blank page staring vacantly at me.

'I'm glad I caught you. I was getting a bit concerned when you didn't reply to any of my messages.'

There is a jolt inside my head, a brief fissure in time in which the past and the present collide, and I cannot make sense of them. 'What messages?'

There is a pause before Carla speaks. 'I've left a couple of messages on your answerphone. It's completely fine if you've changed your mind about coming to therapy, but I do always like to speak to a patient directly if that's the case.'

I try to arrange the therapist's words into a meaningful explanation, but they skid and slide as if skating on ice. 'I don't understand.'

There is another momentary silence. 'Your husband left me a message to say you were feeling better and no longer required therapy. I just wanted to check in with you before discharging you. It's entirely your decision, of course, but most patients who've suffered amnesia do find a course of therapy helpful.'

The words swirl in my head as though circling around the edge of a whirlpool. 'When did he phone?'

There is a rustle of paper. 'On Tuesday, I believe. As I say, I've left a couple of voicemails on your answerphone since, so I'm glad I've got hold of you.'

I am aware of lowering myself onto the edge of the sofa, phone clutched in hand, knuckles aching with the ferocity of my grip. My head feels light, as though I have been spun too fast on a roundabout, cannot now re-orientate myself to solid ground.

I close my eyes, replay the therapist's words in my head, my thoughts curving, looping, like stars in a distant spiral galaxy. I think about Stephen telling me that Carla had cancelled my appointment, about his reassurances that I would get another

238

one soon. I think about the messages Carla says she has left this week, do not remember seeing the notification light flashing on the answerphone. Suspicions trip inside my head as Stephen's voice echoes in my ear: *I can access it remotely. I often check it during the day, see if there's anything important. I don't want you worrying about messages from the landlord or anything like that.*

'Like I say, it's entirely your decision, but perhaps just come along for one session and see how it goes? You don't have to come back if it's not for you. But most people do find it helpful.'

I am aware of nodding before realising that Carla can't see me. I open my mouth to reply but my voice seems to have got lost and I have to dig deep for it. 'That would be great, thank you.'

'Good. How about next Friday. Two p.m.? Do you want to take the address again or have you still got it?'

I ask her to tell me both the address and telephone number again, write them on the notepad, tear off the piece of paper and slip it in the back pocket of my jeans.

Carla is about to end the call when a thought barges into my mind, demanding to be heard. 'Can I ask you something?'

There is a fractional hesitation and I wonder if she is looking at her watch, glancing at her list of appointments, thoughts already segueing to her next patient. 'Of course.'

'If someone has amnesia like mine – where they can remember things day-to-day but not about their past – should they be told about their life before the amnesia, or is there a danger in finding out too much, too soon?' The words come tumbling out as though they may lose courage if they stall too long.

'Well, obviously every case is different and it's difficult – and often unhelpful – to generalise. But if a patient is coping well day-to-day, then learning about their past shouldn't be disadvantageous. It's all about the brain rediscovering old neural pathways and making new ones.'

She pauses, and I try to absorb what she is saying, try to match it to what Stephen has told me, but it is like trying to slot squares into a tile puzzle when all the pieces are different sizes.

'So if I want to find out more about my life before the accident, I should? It won't cause me any harm?'

'I wouldn't want to say anything definitively until I'd spent time with a patient, but generally my work is about trying to help patients remember, within a safe environment.'

I can hear she is on the verge of ending the call and I need to slip in one last question. 'So is it likely that a doctor – in a hospital, say – would recommend not finding out about your past if you're suffering from amnesia like mine?'

There is another pause, pregnant with speculation. 'Obviously I wouldn't want to second-guess another medical professional's diagnosis, but in most cases of episodic memory loss, a gradual reacclimatising to familiar people and places is helpful.' I hear the click of computer keys, wonder if it is my notes she is accessing or her next patient's. 'But I really would rather discuss this in person, when we meet. I think that will be much more productive.' Her voice is warm, and she tells me she is looking forward to meeting me. I thank her, tell her I am too.

We say goodbye and the phone call ends. My thoughts scramble over one another, each eager to be heard, but there is one louder than all the others, looping around my mind like a music track on repeat: why would Stephen lie to me about the therapist cancelling the appointment?

I'm not sure I understand the rationale in telling you so little about the rest of your life. It's almost like he doesn't want you to remember.

Three days ago, I thought Zahira's suggestion absurd. I felt certain that all Stephen's decisions were in my best interests. Now I do not know what to think, what to feel. Where to turn.

If a patient is coping well day-to-day, then learning about their past shouldn't be disadvantageous . . . In most cases of episodic memory loss, a gradual reacclimatising to familiar people and places is helpful.

Carla's words hum in my ears, somewhere between a response and a challenge, and as I replay them, an idea takes shape in my mind: curves, forms, solidifies.

I know what it is I need to do.

LIVVY

BRISTOL

Leo sat on the sitting room rug next to her, watching her twist the button on his pop-up toy until the brightly coloured elephant sprung from its hiding place. Pressing his chubby palm down on the lid to close it again, he looked up at Livvy, smiled, and Livvy tried to reciprocate.

It had been over an hour since Dominic had stormed out, slamming the front door behind him.

Sitting up on her knees, Livvy pulled a tissue from her pocket, wiped the sleep from Leo's eyes, while the argument with Dominic repeated in her head like a film caught on a loop.

Anger burrowed its way under her skin as she remembered the feel of Dominic's fingers tightening around her wrist. The recollection had an unreal quality to it, as though it belonged to a different time, a different marriage. She kept recalling the expression on his face – something beyond anger – but the memory was too painful to handle, like shards of glass. The soundtrack of their row recapitulated in her head, but still she couldn't understand how they had segued into this: Livvy sitting at home alone with Leo, a quintet of angry red welts encircling her wrist.

The sound of a key in the front door made Livvy jolt. She stroked a finger across the plump roll of flesh at Leo's ankle, pre-emptively reassuring him that it would be okay, even as dread churned in her stomach.

The hall door opened and then closed, and Livvy did not turn around.

'I'm sorry.'

Dominic's voice behind her was full of contrition, but Livvy was not yet ready to face him. A part of her feared that, when she did, she would find a different man to the one she had married.

'I know what I did was wrong. I was angry with Bea, not you. I shouldn't have taken it out on you.'

A hand rested on Livvy's arm and she shifted her body away from it.

'What can I do to make this better? I love you. You know that. I'm sorry I let my frustration with your sister get the better of me. You know I'd never intentionally hurt you.'

He sat down beside her, close but not touching. Leo looked up at him, eyes wide and unsuspecting, and Dominic kissed the top of Leo's head, ran his fingers across their son's dark hair.

'Talk to me, please.'

She could feel his eyes on her face but could not turn to look at him. 'I don't know what to say.'

'Scream and shout at me if you want. It's only what I deserve.'

Livvy said nothing. She had no desire for another row, felt exhausted by their earlier conflict.

On the periphery of her vision, she saw Dominic reach out towards her. His fingers ran across the scarlet weals on her wrist, raised from her skin like miniature mountains, and she withdrew her hand.

'Does it hurt?'

'What do you think?' She swallowed against the tightness in her throat.

'I didn't mean for it to happen. I'm sorry. It'll never happen again, I promise.'

There was such remorse in his voice that Livvy experienced a moment's dislocation, unable to inhabit two worlds at the same time: the world of conflict, anger and unexpected violence; and the world of contrition, solicitude, affection. It was as though she were straddling two different versions of her life, trying to figure out which was real. 'It shouldn't have happened once, Dominic.'

'I know. And I feel wretched about it. I wish you could know how sorry I am.'

Neither of them spoke for a moment, Livvy's need for the truth demanding that she ask the question. 'So, this Daisy woman – she's real? You were together?'

Seconds passed, Dominic's breaths slow and steady. 'It's true that I dated Daisy, though not for very long. It was only a couple of months. But she's totally twisted everything that happened. *She* was the one who dived in head first, who started talking about moving in together after a few weeks. She was the one who became obsessive when I broke up with her. She's twisted the entire narrative to cast herself as the victim. It's so galling that your sister believed it.'

Livvy thought about what Bea had told her, tried to rearrange the story in her head, swap the key protagonists. 'Then why have you never told me about her?'

Dominic exhaled a long stream of air. 'Honestly? I was embarrassed. I should never have dated someone so young. It's such a middle-aged cliché and I should have known better. The whole thing . . . I just felt foolish. I wanted to put it all behind me, pretend it had never happened.'

'And all this was just before we got together?'

'Not right before. But a few weeks, yes.'

Livvy paused, thought back to the beginning of their relationship. 'So you lied to me. When we met, you told me you'd been single for over a year. That was a lie.' She sensed her words stiffen, as though they had been dipped in resin and left to dry.

'You're right, I did. And I'm sorry. I don't know what to say. I felt ashamed that I'd got myself in that situation in the first place. It was a complete lapse of judgement on my part. And it was so short-lived – it really was just a couple of months. But I should have told you. I'm sorry.'

Livvy looked down to where Leo was trying to pull soft rings from a stacking toy, his fingers too uncoordinated for the task. 'So all that stuff about her going to the police – this woman just fabricated the whole thing? Why would she do that?'

Dominic sighed, shrugged his shoulders. 'I honestly don't know. Maybe she's embarrassed about the way she behaved. Maybe she's still angry that I broke up with her and this is her way of getting back at me.'

Neither of them spoke for a moment.

'So you never asked her to marry you?'

'What?' Dominic stared at her, mouth agape. 'Of course not. Is that what she said?' He shook his head. 'I told you, we were only together for a couple of months and it was all pretty casual as far as I was concerned.'

Livvy tried to slot Dominic's explanation into place with the other things Bea had told her. 'Daisy told Bea you said you were adopted.'

For a moment, Dominic seemed speechless. 'Jesus. I knew she was unhinged but that's insane. She's a complete fantasist. And your sister really believed her? I honestly thought Bea was smarter than that.'

Leo let out a frustrated cry as the fabric rings refused to be pulled off, and Livvy bent forward, removed them for him.

When she sat back up, Dominic took hold of her hand, looked down at her wrist. 'How's it feeling now?'

Livvy followed the direction of his gaze to the line of livid red welts. 'Pretty sore.'

Dominic breathed slowly, his shoulder blades rising and falling. 'I think I know why I got so angry. I know there's no excuse for the way I behaved, but I was just really hurt that after all I've confided in you, you still believed a pack of lies. I've told you things I've never told anyone before and I was disappointed that there are still ways you doubt me, even after all that.' He looked away, eyes narrowing as they grazed the room with its depleted bookshelves, boxes stacked against the wall, ready for the move.

Livvy allowed herself a moment's pause. 'I didn't mean to make you feel like that. But you must be able to see it from my point of view? My sister tells me about a woman she's met, who clearly did date you at some point and who you've never mentioned. What was I supposed to think?'

Dominic shifted position, turned to face her. 'I know. I understand. If I could turn back the clock, I'd do it all differently. Especially today. It's just been such a stressful time, with my dad and the job and the move.' He pulled his mouth into a tight, sad smile. 'Can you forgive me?'

The events of the afternoon spooled through Livvy's mind in accelerated time. A part of her feared she might never be able to forgive him, not fully. But then she thought about all that had happened in recent weeks – Imogen's appearance, John's death, the unattended funeral – and found herself nodding.

'Thank you. Really. I promise it will never happen again.' Dominic's fingers followed the contour of her wrist along the tender ridges of her skin. 'What are we going to do about your sister?'

'What do you mean?'

'It's going to be hard, getting beyond this. It's such a destructive thing for her to do. I don't know how I'll be able to pretend nothing's happened.'

Livvy panicked at the prospect of her husband and sister at loggerheads, Livvy stuck between them, torn one way and then the other, like a character in an ancient proverb. 'She's my sister. If I can forgive you, then you need to forgive her. She was only looking out for me. That's what sisters do.'

Dominic said nothing for a few moments, before lifting Livvy's hand to his mouth, brushing his lips along her skin. 'Fair enough. It just might take me a little time, that's all.'

He pulled her into his arms, his breath hot against her scalp. And yet, in spite of the resolution to their conflict, somewhere beneath the wall of Livvy's chest, a caged bird flapped its wings.

ANNA

London

I stand in the small space at the top of the stairs, look up at the hatch above my head. I know what I need to do, even if a part of my brain is cautioning against it.

Since the call from the therapist yesterday lunchtime, I have scoured the house, searching for something – anything – that might tell me more about my life. Every box piled up in the spare room has been opened, rummaged through, discarded when it revealed nothing of interest. I have felt like a scavenger, hunting for scraps of information and repeatedly going hungry.

When Stephen telephoned yesterday evening from his hotel room in Southampton, I told him nothing of what I was doing, nothing about the call with the therapist that had revealed his lie to me. For most of last night I lay awake, thinking the same circular thoughts, wondering if I was a coward for not confronting him. Because whichever way I turn the facts over in my mind I cannot seem to fashion them into a viable explanation. They are like lumps of parched clay: too tough, unyielding, to mould beneath my fingers.

I look up at the small brass padlock, wrack my brain, try to think where Stephen might have hidden the key. I think about where he is often most furtive and head into our bedroom, pull open his bedside drawers. They are neatly arranged as though nothing dare leave its designated spot: cufflink boxes, a clip-on reading light, a pack of ear plugs, a small notebook which I flick through and find empty. No key.

I open the chest of drawers where Stephen keeps his underwear, rifle through it, scrunch each ball of socks inside my fist in search of anything sharp or metallic, run my fingers along the edges of the wooden drawers, but find nothing.

Lifting the edge of the duvet, I discover a collection of transparent plastic tote boxes under the bed. I pull out the first one, lift the lid, find it full of old audio cassettes. Taking them out, I pile them onto the bed, checking each one to see if a key may have been slipped inside. But there is just Mahler, Wagner, Strauss. I reach for the next tote, drag it across the floorboards, open it. Inside is a collection of plugs and cables: phone chargers, camera batteries, endless USB leads. I lift them out, one by one, careful not to entangle them so I can replace them later as though they were never disturbed. Placing them next to the cassettes, I wonder what they are all for, why we have so many when there is just a single laptop in the house. At the bottom, I find a small square ring box tucked in the corner, take it out, prise it open. Inside is a small silver key, the right size for a padlock, and I hold it in my palm, hope inflating in my chest.

Dragging a hardback chair from the spare room, I place it under the opening to the loft, step onto it, ignore my pounding heart reminding me what happened the last time I attempted to venture up here. Reaching above my head, there is a momentary wobble, and I launch my arms to the side to steady myself. I breathe deeply, stabilise myself, and when I am sure my footing is secure, I lift my arms again, take hold of the padlock with one hand, slip the key inside, fingers fumbling.

The key turns and I hear myself exhale a sigh of relief.

Opening the hatch and lowering the loft ladder, I guide it slowly until it reaches the floor.

The loft ladder's pretty treacherous – I need to get someone to come and fix it – so don't venture up there if I'm not here.

Stephen's words reverberate in my ears and I do not know if I am being foolish ignoring them. I only know that I have foraged through the rest of the house and found nothing. The loft is the only place left to search.

Placing one foot on the bottom rung and holding on to the ladder firmly with both hands, I test my weight on it, feel its steady grip against the floor. Tentatively, I take a second step and then a third. The ladder feels solid beneath my feet and I make my way to the top without a hitch. I think about Stephen's note of warning, cannot waste time speculating why he didn't want me up here.

Shining a torch around the dim loft space, I find a light switch, flick it on, a naked bulb illuminating overhead. A throng of boxes are stacked haphazardly, the disorder at odds with the organisation of rest of the house, and there is a moment's dislocation, as though I have inadvertently entered someone else's home.

Pressing gingerly on the plywood floorboards to test their strength, I lift myself into the space, the musty air like a church hall that has been closed all winter.

Turning around, I see it immediately, though it takes me a second to assemble the separate parts in my mind. I step towards it, place a hand on the white wooden frame. My breath catches in my throat, wondering if this was what Stephen was trying to protect me from: the sight of my son's dismantled crib. With unsteady fingers, I trace the wooden slats, imagine Henry sleeping soundly inside: the quiet snuffle of his breathing, the flicker of his dreaming eyes, the soft curl of his fists. Something stirs inside me, a sense that my son is still with me. I feel an intense closeness to him, as though our separation is a matter of days rather than years, as though I can sense an echo of his recent presence.

Forcing open my eyes, I instruct myself to breathe deeply, pull myself back into the present. I know it is grief causing me to imagine such proximity to Henry, but a part of me cannot bear the thought that it is already such a long time since I last held him in my arms.

My hand runs across the smooth edge of the crib and I wonder why we have kept it all this time. Whether, when we moved here a year ago, I refused to part with it, could not bear the thought of being separated from anything that had once felt the warmth of Henry's skin. Whether, somewhere amidst this assembly of boxes, I will find Henry's babygrows, his toys, his blankets, his bedding, as though each inanimate object is impregnated with his essence: particles of his soul held in the fabric of his clothes.

A question emerges from the shadows: why Stephen and I have not had another baby. Whether the grief has been too profound. Whether we have tried and, thus far, failed. Whether the presence of the crib in the attic is not a symptom of my enduring heartache but a signal of hope, of what the future may bring.

I allow my hand to linger on the white wood before stepping away. I know that if I stay close, I will be compelled to keep touching it, as if drawn to it by some gravitational force.

Surveying the boxes in front of me, I am not sure where to begin. Perhaps if I knew what I was looking for it would be easier, but the boxes are not labelled with their contents.

The first box I open contains a pair of old curtains. In the next box I find some crockery wrapped haphazardly in pieces of kitchen paper: a brightly coloured teapot, a quartet of stripey mugs, a large serving plate in Mediterranean blue. They are so unlike the stark white crockery downstairs that I wonder when Stephen and I bought them.

When I open the next box, I'm greeted by a series of cardboard wallets in a variety of muted colours. Lifting the flap of one, I find a collection of letters. On the front of each, in looping font and midnight-blue ink, are written two words: *My darling*.

A voice in my head tells me that these are private, that I have no business reading Stephen's personal correspondence. And yet, even as the voice whispers for me to stop, I watch myself pull a letter from its envelope, begin to read. The feeling of wrongdoing prickles my skin, but as my eyes skim the first line and then the next, I am aware of the world falling silent around me.

Delving into the wallet, I pick another letter, find the same elegant handwriting and blue ink. I read line after line, have the sensation of rolling down a steep hill without anything to halt my fall. Every word is like an assault, an arrow piercing straight into my chest.

I read another letter, and then another, my eyes scanning each word, telling myself that I must be mistaken, that there has to be a simple explanation. And yet I cannot ignore the dates at the top of each one – six weeks ago, eight weeks ago, ten – my stomach churning with a truth that demands to be acknowledged.

I read letter after letter until my eyes are aching. I try to catch my breath, but it is as though a thousand tiny dust motes are trapped in my throat.

Because in my hand is a stack of love letters. Letters containing intimate details about Stephen's life. Letters addressed to 'my darling', filled with outpourings of devotion.

Every letter has been written in the last three months. The most recent, just four weeks ago.

All these letters have been written while I have been married to Stephen.

And yet none have been written by me.

Every single one is signed with the same elegant flourish. The same graceful fountain pen. The same two-syllable name. Signed by a woman I have never heard of before. A woman called Livvy.

LIVVY

BRISTOL

Livvy sat on a park bench, looking left and right, then down at her watch, wondering if it was too late to bail. Pulling out her phone, she sent her mum a quick text to ask if Leo was okay. A reply came back almost instantaneously.

> *He's absolutely fine. Having a whale of a time in the garden with your dad. You take as long as you need. xxx*

She had not told her parents the truth about where she was going, had said only that she needed to run some errands. With two days until the move to London, her parents had required no further explanation. Dominic was not due back from Sheffield until tomorrow afternoon, and Livvy's To Do list seemed to be growing exponentially. She didn't really have time to be here. She didn't know why, in truth, she had orchestrated the meeting. Only that, since last weekend, she had been aware of a constant hum of restlessness and hoped this conversation might help resolve it.

Pulling her jacket across her chest and fastening two of the buttons, she questioned again whether she definitely wanted to do this. Whether she might be lifting the lid on Pandora's jar, releasing something that, once escaped, could never be put back. Because even if she never told Dominic that the meeting had taken place, Livvy would know that it had. She would have to carry that secret and live with the knowledge that she had transgressed a boundary, betrayed his trust.

'Livvy?'

Livvy turned around, saw the person she had come to meet, burgundy leather handbag hooked over the crook of one elbow, a bookshop tote over her shoulder.

'Do you mind if I sit down?' Imogen gestured to the bench beside Livvy, and Livvy tried to pull her cheeks into a smile, reminded herself that Imogen could do no harm as long as Livvy kept her at arm's length. It was one get-together, that was all.

Imogen sat down, rested her bags on the wooden slats, one hand holding on tight to them. 'I was so pleased when you phoned. I hoped you would, but I didn't want to make any assumptions.' Imogen's eyes darted over Livvy's shoulder. 'Where's Leo?'

Livvy kept her voice steady. 'I didn't bring him. I thought it would be easier for us to talk alone.'

Something flitted across Imogen's face, and Livvy watched her swallow her disappointment, rearrange her expectations.

Imogen reached behind her, fished inside the tote bag, pulled out a package wrapped in Beatrix Potter paper. 'I bought Leo a little something. I hope that's okay. It's just a toy bunny. Nothing ostentatious. Dominic always loved bunnies when he was little.' She opened her mouth as if to say more, then closed it again.

Livvy looked down at the package, felt herself hesitate.

'It's just something little. A token, really. You don't have to tell anyone who it's from. I thought he might like it, that's all.' Imogen held out the package, and Livvy, as if on autopilot, reached out and took it from her.

'I wanted to ask—'

'You said you had—'

Their voices collided and they each took a verbal step back.

'You first.'

'No, you please.'

Livvy tried to collate her thoughts, remind herself why she'd phoned Imogen in the first place.

She thought about her row with Bea, about Bea's meeting with Daisy, about the relationship with a woman half his age that Dominic had kept secret. She thought about her fight with Dominic last Saturday, the bruises on her wrist fading but still visible. She thought about her phone call with Imogen a few weeks ago: *There are things I think we should talk about . . . I can't say. Not over the phone. They're too delicate.*

'The last time you came to the house, you asked if Dominic was good to me. Why?'

Imogen studied Livvy's face through narrowed eyes. 'What makes you ask?'

'It just seems like an odd question.'

Imogen looked down at her hands, and Livvy's eyes followed: the manicured nails, neat cuticles, slim gold band on her fourth finger. 'As I said before, we didn't know Dominic had got married or that he had a child. I just wanted to understand what kind of a husband and father he is.' There was something incomplete in Imogen's explanation, like a piece of music from which the last page of the score had been lost.

Livvy thought about last Saturday's argument with Dominic, reminded herself that it was out of character, a one-off. It had been a perfect storm of emotional upheaval, unlikely ever to be repeated. 'He's a fantastic father and a great husband.'

There was a small, fractional nodding of Imogen's head, as though she were just going through the motions of agreement. 'That's good to hear. So he's kind to you both?'

Livvy baulked at the invasiveness of the question. 'He's incredibly kind.'

Imogen nodded vaguely, as though still only half listening. 'So do you think . . . is there any chance he might want to see me? Or that he'll let me see Leo?' A light flush crept into Imogen's cheeks.

'I honestly don't know. He's still pretty damaged by everything that happened in his childhood.'

Imogen squinted. 'What do you mean?'

'I honestly don't want to rake it all up—'

'But Dominic had a perfectly normal childhood.'

Livvy stared at her mother-in-law. Dominic had told her how delusional Imogen could be, but it was still discombobulating witnessing it first-hand. 'I know it must be difficult for you to talk about and I don't want to cause you any unnecessary upset, especially after the past few weeks.' She reminded herself that Imogen's husband had died less than two months ago. Whatever Livvy's feelings about her, Imogen was still a woman in her seventies, grieving. 'When you phoned a few weeks ago, you said there were things I ought to know. Delicate things. I wanted to understand what you meant.'

Livvy reached up, scratched a mosquito bite on her neck that had been bothering her for days. Too late, she saw Imogen's eyes hone in on the marks around her wrist like a bird of prey spying its next victim. Livvy dropped her hand into her lap, pulled her sleeve down towards her knuckles.

'How did you get those bruises?'

Livvy clasped her hands together. 'It's nothing.'

'How did you get them?' Imogen's voice was quietly insistent.

A wave of heat swept up through Livvy's chest, around her neck and into her cheeks, and she could imagine it, pulsing, like an ocean bloom. 'Carrying heavy shopping bags over my wrist. I bruise really easily.' The lie slipped out effortlessly, as if it had been waiting in the wings, ready for its moment in the spotlight.

Imogen's eyes narrowed, and for the first time, Livvy could see Dominic in them: a particular kind of scrutiny that made her feel as though Imogen were looking straight into her soul.

Imogen laid a hand on Livvy's knee, the gesture so unexpected that Livvy was too shocked to remove it. 'I hate to say this, but a man never hurts a woman only once. There's always a second time.'

There was a moment's stillness, as if time itself were holding its breath.

Livvy looked away, could no longer bear the intensity of Imogen's gaze. Imogen's hand was still on her knee, and there was something gentle in it – maternal almost – so out of kilter with everything she knew about her mother-in-law. With a stab of guilt, she wondered whether her parents had been right: whether Dominic hadn't been the only victim of his father's cruelty. Perhaps Dominic had never witnessed his father doling out the same punishments to Imogen. Perhaps he had been too young to notice. But as Livvy looked up and saw the distress in Imogen's expression, she felt certain that John's attacks had not stopped with his son.

She thought about all the stories Dominic had told her about his childhood: the silent mealtimes and lonely bedtimes. Shifting the prism, she looked at the scenes from a different angle and saw the possibility of a woman terrified of the consequences of defying her husband's tyranny.

Livvy's phone pinged and she pulled it from her bag, saw a diary notification reminding her to get some cash to tip the removers, remembered with a panic all she had to do before Saturday. 'I'm really sorry, but I'm going to have to go.'

Imogen took her hand from Livvy's knee. 'Really? So soon?'

Livvy checked the time on her phone. 'I'm sorry, I've just got so much to do before the move—' The words were out before she had a chance to haul them back.

'What move?'

Livvy scrabbled for a feasible explanation but found none willing to rescue her. 'We're moving to London.' It didn't matter, she reassured herself: London was a big city. It wasn't as if Imogen would be able to find them if they didn't want to be found.

'When?'

A sense of strange defiance overcame Livvy. She refused to be cowed by this woman she'd met for the first time only ten weeks ago. 'On Saturday.'

Imogen's face dropped. 'This Saturday? But what about Leo?'

'What do you mean?'

'You have to let me see him before you go. It's cruel not to.'

There was something maniacal in Imogen's tone, and Livvy was aware of unease creeping across her skin, just as it had during their earlier meetings. 'I haven't got to do anything, Imogen. Leo's my son and I'm not putting him in the middle of all this.' She stood up, slung her bag over her shoulder, prepared to leave.

'But he's my grandson. I have to see him. You must understand that, surely?'

Livvy fished her car keys from her bag. 'I don't mean to be unkind and I'm sorry if I gave you false hope, arranging to see you today. But there's too much that needs resolving between you and Dominic before there's any chance of you having a relationship with Leo.'

Imogen opened her mouth to speak, but Livvy cut across her, issued a firm goodbye and walked briskly away.

Heading towards the edge of the park where she'd left her car, Livvy took the Beatrix Potter–wrapped gift and tossed it in a bin. Dominic had been right, and Livvy wished she'd listened to him in the first place: there was something deeply unsettling in Imogen's behaviour, like a rogue missile veering off course, and Livvy knew now for certain that she didn't want her mother-in-law in any of their lives.

ANNA

LONDON

I tear open the lids of one box after another, searching, hunting, digging for clues, anything that might tell me more. Beads of perspiration pool in the small of my back, a matrix of paper cuts lining my fingers.

Glancing down at my watch, I realise that I have been in the loft for almost three hours. I no longer know whether I am foraging for proof that my fears are correct or evidence that I have got it all wrong.

Lines from the letters I've read burn behind my eyes.

I wish you could know how much I look forward to the weekends, when you'll be home, and we're together again.

The bed will be so empty without you.

I hope you know how much I'll miss you.

I love you.

Nausea fills my throat and I swallow hard against it.

Part of me wishes there had been no dates on them, that I could delude myself they are from a time long before our marriage. But those dates, I know, can mean only one thing, even if I am not yet ready to accept it.

I don't have to go away for work very often . . . It's really unfortunate timing.

I think about Stephen's annoyance when he received the message from his boss, how cross he was about having to leave me so soon after my accident. I wonder if it was nothing more than a charade, whether he has been absent every weekend for months, has used the convenience of my amnesia to pretend this is a new phenomenon. My heart thumps with my own gullibility, so trusting that I never even questioned a second consecutive weekend away.

I think about all the furtive phone calls taken in our bedroom with the door closed. All the snapped lids of laptops when I have walked into a room. All the evenings he has been late home. The two mobile phones.

It's my work phone.

Humiliation burns in my cheeks.

I rip open another cardboard box, find board games, playing cards, a two-thousand-piece jigsaw puzzle. At the bottom of the box is a lone novel, an Agatha Christie thriller, its jacket tattered, spine creased, pages curled at the edges. I lift it out, open the front cover, feel the air being sucked from my lungs.

On the title page, in the top-right-hand corner, is a name written in midnight-blue ink, the handwriting identical to the script on the letters.

Livvy Nicholson.

I drop the book back into the box as though it might char the tips of my fingers. My eyes follow it, lying there brazenly, as though it has nothing to be ashamed of. I try to make sense of its presence in our loft, am aware of something on the periphery of my mind. I close my eyes, focus all my attention on it. And then I understand.

The affair between Stephen and this woman must have been going on for at least as long as we have lived in this house. Over a year, possibly longer. It is the only explanation for the book being here.

Stephen has been having an affair while we have been grieving the loss of our son.

The thought wraps itself around my neck, presses down on my windpipe. I double over, mouth open wide, encourage short breaths in and out of my lungs.

I think about the woman's name written in the front of the book, wonder who she is, where he met her, what she looks like. Whether she knows about my existence or whether Stephen has weaved an elaborate web of lies for her too.

And then a new speculation inveigles its way into my thoughts, and I try to ignore it, but it is persistent, determined, demands to be noticed.

What if Stephen had planned to leave me and it is only the aftermath of my accident that is forcing him to stay? What if the only reason he is still here is because his conscience won't allow him to go?

My head throbs, and I know I cannot stay here any longer, breathing this stale air.

Armed with two thick bundles of letters, I make my way down the ladder, realise how sturdy it is, wonder if there are more secrets up there that Stephen doesn't want me to find.

Wrenching open the chest of drawers in our bedroom, I thrust my hand into the far right corner, fingers scrabbling until I have found what I am looking for. Pulling out the mobile phone Zahira gave me, I press a finger on the power button, wait to see if the battery is still charged. The screen lights into life, and I flick through the menu, find the address book and click on the only name in there, hoping and praying that she will answer.

LIVVY

BRISTOL

Livvy stood for a moment in the centre of the sitting room, savouring the silence. She couldn't remember the last time she'd been home alone: probably almost nine months ago, in the week before Leo was born.

Rousing herself into action, she ran through a mental list of the things she needed to do: pack up the bathroom, organise their moving-day necessities, double-check the cleaners were coming before the tenants moved in on Sunday. Her parents had said she could leave Leo with them for as long as she needed today, but given he'd be staying with them for the weekend while she and Dominic oversaw the move, she didn't want to be separated from him for too long.

Packing her toiletries into a cardboard box, she wondered when she might confess to Dominic about yesterday's meeting with Imogen. There had been a moment during their video call last night when she had almost told him, before realising it was a conversation that needed to happen in person. Once they were settled in London, she reasoned to herself, she would tell him then.

Heading down to the kitchen for a glass of water, she saw it straight away: the bag containing Leo's lunch of pureed sweet potato, pureed mango, his bottle of expressed breast milk. Cursing under her breath, she looked at her watch, knew that Leo would need his lunch soon. Mentally calculating the time, she figured it would only be a twenty-minute round trip to her parents' as long as she didn't stay too long.

When her dad opened the front door, his face seemed to race through a flurry of emotions. 'Livvy, what are you doing back here?'

Livvy held up the offending bag. 'I forgot to bring Leo's lunch and snacks earlier.' She stepped into the hallway, past her dad and into the sitting room. And when she saw who was there, relaxing on her parents' sofa, it was as though her heart had lurched into her throat.

Next to her mum, bouncing Leo on her lap, was Imogen.

Livvy swooped Leo out of Imogen's arms, held him tight against her chest. 'What are you doing here?'

Her mum and Imogen jumped to their feet, Hazel's face infused with panic. 'Imogen just popped round, she just wanted to see Leo before you left for London.'

'And you let her in? After everything I've told you?'

'I'm sorry.' Imogen glanced between Hazel and Robert as though waiting for someone to come to her rescue. 'I didn't mean to upset you. But when you wouldn't let me see Leo—'

'Oh, so it's *my* fault that you've wheedled your way into my parents' house?'

'No, of course not, it's just—'

'Let's all try to calm down, shall we?'

Livvy whipped her head around to her dad. 'Don't tell me to calm down. You let a total stranger into your house to play with *my son* and you don't think I should be angry?' She turned back to Imogen. 'How did you even know where my parents live?'

Imogen's eyes darted between the trio of faces, her cheeks the colour of beetroot.

'Of course. You followed me, didn't you?'

'I just wanted to hold Leo. He's my grandson.'

'And he's *my* son. And you don't get to decide if you have access to him.' Livvy's heart thudded in her chest, her hands shaking. 'After everything you put Dominic through, you really think I'm going to let you anywhere near my son?'

Imogen's body became rigid, her voice implacable. 'You shouldn't believe everything Dominic tells you.'

Disbelief surged through Livvy's veins. 'I've had enough of this. It's got to stop. You can't come round here, harassing my parents like this.'

'She wasn't really *harassing* us, love—'

Livvy shot a furious glance at her mum. 'She turns up here, uninvited, having *followed me* to your address, to get access to my son when I've explicitly told her she can't see him, and you don't think that's harassment?' Livvy felt as though she had stepped into an alternative reality where nobody but her could see common sense. She turned back to Imogen. 'You need to leave.'

For a moment, Imogen stood still, like a rabbit caught in the headlights. And then she seemed to gather her senses, collected her bag from the floor, stood up again slowly. 'I really didn't mean to upset you. All I ever wanted was to see my grandson.' She let her eyes drift down towards Leo's face, then back up to Livvy. 'I know you don't want to hear this, but Dominic's always had a habit of making up stories, ever since he was little. I just wish you'd let me explain—'

'There's absolutely nothing I want to hear from you. You need to leave.'

Imogen hesitated for a moment before turning to Hazel. 'I'm sorry to have troubled you. I really didn't mean any harm.'

Hazel nodded, gestured towards the door. 'Let me show you out.'

Livvy did not meet Imogen's gaze as her mum led her out of the room. Indignation blazed in her cheeks and she waited until she heard the definitive click of the front door and her mum had returned before trusting herself to speak. 'What were you thinking? Why did you let her in?'

'What did you expect us to do? Shut the door in her face? She's Leo's grandmother. We were in a very difficult situation.'

'But you know how I feel about her. You know she's been following me. You know Dominic's been estranged from her for years.'

'To be fair, love, we don't really know anything about Dominic's family. It's very difficult making a judgement call when you don't have any of the facts.' Her dad's voice was calm, placatory, but Livvy didn't want to be placated.

'You don't need to know any details. You just have to respect the fact that I don't want her near my son.'

'But she seemed very nice, not at all what I was expecting—'

'That's because she's a manipulator, Mum! She was manipulating you. Can't you see that?' Frustration bled into Livvy's voice as she moved Leo from one hip to the other. 'How on earth am I supposed to leave Leo with you this weekend when you let that woman in the house to play with him?'

'Don't be silly. He'll be fine with us. Now that we know how strongly you feel about Imogen, of course we won't let her in again. We were just caught off guard.'

'Dad's right. We don't want you worrying about Leo on top of everything else. You know what good care we'll take of him.' Her mum smiled. 'Why don't you go back home and get on with your packing. We can bring Leo back later.'

Livvy shook her head. 'It's fine. I'll take him with me now.'

'But you've got so much to do—'

'Honestly, it doesn't make sense you dropping him back later when I'm already here.' She couldn't delete the image from her mind of Imogen sitting on her parents' sofa with Leo on her lap.

'Okay, whatever you think's best. But we'll be over at eight in the morning to collect him.' Her dad sounded hesitant, as though Livvy might feasibly cancel the arrangement even though, this late in the day, she had no alternative.

Livvy left her parents' house, aware of the lingering tension between them.

Driving home, she found herself repeatedly checking her rear-view mirror for the sight of a blue Ford Fiesta. Because after today's encounter, she was aware of a sickening certainty that there was nothing Imogen wouldn't do to get close to Leo.

ANNA

London

'Are you sure you don't want something stronger?'

Zahira places a mug of peppermint tea on the kitchen table, and I shake my head, do not want anything to cloud my already foggy thoughts.

Since arriving at Zahira's flat, I have told her everything: the cancelled therapy appointment, the letters, the paperback book with another woman's name in it. The words have come tumbling out of my mouth as if they have a life of their own.

'What are you going to do?' Zahira stacks the letters into a pile, pushes them to the far edge of the table.

'You definitely think he's having an affair?' I hear the flicker of hope in my voice, cringe that I'm even entertaining the possibility that he might not be.

Something flashes across Zahira's face – sympathy, perhaps, or pity – and she reaches across the table, takes hold of my hand. 'It's hard to think of another explanation, isn't it?'

There is a momentary squawk from the bedroom next door where Elyas is having a nap, and Zahira stills her head, listens, before turning back to me. 'I've been exactly where you are now and

I know how much it hurts. I'm sorry you're having to go through it. I wouldn't wish it on my worst enemy.'

She inhales deeply, and it strikes me that perhaps it was selfish of me to come here and share my suspicions when it may reignite painful memories for Zahira.

'And there's nothing you can remember about any tension with Stephen before the accident? Nothing about him going away or being secretive?'

I shake my head.

'Maybe—' Zahira stops herself, averts her eyes, picks at some dried wax stuck to a candlestick.

'What?'

She hesitates, as if silently assessing what she is about to say. 'I was just thinking about how Stephen hasn't wanted to tell you anything about your family or friends. Perhaps you'd found out about the affair before the accident and had confided in someone. Perhaps that's why he hasn't wanted anyone getting in contact with you.'

The suggestion lands like a sucker punch.

'Sorry, I'm only speculating – I could be completely wrong.'

I open my mouth to reply, but nothing emerges. And yet it all makes sense. It is all so blindingly, humiliatingly obvious. Stephen doesn't want me to remember anything about my past. He is fully invested in my amnesia. Because if I do remember, there is a risk that I will find out, not for the first time but the second, that he is being unfaithful to me.

LIVVY

BRISTOL

All week the forecast had been predicting rain, but as Livvy stood on the pavement with Leo in her arms, the sun was warm, the sky free of blemishes.

'We really are sorry again about yesterday. I promise that if she comes back, we'll send her packing.' Hazel whispered, careful that Dominic – still inside the house, checking the boxes – wouldn't hear.

'You mustn't let her in, whatever she says. And if she follows you somewhere, like the park or whatever . . . just phone me, okay?' Livvy rubbed her eyes, abrasive with lack of sleep. Half the night she had lain awake, unable to escape the image of Imogen with Leo on her knee, like a wicked witch in a fairy story intent on stealing her child.

'Of course we will. But nothing's going to happen. Leo will be fine. It's only a couple of nights.'

Livvy pressed her lips to Leo's hair, couldn't quite countenance that they were about to be separated. It would be the first time she had ever left him overnight. As she held him now in her arms, the thought of handing him over to her mum in a few minutes and not seeing him again until Monday was like someone carving off one of her limbs and assuring her she'd manage fine without it.

'We're going to have fun, aren't we, Leo? And you'll be back with Mummy in no time.' Hazel ran a finger across Leo's cheek, and Livvy reminded herself that her parents had raised two children, that they loved Leo almost as much as they loved her and Bea. And they understood now the importance of keeping Leo away from Imogen's grasp.

'What time are the removal men due?' Her dad peered down one end of the street and then the other.

'Half past eight. Dominic's hoping we'll be done here by late morning and in London by early afternoon.' Livvy shivered in spite of the day's warmth, pressed Leo closer against her chest.

'You know, I'd feel much happier if we had an address for you. I don't like not knowing where you're going to be living. It doesn't make any sense, having to be so cloak-and-dagger about it.'

'There's nothing to worry about, Robert. Everything's in hand.' Behind them, Dominic appeared from the open front door, strode down the short garden path towards them. 'As I've said, I want it to be a surprise for Livvy.' He wrapped an arm around her shoulders, kissed the top of her head. 'Having got this far, I'd rather not give the game away. We'll send you the address later.'

Livvy's eyes flitted between Dominic and her parents. She had told Dominic she felt uneasy, not having seen their new home, not even knowing the address. But Dominic had reiterated the same response each time she'd raised it. '*Please let me do this for you. Don't make me waste all the effort I've gone to. I really want to see your face when we walk through the front door. And remember, it's only our temporary home. Of course we'll pick our long-term place together.*'

There was an infinitesimal tensing of Robert's jaw. 'But you'll call us as soon as you get there?'

'Of course I will—'

'Well, we might not be able to call tonight. But we'll definitely text.' Dominic rubbed Livvy's shoulder. 'You know what it's like on moving day. Suddenly it's almost midnight and you still haven't managed to locate the duvet.' Dominic laughed, but Hazel and Robert's mouths were set in horizontal lines.

'Right, shall we let your parents go? The removal men will be here soon and we ought to do one final check before they arrive.' Dominic kissed Leo's forehead. 'You be a good boy for Granny and Grandad. No wreaking havoc, okay?' Pressing a hand into the small of Livvy's back, he urged her forwards.

Livvy breathed in the smell of her son, wishing she could bottle it, take vials of it with her to London.

'Come on. He'll be fine. It's only two days. I guarantee you'll miss him more than he misses you. He'll be spoilt rotten and barely want to come home.' There was levity in Dominic's voice as he ran his fingers along Livvy's spine.

'Honestly, darling, we'll take such good care of him. And we'll bring him back first thing on Monday morning, just as soon as we know the address.'

'Come as early as you like. We'll be up.' Livvy tried to laugh, but it snagged somewhere in her throat.

Kissing Leo's cheek, she handed him over to her mum. 'You've got his bags? And all his food in the freezer? And you remember what to do with the breast milk?'

'I have had two children of my own. You don't need to worry.' Hazel bounced Leo on her hip as Robert opened the passenger door of their Vauxhall Corsa. She placed Leo in the baby seat, strapped him in, before getting in beside him.

Robert turned in Livvy's direction, skin pinched between his eyebrows. 'You'll text us as soon as you get there? Let us know where you are?'

'Just as soon as I catch my breath, I promise.'

Through the back window, Leo stared at Livvy as if trying to compute why there was a metal door, a glass window, an enormous barrier between them. As Robert got into the driver's seat and started the engine, something seemed to click inside Leo – some awareness of what might be happening – and his face crumpled, his mouth widening into a horrified circle, tears welling in his eyes. Through the glass, his cries erupted in a disbelieving howl. Instinctively, Livvy took a step towards the car to reassure him that everything was okay, that she would be reunited with him soon. But Dominic held on to her shoulders, firm and decisive. 'Leave him. You'll only make it worse if you fuss. Just smile and wave and let him know there's nothing to worry about.' He held up his phone, camera screen facing towards them. 'Come on, one last selfie together on our street.'

Livvy fixed a smile on her face, cheeks aching with the effort, as Dominic took a photo.

'Now, let's wave goodbye to Leo – he'll be absolutely fine with your parents.'

As if on autopilot, Livvy raised a hand and waved to her son. Inside the car, she could see her mum trying to distract Leo, shaking his favourite toy elephant, clapping her hands, her lips moving in song.

With one final glance over his shoulder, her dad pulled the car away from the kerb, and Livvy watched as her son was driven out of sight.

ANNA

LONDON

'I want to know who she is.'

Zahira looks at me through narrowed eyes, and I wonder if she felt the same three years ago as I do now: a burning desire both to know and not to know at the same time.

'What did you say her full name was, that you found in the book?'

I force myself to say it aloud. 'Livvy Nicholson.' Five short, such seemingly innocuous syllables, and yet enough to destroy a marriage.

Zahira gets up from the table, heads out of the kitchen and returns a few seconds later with a MacBook under her arm. 'Let's do a bit of internet digging, shall we?'

My stomach somersaults, thoughts flashing through my mind like a Super 8 film spooling loose from its projector: what she will look like, how old she will be, whether I will understand, immediately, why Stephen is attracted to her.

I catch sight of myself in the vintage mirror on the kitchen wall: my face free of make-up, my hair unbrushed, dark crescents hanging beneath my eyes. I wonder whether, before the accident, I made more of an effort with my appearance. Whether it was grief, two years ago, that stopped me caring about what I looked like. Whether it was that which prompted Stephen to seek fulfilment elsewhere.

'God, there's dozens of Livvy Nicholsons on Google. What shall we do – start with Facebook or Instagram?'

'I don't know. What do you think?'

Zahira pauses. 'Let's be realistic. If Stephen is your typical adulterer, then this woman is probably going to be younger than you.' She looks up from the laptop screen, blanches. 'Sorry, that was insensitive. Let's start with Instagram.'

Zahira taps and scrolls, while my heart canters in my chest, uncertain whether I want her search to be successful or not.

'God, half these Instagram accounts are private.'

I think about the fact that Zahira tried and failed to find me on social media, wonder whether Stephen's mistress is more gregarious than I am. There is a stab of pre-emptive rivalry with her, quickly followed by a flare of anger that Stephen has done this to me, that he is making me compete with a woman I've never even met. A woman I wouldn't recognise if I saw her in the street. A woman who may be as much a victim of Stephen's deceptions as I am.

'Right, I'm giving up on Instagram. Facebook it is.' The keys of Zahira's laptop click with repetitive urgency.

'What on earth . . . ?' Zahira's voice is sharp, staccato, and she stares at the screen, her expression hovering between confusion and alarm.

'What is it?' My heart drums against my ribs, my mouth sucked dry of moisture. A voice in my head tells me that we shouldn't have begun this, that I don't want to know. Once I have seen this woman's face, I know I will never be able to unsee it. But I realise it's too late, I have already leapt off that cliff.

Zahira glances at me and then back at the screen, unable to disguise her distress.

And then she turns the laptop screen towards me, and my eyes are drawn to it like moths to a flame.

I look at the screen, at Livvy Nicholson's name emblazoned across the middle of the page, and then at the photograph gazing back at me. I sense the blood drain from my cheeks, my eyes disbelieving what I am seeing, as my world tips violently onto a different axis.

LIVVY

BRISTOL

Dominic's hand was warm on her thigh, his long, elegant fingers lined up in a neat row on the denim of her jeans. From the car's air conditioning, a cool stream blew onto Livvy's arms, stippling her skin, but she knew Dominic liked the temperature fresh on long journeys, said it helped keep him alert.

From out of the window, cars came into view and disappeared again. Dominic overtook one vehicle and then another, cursing drivers who failed to pull over when he approached. Early on in their relationship – soon after she'd found out she was pregnant – Livvy had asked him to take it easier on the roads, confessed that sometimes she found his driving unnerving. Dominic had promised to slow down, and for a while his driving had improved: Livvy had been able to relax in the passenger seat without constantly pressing her foot down on a phantom brake. But recently, Dominic's driving had become erratic again, and for the past two hours Livvy had felt as though she were on a theme park ride that she wished would come to an end.

Glancing at the satnav, she saw they were only forty minutes from their final destination, realised they must now be skirting the edge of London.

From the radio came the trill of a violin, the heavy bass of a piano, the deep resonance of a cello. The digital guide on the car's dashboard told her it was a piece by Schubert, the Trout Quintet. Turning around, she looked into the back of the car, at the empty space where the baby seat should have been and felt a compression in her chest.

'Stop worrying. He'll be fine.'

'I might just give Mum a quick ring, check he's okay.'

Dominic exhaled sharply. 'Will you *please* just relax? Come on – we're alone for the first time in months. Can't you just try to enjoy it?' He lifted his hand from her thigh, placed it on the steering wheel, hands at twenty-to-four rather than ten-to-two.

'I know. But it's the first time we've left him—'

'And it's the first time we've moved to a new city together. It would be nice if you could feign just a little bit of excitement.'

His lips pursed into a thin, tight line and Livvy turned away, looked out of the passenger window.

From inside the handbag at her feet came the ringing of her mobile phone. Her mind raced immediately to thoughts of her mum, to the possibility that something had happened to Leo. She grabbed at her phone, but as her eyes grazed the screen, where the caller's identity was displayed, her heart leapt into her throat.

A single letter lit up the screen. The letter 'I'. The letter under which Livvy had stored Imogen's number as a means of screening any calls. Except she had never imagined that her mother-in-law might phone while Dominic was sitting two feet away from her in a moving car.

With clumsy fingers, she tried to hit the reject button. But instead she somehow pressed the answer button, and before she could stop it, a voice was filling the car through the Bluetooth system.

'*Livvy, it's Imogen, I just wanted—*'

Her thumb found the cancel icon and she pressed down on it hard, cutting off Imogen's voice, and switched off her phone.

Stealing a glance at Dominic, she saw immediately the icy expression.

'Why is my mother phoning you?' His voice was flat, arctic, the tension in the car thick and viscous.

'I don't know.'

There was a breath of silence. 'How does she even have your number?'

Livvy stared straight ahead. 'I honestly have no idea.'

'Don't take me for a bloody idiot. What's she phoning for?'

'I've said, I don't know.' Guilt blazed in her cheeks.

'For god's sake, Livvy, tell me the truth. Do me the courtesy of that, at least. Is this the first time she's phoned you?'

Livvy felt as though she were standing on the edge of a precipice, blindfolded, with no idea how far the drop would be. 'No.'

'She's been in touch before? When?'

The car suddenly felt icy cold, as if Dominic had turned the air con down to its lowest setting. 'A few weeks ago. She texted, and then she phoned the house—'

'*A few weeks ago?* My mother contacted you weeks ago and you're only telling me about it now? What the fuck, Livvy?'

'I didn't want to upset you. You already had so much to deal with, with your dad's death and all the issues around the funeral. I didn't think she'd turn up again . . .'

For a split second, Dominic said nothing, and Livvy silently prayed that he hadn't witnessed her slip.

'Turn up again? What do you mean?'

Possible deceptions scrambled for prominence in Livvy's head, but none made any sense. Her thoughts were muddled and she couldn't think of a decent way out. 'She came to the house again, about a month ago.'

'What did she want?'

Panic scuttled across Livvy's skin. 'She wanted to give you your dad's watch, she said he wanted you to have it—'

'And what did you say? Did you invite her in? Have a cosy cup of tea and a chat?'

'Of course not—'

'So what happened?'

Livvy remembered Imogen stepping into the house uninvited, creeping up behind her, transfixed by Leo. She couldn't tell Dominic that part of the story, not when he was already so angry. 'Nothing. I told her you wouldn't want it and she left.'

'And that's it?'

Livvy nodded.

'And she hasn't contacted you again until today?'

Livvy hesitated a fraction too long.

'For fuck's sake, just tell me. It's written all over your face that there's more.' His hands gripped the steering wheel, knuckles the colour of chalk.

'I went to meet her. The day before yesterday. I wish I hadn't but—'

'You went to meet my mother?' Dominic's voice hardened. 'In spite of everything I've told you, you still chose to go and meet her? To listen to whatever lies she had to tell?'

Livvy shook her head. 'It wasn't like that. I thought that if I met her, just once, she might stop turning up at the house.'

Dominic banged a fist down hard on the steering wheel. 'This has got *nothing* to do with you. How *dare* you go behind my back.'

'I'm sorry. She said there were things she needed to tell me and I thought it might help me understand—'

'What things?' He was shouting now, his face puce with rage.

'I don't know, I—'

'What did she tell you?'

Thoughts tripped and floundered in Livvy's head. 'Nothing, really. She denied that anything bad had ever happened when you were a child—'

'And you stayed to listen to that? You swallowed those lies?' He pressed his foot down harder on the accelerator.

'No, I was with her for less than fifteen minutes—'

'You shouldn't have been with her at all.' He shouted at her, face tinged with sweat as he swerved into the inside lane, horns beeping furiously behind them.

Livvy's heart thundered in her chest, and she twisted her wedding ring around her finger. 'Slow down, Dominic, you're scaring me.'

He ignored her, turning the steering wheel right and then left, weaving in and out of the traffic.

'Please, let's pull over. We can talk about it. You shouldn't drive when you're this angry.'

There was a splinter of silence, like a hesitation between heartbeats.

'Don't *ever* fucking tell me what to do.' Dominic's voice was flat, carefully enunciated, and Livvy was aware of holding her breath in her chest.

Time seemed to take on a different dimension, to accelerate and slow down in the same moment.

She watched as the skin across Dominic's forehead corrugated into a rigid frown, his jaw clenched, his grip tightening on the steering wheel. She watched as he turned to her, eyes spitting with rage, hissing in her direction. 'Don't you *ever* go behind my back again.' Her head turned just in time to see their car hurtling towards the back of a moving lorry, a shout erupting from her throat. She twisted her wedding ring around her finger, watched it slide over her knuckles and fall to the floor as the car jerked forwards. Her eyes flickered towards Dominic just in time to see the lock of his jaw, the intransigence in his eyes, the twisted fury at the corners of his lips. And just as it flashed through her mind that this was it, that they might both be killed, that Leo would be orphaned, she heard Dominic curse, felt her body lurch to the left as he pulled down hard on the steering wheel, watched in horror as the unrelenting speed of the car took them over the kerb, across the pavement, towards a high, red-bricked wall.

And then everything went black.

ANNA

LONDON

'But that's me. The woman in that photograph is me.'

My eyes dart up to Zahira and then back to the screen, unable to compute what I am seeing. The neurons in my brain are firing in all the wrong directions, unable to connect.

I look at the photograph again, at the name in the middle of the profile, confirm that my eyes are not deceiving me.

It is the Facebook page of Livvy Nicholson. And yet the profile photograph on the account is of me: me with long hair.

I turn back to Zahira, see my own confusion reflected back at me. 'I don't understand. Why has this woman got a photo of me on her profile?'

Zahira brings her chair closer to mine so that we can share the screen. 'I don't know. It doesn't make any sense.'

She scrolls down the profile page – through articles from the World Wildlife Fund and the National Trust – and then her fingers stop and my eyes blur momentarily, unready to absorb what they're seeing.

It is a repost from someone else's account, a woman called Bea Nicholson. It is a photograph of me, standing in a park, a bridge in the distance behind me. Next to me, with her arm around my shoulders, stands an athletic woman wearing shorts and a t-shirt, dark hair cropped close to her head, her strong features both resolute and kind. Beneath the photo there is a caption and a date.

Happy Birthday to my little sis and best friend. I love you!

The photo is dated seven months ago.

My heart thuds. I hear Stephen's voice in my head, patiently answering all my questions, telling me I am an only child, that I have no extended family.

My hand takes over from Zahira's on the trackpad, scrolls through the profile – more articles about the Woodland Trust, the Bristol Balloon Fiesta, an international climate change summit – and then there is another photograph, and I am aware of my throat tightening as I scan one face and then the next, devour the caption beneath.

It is a photograph of four people in front of a Christmas tree. I am standing in the middle, flanked by a man and a woman much older than me. Clicking on the photo to enlarge it, I see it immediately: the resemblance between my face and the woman on my right. It is there in the cornflower-blue eyes, the wide-open smile, the gentle point of the chin.

And in the centre of the photo, cradled in my arms, face out towards the camera, is a tiny baby wearing a blue sleepsuit.

My head swims as I read the caption beneath.

Three generations of the Nicholson family: me, my little boy, and my (very proud!) parents.

The photo was posted nine months ago.

My stomach lurches and my head feels light, as though I have inhaled helium.

I stare at the photo and I know, without any need for confirmation, that these are my parents, that this is my son. I do not remember them and yet I know it is true.

This is the family Stephen told me were dead.

'I don't understand. Why is there a Facebook profile for me under a different name?' My voice is tight, strained, as though it is being wrung from a damp cloth.

Zahira takes hold of my hand, and her voice, when she begins to speak, is gentle. 'Remember when I said I looked for you online and couldn't find any trace of you? It's pretty much unheard of these days. Everyone has *some* online presence, whether they want it or not. I thought it was weird at the time. But now . . .' She pauses, and my thoughts swirl as though being pulled deep into a vortex. 'This profile has to be yours. You must be Livvy Nicholson.'

The suggestion reels in my ears and I shake my head. 'But I'm not. My name's Anna Bradshaw.'

Zahira squeezes my hand and I feel it there in her fingers: the tentative delivery of difficult news. 'I don't know what your husband's playing at, but whatever he's been telling you, it's clearly not true. That's you there, with your family, less than a year ago.'

I know she is right, but it still makes no sense. 'But if I'm Livvy Nicholson, then all those letters to Stephen would be from me? And I don't remember writing any of them.' My voice feels shrill in my ears.

'But would you remember writing them even if you had?'

I scour my brain, in search of a crumb of memory, however small. I try to recollect having once been a woman called Livvy Nicholson, of having written those letters to Stephen. But my memory is a dark, hollow cave and there is nothing to light my way.

And then a thought splices into my mind, at once hopeful and terrifying. Nine months ago I had a son who was alive. Whatever story Stephen has told me about a child of ours dying two years ago, there has to be another truth.

'But if that's me – if I'm Livvy Nicholson, and that's my child – then where's my baby now?'

ANNA

Neither of us speaks for a moment. The thought of my child, possibly still alive and yet separated from me, claws at my heart.

'I think we should call the police.'

I tear my eyes away from the photograph on the screen, look at Zahira. 'And say what? That I can't remember who I am but there's a profile of me on Facebook with a different name? What are they going to do?' I hear the hysteria in my voice, panic ballooning in my chest.

'Something's really wrong here. All these photos . . . They suggest you have a whole life Stephen hasn't told you about. A whole family he's deliberately kept you from.'

The words sink in and I know Zahira is right. Pulling the laptop towards me, I scroll through the profile, see that Livvy Nicholson has uploaded very little about her life in the past year apart from that single family photograph. But posted just before that, there is a selfie, standing on a bridge, a wide river beneath. And, beneath it, a caption.

> *As if I need any other reason to love being a born and bred Bristolian. Just look at that view!*

Bristol. Not London.

A year ago, I was living in Bristol. And yet Stephen has never mentioned Bristol to me. He told me I was brought up in Gloucester.

I scroll some more, find a photograph of me from eighteen months ago, standing on a stage behind a podium, a picture of a rainforest filling a screen behind me. I read the caption, feel as though I am falling from a great height.

> *Delivering a speech at this weekend's climate conference in Manchester. I've been working in environmental policy my entire career and things have only got worse, not better. Let's hope the world starts listening soon.*

I swivel the laptop so Zahira can see the screen, watch her face as she absorbs the information.

'He told me I was a librarian, that I'd left my job two years ago, after Henry died.'

Zahira pauses, the silence suffocating. 'All these lies. How do you even know Stephen is who he says he is?'

The question seems to suck all the oxygen from the room. 'He must be . . . Who else would he be?'

'Where did you say he worked?'

I tell her the name of the university, the engineering faculty, watch her tap rapidly at the keyboard.

'And he's got the same surname as you – Stephen Bradshaw?'

I nod, a voice in my head pleading for this not to be another betrayal.

My eyes train themselves on Zahira's face, searching for a clue as to what she might find. Her fingers scroll down the trackpad and then she squints, clicks, frowns.

'What is it?'

She turns to me and there is a beat of silence, a thousand possible permutations tumbling into it. 'Is this him? Is this Stephen?' She swivels the laptop towards me, and Stephen's face stares back, enlarged on the screen, the banner of the university's name strapped across the top of the page. I feel a rush of relief that he is there, it is true, he has not lied to me about that too. But then my eyes scurry across the text, and I see it, in bold font beneath the photo: *Dominic Bradshaw, Associate Professor in Civil Engineering*. Something seems to slip inside me, like shifting tectonic plates. 'But that's Stephen. Why does it say his name's Dominic?'

Zahira shakes her head. 'I don't know. But I honestly think we should go to the police.'

I push back my chair, the legs scraping against the white ceramic tiles. 'I have to talk to him.' The urgency is immediate, like flames bursting into life, licking their way across my thoughts.

Zahira places a hand on my arm. 'I don't think that's a good idea. Not on your own.'

The alarm in Zahira's voice makes me sit back down, and it takes a few moments for me to understand the cause of it. 'Stephen's not *dangerous*. He wouldn't *hurt me*.' Even as I say it, there is a voice inside my head, whispering, probing, like a finger jabbed into the flesh of an arm: *Are you sure?*

'What time did Stephen say he'd be home?'

I try to straighten out my thoughts, rewind my memory. 'About five o'clock.' I glance down at my watch, see there are still three hours to go, do not know how it will be possible to fill such a great gap of time.

'Call him. Ask him to meet you in the park when he gets home.'

'Why?'

'Because I think if you want to see him, you should meet him in a public place. I'll come with you, sit nearby with Elyas, be on hand in case you need me.'

I feel myself hesitate. 'Do you really think that's necessary?'

'Maybe not. But just indulge me on this, okay?'

I release a breath I was not aware of holding. 'Thank you.'

'No need to thank me. Just phone him before I change my mind and insist you go straight to the police.'

I pick up my bag from the floor, empty save for a packet of tissues and the phone Zahira gave me, retrieve the folded piece of paper that has Stephen's number on it, and dial.

ANNA

LONDON

I press a finger down on the speaker button, do not feel I have the fortitude to manage this call alone.

It takes four rings for him to answer. 'Hello?' His voice is suspicious, guarded, and I realise he will not recognise the number.

'It's me.' The words catch in my throat. It's only in saying them aloud that I understand I do not know who 'me' really is.

'Anna? Where are you? I've been calling home for ages and you haven't been answering.'

I peel my tongue from the roof of my mouth. 'What time will you be home?'

There is a pause at the other end of the line and I hear the click of an indicator, realise he must already be driving.

'That's why I've been trying to call. I managed to get away early. I'll be home in half an hour.'

An involuntary gasp escapes my lips and Zahira catches my eye, mouths silently at me. *It's okay.*

'Anna, where are you? What's this number you're calling me from?'

Zahira shakes her head, forms a silent 'no' with her lips.

'Can you meet me in the park when you get back?' My heart pounds in my chest and I have a sense that Stephen will not appreciate my evasion of his questions.

'What's going on?'

There is concern in his voice, and for a second I feel myself falter, think of all the kindness and patience he has shown me since the accident. But then I glance at the laptop, see the photo of Stephen with a different name, think about the photo of me with my parents and my son. 'I just need to talk to you. Can you come straight to the park?'

The line goes quiet and I wonder, if I were watching his face right now, what expression I would see: whether it would be forbearance, irritation or something else entirely.

'This is ridiculous. I've had a hectic couple of days at this conference and I've managed to leave early to see you. I just want to get home. I'll see you there in half an hour, okay?'

This conference. I have no idea whether it is real, can no longer locate the dividing line between Stephen's truths and his lies. 'I won't be at home. I'll be in the park, on the benches near the playground. If you want to see me, that's where I'll be.' I don't know where this assertiveness is coming from, just that this is what I need to do.

Zahira smiles, nods, gives me a thumbs up.

There is a sigh on the other end of the line, filled with barely contained frustration. 'Okay. But I wish you'd tell me what's going on.'

Across the table, Zahira shakes her head, gesticulates for me to say no more. My fingers ache from gripping the phone so tightly, and I steel myself to reply. 'I'll see you in about half an hour.'

'Fine.' He hangs up before either of us has a chance to say anything more.

'Well done. You did really well. Are you okay?'

I nod in spite of the thrumming in my chest.

Zahira stands up. 'Right, I'd better get Elyas up from his nap.'

As Zahira leaves the room, I sit at her kitchen table, trying to imagine meeting Stephen in half an hour's time. I think about everything I've uncovered and I do not know how, when I come to face him, I will know where to begin.

ANNA

LONDON

My heart hammers against my ribs. On a bench a few yards away, Zahira blows bubbles through a plastic stick for Elyas, who runs after them, trying to catch them between his palms. Her eyes flit towards me and I wonder if I would have the courage to do this without her. Above my head, streaks of sunlight vein the sky, punctuated by thin shreds of cloud like cigarette smoke.

I pivot my gaze, look towards the entrance, scan the road encircling the park. For a moment I think perhaps he is not going to come, but then I spy Stephen's Toyota Prius reversing into a parking space that is only just big enough, watch him inch back and forth as he squeezes into the spot.

I watch him get out of the car, close the door, thrust an arm behind him to activate the alarm. I keep watch of him as he strides through the black metal gates and into the park, my fingers curling into tight fists, nails digging into my palms. I realise I am scared of him – of who he is, who he might be – and I have no idea where the feeling comes from, only that it is coiling in my stomach like a threatened snake.

And then he is there, standing next to the bench, towering over me.

'Are you okay? You've had me seriously worried for the past half an hour.'

He sits down, takes hold of my hand, and I snatch it free.

'Anna, what's the matter?'

I turn to him, my throat burning. 'Don't you mean Livvy? What's the matter, *Livvy*?'

My eyes do not leave his face as I search for any sign of derailment. But his expression is impassive, no flicker of unease. 'What do you mean?'

I breathe slowly, in and then out, remind myself of the photographs. 'I've seen the Facebook profile. *My* Facebook profile. I've seen your page on the university website. I know your real name is Dominic.' My voice is steady, unwavering, and I do not know where my confidence is coming from.

'Listen, whatever you think you've seen, it sounds like you've got the wrong end of the stick—'

'So you can explain the photograph of me with my parents and my son, posted nine months ago, can you? Parents and a child that *you told me were dead*.' A crack opens up in my voice, a fault line between conflicting versions of my past, and I swallow it down, will not capitulate to it.

'My love, I think you must be confused. I don't know what you're imagining, but you're still very fragile—'

'I'm *not* fragile. I'm not imagining anything. I saw the photos on Facebook.'

Stephens sighs as though corralling every ounce of patience. 'Social media has all sorts of fake nonsense on it. That's why we never use it. Come on, let's go home, where we can talk in private—'

'I'm not going anywhere with you. I found the letters in the loft. All the letters from Livvy, declaring her love for you. Either you're having an affair, or you've been lying to me about who I really am. Which is it?'

Stephen holds my gaze, eyebrows raised. 'Please, Anna, I can see you're upset, but you know how unstable you've been since the accident. You can't let your imagination run away with you.'

He reaches out, places a hand on my arm, but I shake him off, do not want him touching me.

He sighs. 'Please don't make a scene. You know how erratic your emotions have been. Think about how you overreacted when you couldn't find the piece of paper with the therapist's number on it.'

'You mean the appointment with the therapist that you cancelled and then lied about?' I stare at him, will not be intimidated.

Stephen frowns. 'What are you talking about? The appointment was cancelled. Has she been in touch to arrange a new one?'

There is such nonchalance in his voice that for a second I'm destabilised, as though I'm in a parallel reality where everything is distorted and I cannot trust what I know to be true. But then I think about my call with Carla, about the letters in the loft, about the Facebook page, and I know these doubts aren't just figments of my imagination. 'Stop lying, Stephen. I just want the truth. All I care about are my parents and my son. Just tell me where they are.'

There is a weighted silence, heavy with anticipation.

'It's always the same, isn't it?'

Stephen's quietly accusatory tone throws me off balance, a misstep from which it takes me a moment to find my footing. 'What do you mean?'

He turns to me, eyes flickering with something between disappointment and contempt. 'They *always* come first.'

He pauses, as if waiting for me to speak, but there seems to be a lag between my ears and my brain.

'Can you imagine what it's like, coming home from work to discover you're with them yet again? Just wanting a bit of time and space with my wife and child but *always* having to share you with your bloody family?'

His words are like glue in my ears. 'What are you talking about? Just tell me where they are.' My voice is steadfast, unflinching, and I do not know where my courage is coming from. All I can think about is that photo, my baby in my arms, my desperate need to find my way back to him.

Stephen continues as though I haven't spoken. 'You were *so* unhappy when I met you. You don't remember, do you? Dumped by your last boyfriend, desperate for a baby, biological clock ticking loudly in your ears. I've given you everything you wanted – *everything* – and still it's not enough.' His voice is bitter, and it evokes something in me, an instinctive tightening in my chest, like a muscle memory learnt from experience.

'Do you know what it's like, always feeling like you're second best? Always feeling like you'll never be enough, however hard you try? Have you ever stopped to think what that's like for me?'

He is unrelenting now, his grievances all-consuming, and I do not know what he is talking about, what has prompted this tirade, only that it seems futile to try to stop him.

'Your family *always* breathing down our necks. Your sister muscling in, so sanctimonious, so bloody jealous that we were happy when her life was so small, so lonely. And yet you couldn't see it. You just wouldn't see it.'

His accusations are dense in my ears, but I try to find my way back to the only question that matters. 'What about Henry? He's still alive, isn't he?'

There is a pause. A slight twitch at one corner of Stephen's lips. 'Henry? You mean Leo.'

The words are spoken dispassionately, as though they have no greater significance than the correction of an item on a shopping list. And yet they strike me as if I have been physically assaulted, as if someone has thrust a knife deep into my stomach and twisted it full circle.

Leo. The name resonates in my ears and with it comes a mighty heave of longing: a primitive connection to my little boy through the simple truth of his name. Something shifts inside me, every muscle in my body focused with singular ferocity on the well-being of my son. 'Just tell me where he is.'

Stephen glares at me, frustration tunnelling into the lines around his eyes. 'Why has *everything* got to be about Leo? Has it ever occurred to you that we're a couple first and parents second? Our son doesn't have to be the centre of our entire lives. But even now, even after everything that's happened, that's *all* you want to know.'

Thoughts stagger in my head. 'He's my *son*, Stephen. I want to know he's okay.'

The corner of Stephen's top lip curls with condescension. 'He's fine.' The words are flat, impassive, as if of no consequence at all.

I try to grasp hold of those two short syllables, allow myself to ingest their meaning, but it is as though I am being buried beneath the rubble of too many revelations. 'Why did you tell me he was dead?'

'You shouldn't have put me on the spot like that.'

I think about the lies Stephen's told, about the heinous web of deceit he has spun. My head reels, fingers curling around the edge of the bench to stop myself from falling. 'How old is he?'

Stephen scowls, irritation striating his forehead. 'What?'

'Leo. How old is he?' It takes every ounce of my self-control not to pummel Stephen with my fists.

Stephen sighs as though my questions are testing his patience. 'Nine months.'

Nine months. The photo on Facebook must have been taken just days after Leo's birth.

My son is almost a year old and yet I do not remember him.

'So Henry never existed? We never had a son who died?'

Stephen rolls his eyes as if I am stating something so obvious it's barely worthy of a response. 'Of course not.'

My heart stutters as I pull the Facebook photo to mind, try to fast-forward time, imagine what Leo might look like now. Whether his hair is still dark, his eyes still bright. Whether he has begun to walk or talk. Whether he is missing me. 'Where is he? Where's Leo now?'

Stephen raises his eyebrows, looks at me with disdain. 'So now you're suddenly concerned about Leo, are you?'

'What are you talking about? You told me our son was *dead*. That he died two years ago. How could I be concerned about him when I didn't even know he existed?'

Stephen exhales slowly, and it takes every scrap of self-restraint not to scream into his face. Whatever twisted game Stephen is playing, I know I have to keep hold of my anger, that he is the quickest route back to my little boy.

'For weeks before your accident all you talked about was going back to work. As though some tinpot think tank was going to change the world. And yet now you want to play the part of the devoted mother.' There is derision in his voice, like a smear of grime on a pristine windowpane.

As though some tinpot think tank was going to change the world. A think tank, not a library. There is too much to take in, an avalanche of information I fear may bury me beneath its weight.

'Where is he?' I do not know where the ferocity in my voice comes from, only that it is blazing and will not be extinguished.

Stephen does not reply, gazes at me unperturbed.

The rage in me is so sudden, so violent, I know that if Stephen doesn't tell me, right now, where my son is, I may do something I'll live to regret.

ANNA

LONDON

'Where's my son?' My hand grabs the sleeve of Stephen's jacket, yanks at his arm.

Stephen shakes me off, hisses in a low whisper. 'For god's sake, stop being hysterical. You're embarrassing yourself. Leo's fine. He's with your parents.'

Relief floods my veins. I think of my son, safe with my parents, and it is as if prayers I hadn't known I was reciting have been answered.

And yet there is something niggling at me, like a concealed splinter, tender to touch but invisible to the naked eye.

And then, suddenly, it reveals itself. 'Why haven't my parents been to see me? Or my sister? Why has nobody come to visit?' It is three weeks since my accident. It doesn't make sense that none of them have come, that they haven't brought Leo back to me.

'They know you want to settle into the house, start building our new life together.'

'What are you talking about? What new life?'

Stephen gazes at me with something approaching pity and I feel myself squirm beneath his scrutiny, like a specimen in a Petri dish.

And then I think of the photos I saw on Facebook. *As if I need any other reason to love being a born and bred Bristolian.* I think about the boxes unpacked in the spare room, about Stephen's justification for them: *I know, you don't have to say it. How have we still not got around to unpacking all these boxes despite having lived here for over a year? . . . Every weekend we promise ourselves that we'll finally tackle all this . . . and every weekend we somehow manage to find something more interesting to do.* I recall the sense of disorientation I had coming home to our house, as though I had never been there before.

As though I had never been there before.

Suddenly it is clear, like a view over the hills after the morning fog has evaporated. 'We haven't lived in that house for over a year, have we? We've only just moved here.'

Stephen picks at a piece of loose lint on his trousers, flicks it to the ground.

I want to scream at him for his indifference, but I know I have to contain my fury, extract every piece of information from him while I can. 'Why did you tell me we'd lived there all that time?'

When Stephen replies his words are steady, deliberate, every syllable carefully enunciated. 'I did it for you.'

'What do you mean?'

Stephen sighs – slow, languorous – as though I am a dim-witted student. 'To give us some time together without your family's interference.'

None of what Stephen is saying makes any sense. 'But why has *nobody* been to visit? Why isn't Leo with us? Why's he with my parents?'

Stephen looks at me, unblinking. 'You told them you didn't want them visiting for the time being. You've been busy.'

Somewhere overhead a plane's engine rumbles, but my eyes remain fixed on Stephen, focused on the dislocation between his words and my understanding. 'What do you mean, I told them? I haven't spoken to them.' For a moment I doubt myself, wonder whether my memory is betraying me, whether Stephen is right and I simply can't remember.

'They know you don't want visitors at the moment. They understand you don't have time right now.'

There is a chill in Stephen's voice, and something slots into place like a missing word in a crossword puzzle.

I think of the surreptitious phone calls, the snapping shut of the laptop, the startled expression on Stephen's face when I have interrupted him. For the past few hours, I have attached those moments to a different story: a story of infidelity and sexual betrayal. Now I realise it is a betrayal of a different kind, altogether more malign. 'You've been telling them I don't want to see them, haven't you? Telling them not to come.'

Stephen doesn't contradict me, and the confirmation of my suspicion is loud in his silence.

'Why would you do that? You know how lonely I've been. Why would you cut me off from my family when I needed them most?'

Stephen lifts the cuff of his sleeve, glances down at his watch as though perhaps I am keeping him from more pressing business. The desire to throttle him is overwhelming.

'You've had the support of your family. You've had me.' He stares at me phlegmatically, and for a few seconds neither of us speaks.

I think about my son, about our three-week separation, feel a burning need to get back to him. It is a feeling beyond tangible memory; it is instinctive, primeval.

I think about my mum, about why she isn't feeling like this about me. Why she hasn't come to see me in spite of Stephen's insistence that I don't need her to visit. It strikes me that if a child of mine had been in a serious car accident, I would be by their side, whatever their husband said, whatever reassurances he gave.

And then a thought occurs to me, so monstrous that I almost dare not release it into the world for fear that, in doing so, I will make it real. 'You haven't told them about the accident, have you? They don't know about the crash?'

Stephen stares at me, doesn't blink. 'I can take care of you. We don't need anyone else.'

The ground seems to shift beneath me, as though there is a rupture in the earth and I am being pulled deep into a sinkhole. 'They're my *parents*, Stephen. *I* need them. They must be worried sick if they haven't heard from me for weeks.'

'I already told you. They have heard from you. There's no need to worry.'

'What are you talking about? Why do you keep saying I've been in touch with them when you know I haven't?'

Stephen says nothing, stares across the park as though he is not even listening.

You told them you didn't want them visiting. I cannot get Stephen's words to settle in my head, know there is a misalignment somewhere but cannot understand what it is. His words are like water on damp soil, dissolving before I can touch them.

A sudden breeze unfurls across my shoulders and I pull my jacket tighter across my chest. I feel the mobile phone Zahira gave me in my pocket, and a thought slips into my mind, quietly, surreptitiously, as if unsure it wants to be seen.

My mobile phone. I must have had one, before the crash. I wondered where it is.

It got broken in the accident.

I think about the fact that I don't have a laptop, about Stephen's reticence to let me use his. I think about my lack of contact with the outside world: no mobile phone, no computer, no access to the internet. The suspicion snowballs in my head until it is gathering pace, has a momentum of its own: preposterous and yet, at the same time, horrifyingly plausible. 'You've been contacting my family, haven't you, pretending to be me?'

ANNA

London

The accusation sounds outlandish, but then I turn to face Stephen and see it immediately: expressions of self-righteousness and defensiveness chasing each other across his face.

'You can't have been speaking to them, impersonating me. So, what – texting from my phone, emailing from my account, saying I'm fine and I don't need to see them? Is that it?'

He looks at me, nonchalant and unsentimental. 'It was the right thing to do. We need to focus on us, on our marriage, without any distractions.' The self-justification is inconceivable and yet Stephen's tone is matter-of-fact, unapologetic.

'Distractions? My parents aren't a *distraction*. My son isn't a *distraction*. They're my *family*, for god's sake.' My voice gets louder, the unreality finally catching up with me. 'What were you planning to do? Hide me away forever? Carry on pretending that my parents are dead, that I have no other family? Keep me from my son?' I do not know where my disbelief ends and my anger begins. 'Why would you do something like that?'

Stephen shakes his head, impatience spilling from his voice. 'I did it for you. For us. I just want you to be happy. Why is that so difficult for you to understand?'

'Because it's insane. You've been contacting my family, pretending to be me, telling them I don't want to see them. Why on earth would you imagine – *for a second* – that I'd be happy about that?'

Stephen's face hardens, as if set in concrete. 'I just wanted to give you enough time to realise that we don't need anyone else. We're better on our own.'

'Without our son?'

Stephen groans, loosens the tie from around his neck. It dawns on me that he is wearing a suit, that perhaps he has been at a work conference after all. Perhaps it is the only true thing he has told me.

'Of course not without our son. I was going to get him back, just as soon as you understood that we're happier without constant interference from your family.' He looks at me, eyebrows raised, as though it is the most logical plan in the world.

'How can you possibly think I'm better off without any contact from my family? It's *inhuman*.'

The muscles in Stephen's jaw clench. 'I did it because I love you.' He holds my gaze and it is written clearly on his face: the deluded belief that it is true.

'You *love* me? You tell me my entire family's dead – that my *son* is dead – and you call that love?'

The expression on Stephen's face shifts, like an actor in a Greek tragedy swapping one mask for another. 'I should have known better. It's always about you, isn't it? Other people's feelings just don't matter. I used to think you were ungrateful, but now I think you're just plain selfish.'

There is something in Stephen's scathing tone that snakes between my ribs and I know I have heard it before. I know – somewhere beyond palpable memory – that this is not the first time Stephen has tried to twist the narrative, cast himself as the victim. I do not know how I have reacted in the past. All I know is that I won't tolerate it now.

'This isn't what love looks like, Stephen. Love is about wanting the *best* for somebody, not imposing your will on them. It's not about cutting them off from everything and everyone they care about. You don't *love* me. You don't know the meaning of the word.'

Stephen scowls. 'You really don't have a clue, do you—'

'No, *you* don't have a clue. You've stolen my entire life from me. You've stolen my parents, my sister, my son, my home. You've stolen my identity, for god's sake. And you call that love?'

'Stop being so melodramatic. I haven't stolen anything from you. Let's go home and we can talk things through when you're less hysterical.'

He grabs hold of my arm, fingers digging into the flesh above my elbow, and it is like a physical memory rushing back to me. I know he has done this before, that this is not the first time his violence has imprinted itself on my skin.

'Let go of her.'

I whip my head around, see Zahira standing beside me, cheeks flushed with adrenaline.

'Who the fuck are you?'

'Take your hands off her or I'm calling the police.' With one hand Zahira holds the hood of Elyas's coat. With the other, she pulls out her mobile phone, holds it up in front of Stephen, unblinking in the face of his fury, daring him not to believe that she will do it.

'This has got nothing to do with you.' Stephen spits the words at Zahira, his grip tightening on my arm, needles of pain shooting into my flesh.

Courage finds its way into my throat. 'She's here because I asked her to be.' My voice threatens to waver and I breathe fiercely against it, harden the edges of my consonants as if sharpening the tip of a blade. 'Now *get your hands off me.*'

There is a momentary pause, like the silence before a storm.

And then Stephen opens his mouth to speak and I notice tiny globules of spit at the corners of his lips as he takes a deep breath, his hand still firmly on my arm, fingers pressing into my skin. 'You know you're nothing without me, don't you?'

His words hiss at me through the cool September air and there is a split second when I sense my whole body flinch, like a visceral memory trained to react in a certain way. Something inside me is paralysed, as though I dare not act for fear of the consequences, numbed by whatever has gone before.

And then I think about Leo, about our enforced separation. I think about my parents and my sister, unaware of what has happened to me. I think of the life I must have led before Stephen tried to mould my personality to fit his twisted needs.

I yank my arm free from his grasp, flesh stinging as if pricked by a thousand pins. 'Whatever I am without you, it's got to be better than whatever you're trying to turn me into.'

He glares at me – such hatred in his eyes – and I force myself to stare back, hold his gaze, refuse to surrender. And it is he, in the end, who looks away first.

I make myself study his face for a few seconds, to be clear in my mind who he is, what he has done. To commit this moment – this feeling – to memory. And then I turn around, link my arm through Zahira's, breathe against the hammering of my heart, and I start to walk away. I ignore the sound of Stephen's voice calling behind me, telling me I'm rubbish, I'm hopeless, that I won't last five minutes without him. I ignore him shouting at me that my life is empty, pointless, that I am weak, pathetic, that I will soon be begging him to take me back. Putting one foot in front of the other, I distance myself from Stephen's control. I walk away, towards whatever my old life looked like, whatever the past may have held and the future is yet to reveal.

I walk away and I don't look back.

EPILOGUE

FIVE MONTHS LATER

Snowdrops line the path as I push the buggy through the park. The air is cold, but the February sun is making a valiant attempt to penetrate the chill.

'Mama! Bir!'

I follow the line of Leo's pointed finger to the wood pigeon flying overhead, watch it land on a branch ahead of us.

'Bir-bir!'

Crouching down beside the buggy, I squeeze Leo's thigh beneath his padded snowsuit. 'Clever boy. They're birds, aren't they? Pigeons. They go coo, coo.'

Leo mimics the shape of my mouth, his lips a perfect circle. 'Coo! Coo!' His tongue finds the roof of his mouth and the sound emerges, his face breaking into a wide smile of achievement.

'That's it, sweetheart. You're a pigeon!' I lean forward, kiss the soft skin of his cheek, the ferocity of my love for him hot in my chest. And yet, even as I watch his wide, trusting smile, I cannot help but worry about the effect on him of the past few months, what implications they may have for his future. Whether those three weeks of my absence will stay with him forever, a fear of abandonment he will never quite lose.

A plane flies overhead and it takes me back in an instant to sitting on the bench beside Dominic as the whole, ugly truth emerged. I think about how the rest of that day unfolded and, even now, I find it hard to recall the details, as though a part of my brain is not yet ready to paint the whole picture.

I remember being back at Zahira's flat, Zahira sleuthing through Bea's Facebook profile and finding the veterinary practice where she worked. I remember Zahira phoning Bea, explaining what had happened, and the arrival of Bea and my parents with Leo a few hours later; the rush of tears, embraces, questions, answers. I remember, most of all, the feeling of Leo being placed in my arms: a feeling beyond words, beyond language, my heart expanding like a giant red star until I thought it would explode. So much love, such a fervent desire to protect him. I hadn't known, until that moment, there was such capacity within me.

'Swi-, Mama, swi-!' Leo points a finger in front of him, as though he has every confidence that he knows the way.

'You want to go on the swings? We're heading to the playground now, sweetheart.'

He kicks his legs with excitement, claps his hands, and I take hold of the buggy, continue our journey.

It wasn't until the day after I got home to Mum and Dad's, when the police came to take a statement, that the full story began to emerge. How I had been born Anna Olivia Nicholson but that everyone had always called me Livvy. How my married name was Anna Olivia Bradshaw, that this was the name on my driving licence, my bank cards, the NHS register. How all Dominic had to do was allow the doctors to call me by a first name I had never used and thereby compound the confusion from my amnesia. My Facebook profile was still in my maiden name because I had used it so rarely since getting married that I'd found no cause to update it. It was one of the police officers who pointed out that Dominic had managed to create further disorientation by copying what I'd been doing most of my life: swapping his second name for his first. Dominic Stephen Bradshaw. Making me call him by a name that would have felt foreign on my tongue. He'd known there was little chance of me uncovering the truth, given how vigilantly he was isolating me from the rest of the world.

It did not take the police long to uncover the extent of Dominic's deceptions. My parents and Bea showed them the emails and texts he had been sending from my accounts, pretending to be me. There were messages to Bea smoothing over the conflict we'd had before I left Bristol, telling her what he knew she wanted to hear: that I was looking for a job, that Dominic had opened up to me about his relationship with Daisy, that our marriage had turned a corner. Messages to my parents describing how busy I was, visiting nurseries, getting the house sorted, attending job interviews. Messages asking them to look after Leo for just a few more days, each message extending the time I would be apart from him little by little so as to arouse the least suspicion. Messages obfuscating the requests for our address, continuing the pretence that we wanted it to be a surprise for them too, that we didn't want to share it with them until the day they'd be visiting. Every message innocuous in itself, the collective impact only visible once you surveyed them from a distance, like a pointillist painting whose image becomes clear only when you step back from the canvas. And yet, both Bea and my parents had been worried, had sensed something was wrong; but while I seemed to be insisting everything was fine, there was little they could do.

It took a few days to pluck up the courage, but when I read Dominic's messages to my family, masquerading as me, it was like someone stepping over my grave. The language was so familiar, the tone so authentic. I could hear myself in every single one and yet I knew I hadn't written a word of them. It was like seeing myself in a photograph at a scene for which I knew I hadn't been present.

The police have since told me it is likely Dominic had been reading my private correspondence for months, that the reason he'd been able to mimic me so accurately was that he'd been snooping through my accounts for some time, until my writing style was almost as familiar to him as his own.

I have thought so much about it since: Dominic reading my private texts and emails without my knowledge. It has left me with a sense of violation, knowing that the liminal space between us – between myself as an individual and myself as a wife – has been breached.

The police are also, they have told me, reinvestigating the circumstances of the car crash. Something Dominic said in one of his police interviews – they wouldn't tell me what – aroused suspicion that the accident deserved re-examination. But a part of my brain won't allow me to think about that, is not yet ready to brave the implications of what it would mean.

A chocolate Labrador runs up to the buggy, tail wagging, and Leo squeals with glee. He leans forward, strokes its fur. 'Doh doh.'

'That's right, it's a doggie.'

We stroke the dog and I'm reminded of something Dominic told me when I first came home from hospital: about being on Hampstead Heath on Christmas morning, a cocker spaniel scampering around my ankles. It was, I realise, just another of his lies. I had never been to Hampstead Heath before Dominic took me there the weekend after the accident.

Over the past five months, I've come to realise that so much of what Dominic told me were pure fabrications. Not just the seismic lies: the deaths of my parents and our son, my job as a librarian, our twelve-year marriage, our life in London. Equally insidious were the subtle, day-to-day lies: my supposed love of nineteenth-century novels, Wagner operas, Wes Anderson films. My affinity for the sculpture gallery at the V&A, a building I had never even visited before Dominic sent me there on a fool's errand. My choice of chicken salads over plates of pasta. Each twisted preference designed to destabilise my sense of identity, to shape me into the wife he wanted me to be: compliant and isolated, uncertain and dependent. A wife who mirrored his interests, as though he were Pygmalion and I Galatea, carved from ivory, every sweep of my desires a product of his creation. A woman who didn't dare leave the house for too long in case I missed his calls: those regular daily interactions designed to keep me at home, entirely reliant on him. I remember all those mornings desperately trying to read *Our Mutual Friend* and the crushing sense of failure when I couldn't seem to enjoy it. I remember the anxiety that I had lost a part of myself in the crash, the part of me that had loved Dickens and Trollope, Strauss and Mahler. And yet, all along, that version of me had never existed.

There are still mornings when I wake up with a sense of horror that someone could be so single-minded, so manipulative, so pathologically controlling. Days when I cannot imagine what he thought the end point might be.

With the help of my parents and Bea, I am slowly beginning to rebuild myself, to rediscover the person I was before. The person I really am. Fragments of memory began to reappear soon after I returned to Bristol: familiar people and places were like daily sparks, igniting fresh memories. Sometimes, just little things: the waitress in the café where I always met Bea for coffee, the church hall where I took Leo for baby sensory classes, the swing seat in my parents' back garden. Other times, the memories have been more profound. On Leo's first birthday in early December, I suddenly remembered giving birth to him, the memory so visceral it was like being handed back an absent limb.

My therapist, Lena, has said that regaining my memory is a bit like gluing back together the broken pieces of a china cup: there may always be the odd hairline fracture if you look closely enough, but with sufficient care in the reconstruction, those chinks should be barely visible to the naked eye.

'Bye bye, doh doh.' Leo waves to the dog's swishing tail as it tires of being petted by a fourteen-month-old with gloved fingers.

I pull Leo's hat down where it has risen over his ears, defend him against the winter breeze nipping his skin. He smiles at me with such guilelessness that the muscles in my chest tighten with a determination to protect him.

Dominic is not allowed to see either Leo or me. He was interviewed four times by the police before being charged with controlling and coercive behaviour, and offences under the Computer Misuse Act. The first magistrates' hearing is next week and we do not know yet whether he plans to plead guilty or not, whether he hopes to diminish the possibility of a full jury trial by acknowledging what he has done. But in the meantime, his bail conditions stipulate that he cannot contact me, cannot come within a two-mile radius of my parents' house. A panic alarm has been installed by the front door, fitted by the police after they relayed a set of statistics to me: how two women every week in the UK are killed by a partner or ex-partner. How over half of all women killed are the victims of someone with whom they've been in a relationship. They are the kind of statistics I wish I could unlearn but know I never can.

And yet, even with these precautions in place, I still worry about what might happen in the future. Whether, if Dominic is not found guilty, he will be back in our lives. I have studied the conviction rates, know the rarity of success. I have read the newspaper articles about men who escape justice, again and again, only to seek out new victims, abuse more women. I have spent hours scouring the forums of domestic abuse charities, horrified by the familiarity of the stories people share.

Peering over the handlebar of the buggy as I push onwards through the park, I look at Leo's face: at his dark hair, arresting grey-green eyes, dimpled chin. It is impossible not to see the echo of Dominic in him. More than an echo. An imprint, as if someone has taken the mould they used for Dominic and created a smaller version in the shape of his son. It is hard, sometimes, to look at Leo and not be reminded of all that has happened, all that could still happen. It is hard not to fear what Leo may have inherited from his father beyond their physical resemblance: something malign, intangible, unseen. The desire to control, to domineer, to intimidate.

It is something I have talked about a lot with Imogen in recent weeks. She has given me an insight into Dominic's childhood, the truth so different from the picture Dominic painted: two parallel tales joined only by the thread of his lies. I have learnt that everything he told me about his childhood was untrue. There was no tyranny, no abuse, no eradication of his childhood possessions. Just a perfectly normal childhood. Imogen has told me it wasn't until Dominic was in his early twenties that his personality began to change. Having failed to achieve the level of academic success he thought he deserved at school and university, Dominic had become angry, resentful, contemptuous of the world around him, convinced he was being overlooked and undervalued. He'd become increasingly rigid in his outlook: distrustful of authority, disdainful of women. In his early thirties, he'd physically assaulted a woman on their first date, and when Imogen and John had urged him to seek professional help, he had cut them out of his life, accusing them of disloyalty. When Imogen had first seen me, she'd allowed herself to hope that things had got better, that Dominic had changed.

But when she saw the bruises around my wrist, she had known to worry. She'd wanted to warn me, there and then, but she knew how manipulative Dominic could be, knew it would take time for me to believe what she had to say. She'd hoped that by getting close to my parents she would eventually earn our trust and would be able to tell me what Dominic was really like.

She has since apologised for some of her actions around that time, has acknowledged that some of her behaviour was irrational. Grief had knocked her sideways, made her do things she would never otherwise have done: follow me to the urban farm, turn up at my parents' house. When I asked how she'd discovered my mobile number, she confessed to having used a reverse address site online, that she'd paid a service to find out my full name from where I lived, and then paid another website to discover my mobile number from my name. And then she'd verified it all by chatting with some of my neighbours, discovering that I went by the name Livvy, and that Dominic and I hadn't been together long. It was all, apparently, disarmingly easy.

Now, once a week, Imogen comes to my parents' house to spend time with Leo. And I am constantly watching him for any sign that he has inherited his father's toxicity. But Leo is sweet, affectionate, empathetic. All I can do is love him, nurture him, show him a different way of being and hope it is enough.

I stop the buggy, crouch down beside my son, kiss the tip of his nose. 'Are you okay, angel? You warm enough?'

He nods, grins, his tiny milk teeth like ivory pearls perched in his gums, and I know I have to believe that with love and kindness I can help make Leo a better man than his father. I can help make him a good man.

'Won't be long until we're at the playground. What are you going to go on first? The swings or the slide? Or the roundabout?'

Leo kicks his legs, smiles, too many choices.

'We can go on all of them, can't we?'

My phone pings, and I pull it from my pocket, find a message from Mum.

> *Everything okay, darling? Remember to text and let me know what time you'll be home for lunch. I'm making leek and potato soup. I love you xxx*

I text back immediately, tell her I'm fine, promise to let her know when we're on our way. Tell her I love her too.

It is rare for me to be away from the house for more than an hour without a text arriving from one of my parents. *I just wanted to check . . . I had a quick thought . . . I know you'll be home soon but . . .* Seemingly innocuous messages that disclose their level of anxiety. It is only recently that I've started to understand the ripple effect of Dominic's actions, his impact on so many people beyond Leo and me: my parents, Bea, my friends.

In last week's therapy session, I asked Lena how I would ever be able to trust anyone new again, and she leant forward in her chair, spoke slowly and deliberately. *'No one's saying it's going to be easy. It may take a long time. But when you have a support network as strong as yours, and the determination to overcome what you've been through, I've every confidence you'll learn to love and trust new people again.'* I'm hoping to return to work in a few months' time, just a couple of days a week at first. Christian has been so kind and accommodating, and even though my long-term memory is still fragile, I'm keen to get back, to begin re-establishing my career.

We reach the edge of the playground and I unlatch the gate, push the buggy through. I think about all those mornings in the park, waiting for Zahira and Elyas, not understanding why my need for a friend – for an ally – was so powerful.

Pulling my phone from my pocket, I open WhatsApp, tap out a quick message to Zahira.

> *Can't wait to see you tomorrow. Mum's making enough food to feed an army (as usual). Dad's already got the blow-up bed ready for Elyas. We'll collect you from the station at 11. Bea's got us tickets for the zoo so we'll head straight there. Give Elyas a big kiss from me. Xx*

As I put my phone back in my pocket, I feel a prickle at the back of my neck. My heart beats percussively in my chest and I tighten my grip on the handlebar of Leo's pushchair. I try to breathe slowly, tell myself there's nothing to worry about, it's just my imagination playing tricks on me. I remind myself that this happens a lot, this feeling of being watched, studied, observed from a distance. Lena has tried to reassure me it is only to be expected after all I have been through: moments of paranoia, anxiety, fear. '*You know that if Dominic ever comes near you or Leo, you only have to phone the police and they will be there in a flash. Your case is logged with them. If your mobile number ever dials 999, they will prioritise your call.*' And yet I cannot help envisaging all the scenarios where the police would not be able to help: Dominic appearing suddenly, snatching Leo before I have a chance to stop him, the police arriving too late. Dominic taking my son with him, never to be seen again. It is a fear so real, so potent, that tears begin to prick my eyes, and I stretch out a hand, take hold of Leo's, hold on to him tightly. A voice in my head tells me not to worry, Dominic is not here, he wouldn't risk it with the restraining order in place and the magistrates' hearing next week. I instruct myself not to look around, not to submit to my own worst fears. I rub a hand along the back of my neck, as if to brush away the sense of disquiet. But in the end, my apprehension wins, as it always does, and I whip my head around, scan the park, search for any sign of him. My eyes dart from one person to the next – elderly couples, women on bikes, men jogging, children playing – searching for a face I know too well and would be happy never to see again. But there is no one I recognise. Just my own anxiety, lurking in the shadows, refusing to believe he will ever let us be free.

'Hello, you!'

I turn back, see Bea striding towards us. We hug before she bends down, unclips Leo from his buggy, picks him up and showers him with kisses.

I watch them together, my son and my sister, and tell myself to stop worrying. Bea will look out for me. I think of my mum back home making soup, my dad preparing the spare bedroom for Zahira and Elyas, and try to find the reassurance I need in these acts of familial love. I remember what Lena said to me at the end of one of our sessions recently: *'Dominic has already stolen months of your life from you. It's up to you now whether you let him steal your future.'*

Somewhere at the back of my neck a faint prickling persists, but I refuse to turn around, refuse to look back. With one hand, I take hold of Leo's, the other I slip through Bea's arm, and together we head for the swings.

ACKNOWLEDGEMENTS

I'm incredibly grateful to the team at Lake Union for their professionalism and creativity. Thanks to my Lake Union editor Victoria Pepe, editorial director Sammia Hamer, marketing guru Bekah Graham, the ever-patient Nicole Wagner, and Christiana Demetriou in production. The book's jacket was masterminded by senior art director Liron Gilenberg, and the team at Brilliance oversaw the audiobook production.

Special thanks to Sophie Wilson, editor extraordinaire, whose input into this book I cannot overstate; thank you for the brainstorms, the invaluable suggestions, the careful reads and the cheerleading. You have been transformative, yet again.

Fellow authors never cease to amaze me with their generosity. Thanks to Adam Kay for the medical advice and Clare Mackintosh for insights into police procedure. Any mistakes are entirely my own.

My thanks to Ruth Jones and Rachel Joyce for the book chats, life chats and everything in between. Thanks to Katie Leah and Georg Ell for the dinners, the laughs and the VR expeditions to Antarctica. And eternal thanks to my mum and stepdad, Tania and Jerry Bowler, for their boundless love, encouragement and pride in everything I do. Jerry: you are the stepfather (and grandfather) I always hoped we'd have in our lives. Thank you for bringing such love into my mum's life and such kindness, generosity and care to the whole of our family. Mum: thank you for always being on the other end of the phone, for your endless support and for yet another superlative proofread.

Beginning to write a new novel during a pandemic was never going to be ideal timing, so my deepest thanks, as ever, are to the only people with whom I could spend months trapped inside a house and yet still love them more at the end of it; Adam and Aurelia, I know we always say that there's no such thing as perfection, but our trio comes pretty close. Thank you for being my perfect family.

AUTHOR'S NOTE

I'm indebted to many books, documentaries, online resources and internet forums in the research for this novel.

If you're affected by any of the issues raised in the book, help and advice is available from the organisations listed in the Online Information section below.

Books

Look What You Made Me Do: A Powerful Memoir of Coercive Control by Helen Walmsley-Johnson
I Forgot to Remember: A Memoir of Amnesia by Su Meck
Coercive Control: How Men Entrap Women in Personal Life by Evan Stark
Remembered Forever: Our Family's Devastating Story of Domestic Abuse and Murder by Luke Hart and Ryan Hart

TV / Radio / Press

Panorama: Escaping My Abuser (BBC, 2020)
Love You to Death: A Year of Domestic Violence (BBC, 2015)
Outlook: The Family Murder That Launched Our Campaign (BBC, 2020)

'Sally Challen on her release from prison: "I'm not sure how I'll cope on my own"' by Anna Moore (*Guardian*, 10 December 2019)

Online Information

Women's Aid UK: https://www.womensaid.org.uk/
Women's Aid Survivors' Forum: https://survivorsforum.womensaid.org.uk/
Refuge: https://www.refuge.org.uk/
National Domestic Abuse Helpline: https://www.nationalda-helpline.org.uk/

ABOUT THE AUTHOR

Photo © 2018 Adam Jackson

Hannah Beckerman is an author, journalist and broadcaster. She is a book critic and features writer for a range of publications including the *Observer*, the *Guardian* and the *FT Weekend Magazine*. A regular chair at festivals and events across the UK, she has interviewed a host of authors and celebrities, as well as appearing as a book pundit on BBC Radio 2 and Times Radio. Prior to becoming a full-time writer, Hannah worked in television as a producer and commissioning editor. *The Forgetting* is her fourth novel.

Printed in Great Britain
by Amazon